DARZINS MILL TRILOGY
BOOK ONE

SANCTUARY

ELIZABETH BIEHL

CITY PARK PUBLISHING COLLECTIVE
DENVER CO

First Printing, 2017
ISBN-13: 978-0692874134 (City Park Publishing Collective)
ISBN-10: 0692874135

City Park Publishing Collective
1559 Vine Street, Suite #3
Denver, CO 80206

For John, forever.

ACKNOWLEDGEMENTS

Thank you so much to my immensely talented and patient editor Debbie. Em-dashes and hurricanes and "I think I broke it," right to the bitter end.

To my fantastic beta readers: you guys saw something in the hot mess that I handed to you when I didn't know any better, and you didn't laugh, but you did point me in the right direction, and for that I am so grateful.

To Gail for the anthropology geekery.

To A.J. for the tough questions.

To Kaitlin and Meghann, for so many things.

To so, so many other people for one answer, one insight, one idea. So many.

To Chuck Wendig and the commenting community at terribleminds, who brought me back to writing when I thought I would never write again, and made me laugh and kept me honest and taught me a lot, and continue to, every day.

Thank you most especially to my kids, my captive audience; and to my best friend Andi, who listened when I called her up three days and ten thousand words in and said, "... I kinda think I'm writing a novel." And who has been there every step of the way, ever since.

BOND AND FREE

Robert Frost

Love has earth to which she clings
With hills and circling arms about—
Wall within wall to shut fear out.
But Thought has need of no such things,
For Thought has a pair of dauntless wings.

On snow and sand and turf, I see
Where Love has left a printed trace
With straining in the world's embrace.
And such is Love and glad to be.
But Thought has shaken his ankles free.

Thought cleaves the interstellar gloom
And sits in Sirius' disc all night,
Till day makes him retrace his flight,
With smell of burning on every plume,
Back past the sun to an earthly room.

His gains in heaven are what they are.
Yet some say Love by being thrall
And simply staying possesses all
In several beauty that Thought fares far
To find fused in another star.

First published in *Mountain Interval* (1920). This poem is in the public domain.

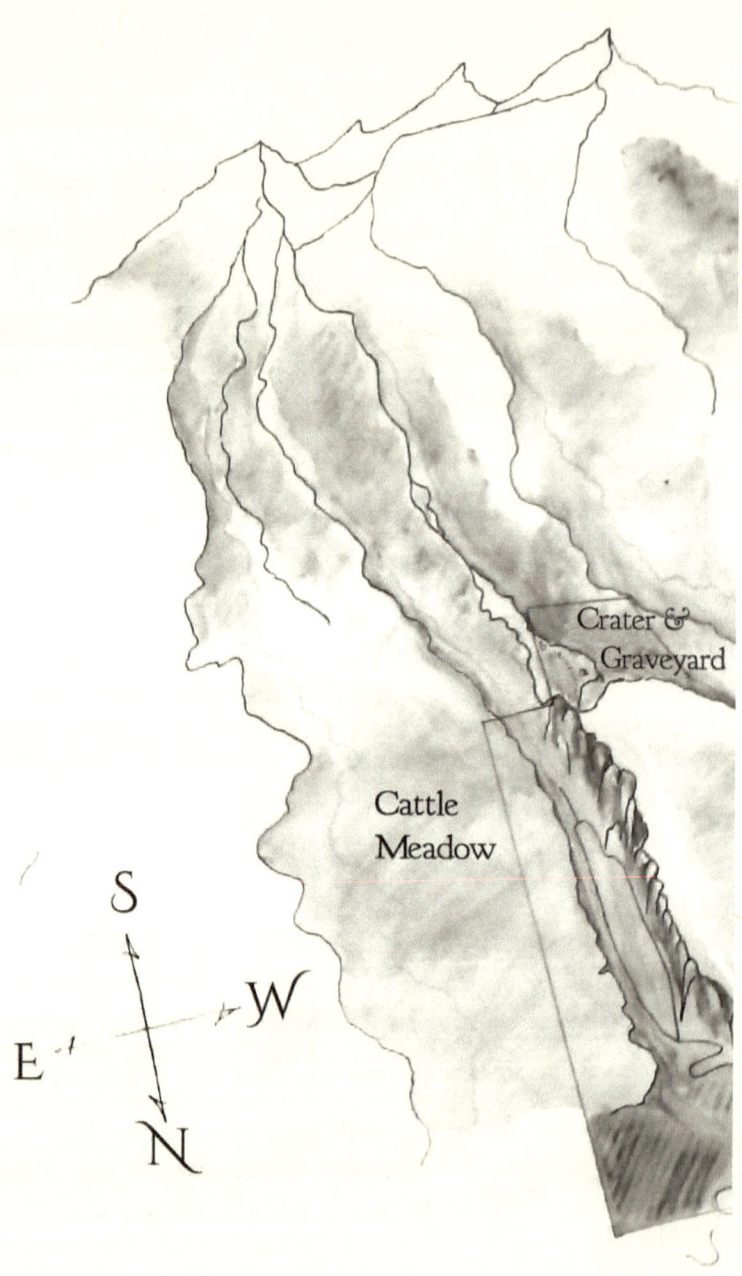

DARZINS' MILL
and the north slope
of the
Uncompaghre

Sheep
Meadow

Property Line

CHAPTER ONE

Just drive, Kate thought, and checked the map. Halfway to Durango. She could make it if she drove half the night, drove until she was too tired to think.

She left the interstate behind, crossed the Colorado River just above the confluence of the Roaring Fork and headed out across the backcountry, the braided river meandering in and out of shadows alongside the narrow state highway. In this clear evening light, the mountains were achingly beautiful, blood-red and violet, still snowcapped in high summer, their lower reaches carpeted by shimmering aspen groves just beginning the turn from green to gold. If there was a fine line between a change of scenery and running away, then on this road, just now, she didn't much care which side of that line she was on.

She rolled down the window, and the air smelled of goldenrod and new-mown fields, and rain.

One highway led to another, south and west, up into serious mountain country dotted with small towns and farms. The first drops hit the windshield as the sun slid below the ragged horizon. The visible world narrowed, steep hills on one side, chop-frothed reservoir on the other, and the winding stretch of highway in front of her. Then the canyon flattened out, the horizon opened up, and she crossed the long, low bridge at Sapinero just as the full force of the storm hit.

She settled right down into it, feeling the buffeting of the wind and rain through the steering wheel, reveling in the body rush, and she had the road almost entirely to herself.

Kate flew through long, flat stretches of farmland, fields and pastures a grey-green blur in the twilight, and started climbing again as dark descended. The road worsened, winding, folding back on itself, the surface gravel and clay, slick and narrow and no edge to it at all. She had somehow gotten off the highway; she started looking for a place to turn back. Over a hill, around a bend; as a great, harsh strobe of lightning filtered through the giant old-growth Douglas fir, she saw the livestock gate half a second too late.

* * *

Just done washing up from dinner when the phone rang, Jake dried his hands and answered. "Alarm at the Mill Creek gate," his uncle said, brusquely. "Go check it out."

"Jā, Tēvoci." He gave Robbie a light play-punch on the shoulder. "Come on, little brother."

He waved at the gatehouse as they passed by, drove slowly for the two tense miles down the dirt road. Lightning up on the mountain threw crawlers near enough to make the hair on his arms stand up, filling the sky with vast rolling sheets of light, casting disorienting shadows through the trees. It was as ugly as this road ever got, and probably all for nothing: just a deer crashing into the fence in the storm, and Robbie said so. Then said, "Huh."

A car sat on the other side of the fence, front end trashed and a solitary figure inside.

The rain was easing off some. Jake pulled over and jumped out, watching the car as he flipped open the panel and entered the code. As soon as the gate started to swing open, the driver's door did too, and a woman stepped out. He frowned, uneasy. A stranger alone, on this road, in this weather, was nothing but trouble.

In trouble. He approached her with a steady gaze, a slow nod, and his hands visible, intentionally unthreatening. "Hey, there, ma'am. You all right?"

"I'm fine, thanks." She made a face at her car. "That, not so much."

"I see that." He stuck out his hand. "Jake Kelley. This is my brother, Robbie."

She shook. "Kate Hutchins. It's a relief to see you boys. I was figuring I'd hike out in the morning."

"The crash set off our alarm, thought we'd better come down and see. Good thing we did." He looked her over. She was older than him, not by much, early forties. Button-down shirt and jeans, but she didn't look like she lived her life in jeans; even soaked and in the dark, he could see her stylish haircut, her smooth, untanned skin. City.

There was something self-sufficient in her posture, though, and she didn't seem bothered about being drenched. She'd have hiked down the mountain and not thought twice about it. She would have been just fine if they hadn't come.

They had, and that changed things. "Well, you can't stay down here," Jake said. "How about you come up to the house for the night? Do you have anything you want to take with you?" Robbie watched, following his cues.

The woman looked at him for a long moment, and seemed to consider her options. Out here for the night,

soaked and cold, and a long walk in the morning, or
through that locking gate with two strangers. He got the
hesitation, sure. But then she nodded. While Robbie
followed her around to the back of the car, Jake memorized
the plate number. Washington State. She was long way
from home.

The drive back was quiet; he focused on the road.
She started to speak a couple of times and stopped, as if she
had questions but couldn't quite puzzle out how to frame
them. Then they came out of the orchard and over the
ridge, and she caught her breath.

Jake glanced at her and grinned. Yes, it was a
stunning sight, all the houses, the outbuildings lit up by
sodium lamps, the rain scattering light everywhere, the
great cliffs rising up and vanishing into the black. A movie-
set village inside a kaleidoscope, all in shades of orange and
midnight blue. "My family has been in this valley for more
than a hundred years," he said. "We've built up a decent-
sized outfit here. We're going to stop and let our uncle
know what's going on, and then take you up to the main
house. We don't have much call for guest quarters, but
there are a few empty rooms up there."

He pulled off in front of the gatehouse. Tẽvocis
Conrad was waiting, frowning at the sight of the new
arrival. "Company?"

"I wasn't going to leave her out there to freeze.
Someone can tow her car out in the morning. No harm
done." Jake glanced at Kate, shrugged a quiet apology.

Conrad stared at her for a minute, frown
deepening, and then shook his head. "You see to it." He

stomped back into the shack, and Jake sighed. They drove
in silence past the dark vineyards and big barns, over a mile
up the hill to the big, ancient farmhouse set against the
edge of the forest.

He pulled around to the side of the house, parked.
"I'm sorry about that," he said, and nothing further.

"Is it going to be a problem for you? That you
brought me up here?"

"Nah." A dismissive shrug, but he was unsure.
There would be a conversation, anyway, before the night
was out.

Robbie spoke up from the back seat, startling them
both. "It's all right. We don't get many visitors out here, is
all." He jumped out, grabbed her suitcase, made for the
door. "Come on!"

Jake laughed out loud, watching his young brother
dash up the stairs out of the rain. "He's right. Let's get you
settled."

* * *

He left her in the kitchen with Robbie and went to the
study, hoping to find his mother. There was no one
around, so he called down to town. A bored voice
answered. "Gunnison County Sheriff's Office, Deputy
Darzins speaking."

"Hey, cos."

"Hey, Jake." Tommy was alert now. "You all okay
up there?"

"Well, that's what I'm trying to figure out. Can
you run a license plate for me?"

"You got company? In this weather?" He sounded

just like his father. Jake could hear the frown.

"Jā"

"Weird. Even the local wildlife is staying holed up tonight. Sure, give it to me."

His mother came out of the inner room, looking tired, just as he was finishing the call. He hung up. "How is he doing?" he asked quietly, nodding at the door.

She shrugged. "It's rough right now. You know. What's going on?" He told her about the crash and the woman. "Where is she? Does she need any first aid?"

"Robbie's feeding her some pie and coffee. She said she didn't hit her head; she's just shaken up. Might have some bruises in the morning."

"All right. Put her up in Irena's old room." She smiled a little at the concern that must be showing on his face. "You did okay, kiddo." The phone rang. "Jā Droša, go ahead." She scrambled around the big desk for a pen, started taking feverish notes. Glanced up. "It's your cousin."

"I puzzled that out." Amused, patiently waiting for her to hang up. "What's he say? Trouble?"

She was already booting up the laptop. "Maybe. I need to check a few things out here. Go get her settled," she said again, absently. "Then tell your dad I need him down here. Family meeting."

* * *

Kate woke just after dawn, stiff from the crash and the long days of driving, and disoriented from dreams she couldn't quite recall. Not quite rested – she was never well rested anymore – but as the fog of sleep cleared, she found herself less jangled than she expected. She stood at the west window for a few minutes, watching swallows flicking in and out of the deep shadow cast by the sculpted cliff face. There was a low-lying mist in the valley, thinning out higher up near the house. It was serene, soothing.

The boys had given her a small upstairs room, tidy and spare, stripped of most of its personality and belongings. The bed she'd slept in was a white four-poster with a green and white hand-woven coverlet. A nightstand and shelf held a few abandoned mementos and books. She thumbed through those, finding teen romances, ten, fifteen years old, wondering about the girl whose room this had been. Then, restlessness taking hold again, she dressed and walked out into the hall, quiet and careful on the wide stairs, and found her way back through the spacious parlor and dining room to the kitchen.

The room was as big as her apartment, cheery and functional. One wall was stone, with a big fireplace set into it; the other walls were whitewashed wood. The appliances were modern, but the two big porcelain sinks were antique, as was much of the cookware. Steel, enamel, and copper, hung on wrought-iron hooks on the walls and stacked on tall open shelving by the back door, not artfully, but with access in mind. Morning sun filtered through white lace curtains on expansive windows.

A massive oak table dominated the room, at least ten feet long, its oil-finished surface pitted and scarred and sanded smooth again, over decades. A man sat at the giant table alone, reading a stack of papers, working on a cup of coffee. He looked up and smiled. "Good morning. You must be Kate. The one the storm blew in."

"Oh, I didn't expect anyone to be up yet. Yes, that's me."

She studied him: thick black hair, a little long and going grey, curling against a lined, narrow, porcelain-pale face. Eyes grey at first glance, but when he looked full at her she realized they were very light green, a startling, catlike color. On the back of his right hand, curled around his mug, was a faded tattoo, elaborate circles within circles and something that might have been text.

She mentally aged young Robbie by forty years, and recognition clicked.

His smile deepened. "This is a working farm. Everyone's up. I'm the straggler." As he unfolded himself, she realized how tall he was – a big man despite his slim build, six-three or more. He crossed stiffly over to the stove, topped off his mug from a half-full French press, and pulled another from the cupboard.

"I'm Goban. I'm the head of this outfit. Please, come, sit down. Do you want a coffee?"

She took the mug he offered, and noticed the faint tremor, the way he rested his hip against the counter. She turned away, busied herself adding the sugar and cream, discreetly not noticing as he worked his way around the table and settled, the slow care of his movements masking pain. Pride or habit, she thought, or some combination of the two.

She sat next to him and wrapped her hands around the warm cup. "You have a beautiful piece of land up here."

His eyes lit. "Yes, isn't it? We've been here... a long time." A complex emotion crossed his face, deep and genuine joy shot through with something darker. "A real diversified outfit – livestock, vineyards and orchards, apiary. And kitchen gardens and things, you know. We're pretty well self-sufficient."

"How many people live here?"

"Around eighty. Mostly family, some hands. Folks passing through who've stayed on, but that hasn't happened in a while."

"Yeah, I got that impression."

A sour note in her voice caught his attention; he frowned. "Right, you would have met Conrad last night. He takes himself too seriously sometimes. I'm sorry for that. I'll speak to him."

Kate contemplated that with dismay. "Oh! Please don't. I – I don't want any trouble for Jake and Robbie. They were very kind to me last night. I understand why everyone was caught off guard, me falling out of the sky into your laps. It's nothing."

That shadow again. "They're good boys. They did all right. And we're wary of strangers here, but caution is one thing and rudeness is something else." He glanced away from her. "Ah, the hero of the hour himself! Morning, Jake, Emmie."

The woman with Jake had the same family look. Bird-boned, more egret than songbird; lightly built, but tall and strong, with dark hair cropped around her ivory face in a practical bob. She dropped a hand on the sitting man's shoulder in passing, placed a light kiss on his cheek. "Good,

you're up!" she said to Kate. "Did you sleep all right? Have
you had any breakfast?" She was looking at Goban,
seeming worried, but he was smiling. He smiled a lot, Kate
noticed, a constant thread of quiet humor running through
his voice and manner.

"We've been having coffee, Emma. I haven't been
exerting myself on our guest's behalf. She wouldn't even let
me fix her a cup. Hostess away." So she fixed plates for
Jake and Kate, from sausage and fried potatoes kept warm
in the oven. Watching her work, Kate thought, *you're the
woman this happy kitchen belongs to*, and instantly liked
her.

Jake came over and sat down across from Kate. "I
just got back from helping my dad hitch your car up to tow
down to town," he said. "Chesterton, not all the way out
to Gunnison, although it might come to that. It's pretty
busted up. Dad was saying it might make more sense to
wait till we hear back from the garage." He watched the
older man, seeming to try to take a cue from him. "To
drive you into town, I mean. Don't want to strand you
down there."

"He's not wrong. Do you need to be somewhere?"
Goban asked.

She shook her head and laughed a little. *Relax, slow
down and enjoy the scenery.* "I'm on vacation. I'm not in
any kind of hurry."

That intrigued him, she saw. *You were in a hurry
somewhere*, his sharp glance said. She met his eyes steadily,
not caring to explain herself, and he didn't push the
question. If anything, it seemed he approved of whatever

he read in her silence.

He stood, and there was a small wince, whitening around his lips and knuckles for an instant, passing as he straightened. *You're good at this*, Kate thought. *You've had some practice at it.* "Well," he said, "you're welcome to stay here as long as you need. Or would like." He nodded, a gesture gracious in its deliberation, almost a short bow. "Emma, walk with me?"

"Of course." The two of them walked out, leaving Kate and Jake alone. He watched her out of the corner of his eye as he ate, seeming amused, waiting for her to speak. She didn't indulge him. They finished their breakfast in companionable silence, and she collected both of their plates and carried them to the sink.

* * *

"Kāda velna tu dari?" Emma hissed, barely past the dining room door.

"Oh, Emmie, settle down." His tone was mildly impatient, but he was laughing. She wasn't.

"You gave her your real name."

"You were listening at the door?"

"It seems like I had reason."

"Anyway, what can it possibly matter?"

"Who taught us how to talk to outsiders? You ..." Emma stopped, hand on the study door, and turned to stare. "You're flirting with her."

"Don't be absurd."

"You *are*, and she's giving it right back. What are you thinking?"

He smirked then, gently mocking her, as he pushed

the door open and stepped past. "Yes. That nice young woman, that Westcoaster, is flirting with a broken-down old farmer. Pity, maybe. More likely politeness."

That was the disease speaking; he knew better. All Emma's life, he had been the most formidable man in any room, able to charm anyone, own any conversation. He still was, when he made the effort.

This business of putting himself down was new. He had never done that, before. It was a sign that he was about to get much worse, and it frightened her, and made her sad, and angrier than she already was. "You were in the room for the conversation last night, weren't you? When Conrad was digging up what she does for a living?"

"The firm she works for does some military contracting. We have no idea what she does." He sat down heavily in the big chair by the fireplace. "Tell me, Emma, what's your impression of her?"

"She's careful. Smart. Not jumping right in with questions, but she's paying attention to everything around her."

"Do you think she's some kind of investigator?" he asked.

"I don't know, and that's the point, isn't it? She seems sincere enough. But if she wasn't on her way here, what was she doing on that road last night? Trying to get herself killed?"

"Maybe not far from it." Morning light and shadow played across the lines on his face, and Emma watched him, trying to puzzle out what was on his mind. "Try again. What is your impression of her?"

She sighed, looked away. Thought about what Jake had said last night, what she'd just observed herself. Reluctantly, she said, "She puts on a good face, but she's exhausted. Looking for a place to crash."

"Give her every opportunity to decide to let this be the place. She wouldn't be the first. We have, perhaps, forgotten where we started." He stretched out, put his head back, and closed his eyes. He looked so tired. "Look, think it through. If this is all some grand coincidence, then she's in some kind of difficulty, and what can we do but help? But if she's here looking for me, if she knows, then we're already lost. Our best shot is to buy some time to win her over, and having lied to her at the start won't make that any easier. So. Either way — decency and hospitality, truth where we can, and silence otherwise. No lies. Doing what's right bears its own rewards, you know that."

* * *

When Emma got back to the kitchen, the stranger was washing up. Relieved of guest-wrangling, Jake gave his mother a quick hug and a peck on the cheek and headed out the door.

Who are you? What do you want from us?

She started putting away the last of breakfast, not looking at the younger woman. Calming her nerves with familiar work gave her a space of breath to organize her thoughts. "So," she asked, "what do you think of our patriarch?"

Kate considered her words carefully. "He's absolutely charming. He doesn't seem well, though. Is he your brother?"

Emma laughed, startled. "Ah, no. No, he's not. Conrad's my brother. I heard you met him last night. How in the world did you end up on the mill road?"

"I'm not sure." Kate frowned, looking confused. "I must have turned at that town – Chesterton? – thinking it was another highway. Trying to head south, on my way to New Mexico."

"You were lucky then; you turned a couple of exits too soon. Red Mountain Pass was where you wanted to be. Do you know it? People call it the Million Dollar Highway. 'Wouldn't drive that road in bad weather if you paid me a million dollars.'"

Kate went ashen. "I've heard of it. I thought that name was because of the gold mines."

Emma tried for a reassuring smile. "Well, that too. I'm glad you found your way to us instead."

The women chatted for a while, and Emma started to relax. "Robbie, sure," Kate said, "but I would not have thought you were old enough to be Jake's mother. Stepmom?"

"No. Just good genes." She smiled.

"They're what, ten years apart?"

About that, she started to say, and then, *no lies.* Kate was trying to orient herself by puzzling out relationships, and that was fine, but down that road were questions Emma didn't want to have to wiggle out of answering just now. Better to leave it vague. "They have a sister in the middle, and I was away for a few years, between Irena and Robbie, working on my second MBA."

"Your second..."

"Ag biz. Purdue." Kate's eyebrows twitched, and Emma laughed.

"I'm not sure what I expected when Jake said *come up to the house for the night*, but this –" Kate made a sweeping gesture – "was not it. Can we take a walk? Show me around a little?" She was smiling, seeming at ease, but there was a tension in her. *Distract me*, it said, desperately, and it tugged at every nerve of Emma's mother-sense. Just a poor lost thing after all.

Emma nodded slowly. "It's shaping up to be a pretty day. Yes, let's."

* * *

They walked out the kitchen door and around to the front of the house, and Kate stopped in the path, stunned by her first full daylight view of the cliffs. Carved and smoothed by water and time into great stone curtains, they rippled in layers of grey and rust. A thousand feet nearly straight up, scraggly trees clung to crevasses, and small waterfalls, like silver ribbons, traced a downward path. The eastern cliff wall was in deep shadow; the western wall caught the sun coming over that near horizon, and the pale gold light reflected and filled and warmed the valley, burning off the last of the morning mist. Below them, the valley stretched out for two miles in the shape of a folded fan — high and narrow to the south, sloping down to rise again at the wider, softer north end into rolling orchard-covered hills.

She took a deep breath, took in the smell of turned earth and fog-damp stone, horses, and resinous conifer forest. Felt long-tense muscles in the back of her neck unknotting.

Two fluffy black-and-white dogs, dozing on the veranda, sat up, vigilant at the sight of a stranger, and padded over. Emma scratched their big floppy ears and made soothing noises as they nosed her in the ribs. They were as tall as St. Bernards, leggier but more lightly built. They watched Kate, calm but alert, as she took it all in.

It was a big house, she could see now; a proper manor, set up on a low slope on the edge of a remnant aspen grove, a dozen yards from the cliff face. The front façade was original, a lovely little Victorian with a turreted northeast corner and fretwork along the veranda, roses around the door. The back of the house had been added later: the huge kitchen and the adjacent dining room, a second porch, more bedrooms upstairs.

A rim of aspen had been left intact all along the base of the cliffs. The whole valley floor had once been wooded, Kate realized. It was cleared and developed now, encircled by a ring road. Smaller houses were tucked in among the edge of the trees between the west loop and the cliff, and a substantial creek tumbled alongside the east loop, dammed in two places. Up above the house, where the valley narrowed into a canyon, the first dam had a small powerhouse attached. The larger pond was down at the other end of the valley, with a two-story building on the shore, and two large companion buildings closer to the road.

There were vineyards, working buildings, corrals and coops, great expanses of gardens, and between the nearest gardens and the house, a sloping lawn. Signs of life scattered here and there: a cat chasing a chicken, a truck pulling away from one of the buildings, a teenager weeding in one of the gardens. But there was less activity than she expected. "A lot of people working up top," Emma said, in answer to her question. "The livestock is the biggest part of our operation. Other people are working indoors by now. It probably looked busier a few hours ago."

The village looked self-contained, almost medieval, but Kate saw traces of modern efficiency everywhere. There was a garage and motor pool and, up beyond the rim of the east cliff, the top of a telecom tower and the turning blades of a bank of wind turbines. There were no power cables strung through the valley; Emma pointed out the discreet markers of buried conduit. The hydro plant had been the second built in Colorado, she said, at the end of the nineteenth century. It had supplied enough power for the valley for a hundred years before they'd had to add the windfarm.

The two women walked down the ring road, through the village, along the edge of the vineyard, and back up through the industrial area. Emma pointed out the big building by the pond as they passed. "The sawmill was shut down when I was a little girl, but one of my cousins has opened it up again as a fine woodworking shop. The old lumber drying sheds are warehouses now — a lot of our income comes from the Internet." There was a textile shop, and an industrial kitchen. "We have a real craft community here. Everything that we sell we started out making for ourselves, and now there are people just clamoring for it all. It's a good balance. The land won't support big cattle running like they have in the lowlands, and we want quality of life, not a subsistence operation. Education for our kids. Top of the line, energy-efficient equipment. We feel pretty strongly about sustainability."

"You could live like this for a thousand years and the land would never know the difference."

"That's the idea." Emma frowned, pensive. "You can see why we're careful about who we invite in here. It's appealing, and it looks idyllic, but really, it's fragile. Everyone has to be committed, and everyone works very hard. It could fall apart so easily. It could be... mistaken for a cult, I suppose, and torn apart by well-meaning outsiders. So you come along, out of nowhere, with no apparent agenda, and it makes people edgy. Some of us want you to go away, as quick as possible. Some of us want to make sure you're who you say you are. If there's no resolution, he'll step in, but we don't want to stress him."

Stay here as long as you need to. Kate had brushed the offer off, thinking it nothing more than a polite fiction. But she found herself circling back to it.

She shook her head. Emma had misread her, earlier, her shock in the kitchen. It had just finally sunk in, at that moment, what a stupid, reckless stunt she'd pulled. Just like the night on the bridge: drifting toward the edge, pedal down, heading right into Lake Washington like a moth to a flame. Coming to her senses and steering away, bare inches from crashing into the low wall. She flinched away from that memory, blinked in the sunlight, took a deep breath.

Yes, she should get away from these nice people as

fast as she could, and take her problems with her; they seemed to have enough troubles of their own. "I just got lost and crashed my car. I'm not here to mess things up for you." Kate looked up the valley, back to the other woman. "I won't," she added, with more conviction than she felt. "I promise."

Emma did not seem reassured. "Maybe don't make promises until you know a little more of what you're taking on."

* * *

Conrad stood on the porch of the big house with his brother-in-law and nephew, watching his sister walk up the ring road with the other woman. *This*, he thought sourly, *is exactly what we put the gate in to prevent. Strangers, wandering around. People with no business being fifteen miles off the state highway in the middle of the night in a summer storm. Took a wrong turn. Sure.*

"*Avete*," he called, as they approached. No breezy *sveiki* or *hey*. A greeting, but also a warning, setting the tone.

Tēvs and Māmiņa had each brought their own language into the valley, all those years ago. They had each learned the other and English too, intertwining like so many vines over the years, growing into a pattern unique to this isolated place. Familiar from the inside, the polyglot texture of day-to-day conversation vanished into the background unnoticed, until a careful choice made a point, signaled an intention, or excluded an outsider. As he did now.

Em got the message, and she didn't look happy. He

continued in the insular language of their childhood. "What are you doing?"

"Following instructions. She asked, and I could not think of any reason to say no. I couldn't imagine what harm it would do for her to see that we, in fact, have a farm here." Emma glanced up at the house. "Have you – "

"I just came from the hospitality lecture, yes."

"He's not wrong."

Conrad snorted. "Is he ever? That's the problem, *sada ve*? He's capricious, and we all scramble around looking like fools until it crosses his mind to let us in on what he's thinking. It might be less annoying if he could deign to be wrong once in a while."

A tiny smile twitched at the corner of Emma's mouth. He frowned and her smile broadened in answer; he glowered, she grinned, and finally he laughed and shook his head. He switched back to English, nodding to the stranger. "I'm sorry I wasn't here earlier. I should have checked in with you first thing. Reg and Robbie here just got back from taking your car into town. It's going to take a couple of days to get it fixed. We'd like to offer you a place here in the valley while you're waiting."

She took her time. Glanced over at young Robbie, at Emma. Finally she gave a little shrug and a little smile. "I'd be delighted to stay, thank you." Conrad slowly exhaled his relief, and so did Reggie, standing next to him. "I'm no farmer, but I spent some summers on my grandpa's place when I was a kid. You could put me to work if you want. Or tell me how to stay out of the way. I don't want to be any more trouble – for anybody." Pointedly.

Conrad's lip twitched. Tough but earnest was a combination that got under his skin. He could find himself liking this woman, if he didn't watch himself. "No, you're our guest. We've moved you into a different room. There are books, and a better view. No Internet, I'm afraid, but a few more things to occupy your mind than in that empty little girl's room." *Stay out of the way.*

The room was a suite, in fact, in the original structure, on the other side of the stairs from where she'd been the night before. A small bedroom with a gabled dormer faced out over the valley. There was a sitting room with a well-stocked secretary desk, and a turret library. All of the furniture was antique and very fine, and the books were turn of the century, collectors' items. First edition Twain and Frost and London. "This was my grandfather's room for many years," Conrad said quietly. "Please be careful in here."

"Oh, I will," Kate breathed. She gazed around, hushed. "It's very gracious of you to let a stranger come in here." Then she surprised him. "I am so sorry for – for being a disruption to your family."

He wanted very much, just then, for her to be nothing more than what she seemed to be, what Emma and the boys seemed convinced she was. A nice young woman lost on the road, a stranded traveler, gone again in a few days, taking with her a pleasant memory of a place she'd passed through on her way to somewhere else.

But the damage control would be on him, if she was something else entirely. He started to say something but changed his mind, nodded a curt silent acknowledgement, and left her there.

* * *

The day passed. No one visited Kate, and she did not venture out. She explored no farther than the limits of the space, but it was rich, and she was not bored.

There were the books, of course, most after 1890, nothing after 1930, filling the built-in shelves of pale, fine-grained wood, lining the turret. This was the mature collection, she imagined, of the founder of this valley, perhaps the great-grandfather. A man at the end of his life, who, having worked hard to carve a piece of civilization out of the wilderness, finally found the leisure to explore the terrain of the mind. There were only a few pieces of clothing of the same era left in the closet, and various domestic objects. One shelf held ledgers; those were newer than the books, some into the early '70s. A trunk held antique linens, handwoven in intricate geometric designs. Another trunk was full of letters, unsigned, written to a woman named Amalija.

She picked up a bundle and started reading, hesitated, wondering if she was intruding, but continued anyway.

Amalija had died young, it seemed, but her lover wrote to her nearly every day, for over half a century. Thousands of letters. He wrote lovingly and at length of the children they should have raised together: Mikels, Nikolajs, Eleonora, Arturs, and Anna. Of orchards and vineyards she had planted, and of others, planted later in her memory. Of the grandchildren born, the sons and grandsons gone off to war. There was an entire stack, months' worth, about a visit to Amalija's childhood home in Latvia with some of the grown children. There were other trips, and homecomings. But mostly, the letters described ordinary days, doing the work of running a farm and mill, working out problems, planning for the future.

She was absorbed, enthralled, when a tap on the door startled her in the late morning. The clock said not quite ten. The woman resembled Emma enough that she must be a sister or cousin; she laughed when Kate asked. "Cousin. I'm Rita. I'm the outfit doctor here. How are you feeling?" Rita checked her for signs over for signs of concussion or whiplash, left a salve for her bruised shoulder and a bottle of aspirin, and reminded her to come down for lunch in an hour or so. But the lunch hour came and went; lost in the letters, she never noticed.

Sometime in the hours before twilight, the emotional weight of them caught up with her all at once. Kate went to the window for a while and watched the workings of the farm unfolding below. *What a thing you've built here*, she thought, awed. *These people, dedicated to your dream today as much as you were at the beginning. Loving this place in the tradition of the love that you had for it. For her.*

As the sun sank over the mountains, the cool settling air bringing another storm, a young woman brought her a sandwich and a glass of superb, deeply fruity red wine. She said she was Emma's daughter, and she stayed and chatted for a little while. When she left, Kate went back to the letters.

It was after midnight when she found the false

bottom of the trunk, and beneath it, threadbare clothing of a strange cut and fabric, and fragile, yellowed journals in an unfamiliar calligraphic language. Wrapped in tissue were two sets of glass pieces, five inches or so square, engraved with tight, tiny lines of text in the same language. Pressed between the glass, preserved exotic leaves and flowers still held some of their wild purple and blue pigmentation. Held up against the warm gold light of the old lamps, they scattered little rainbows across the room, the flowers casting suspended shadows like mothwings.

These strange objects filled Kate with foreboding and wonder. She put them away as she'd found them, love letters and all, tossed back the last of her wine, stumbled into bed, and slept hard, without even pulling up the covers.

* * *

CHAPTER TWO

Kate woke early again, and this time it was Robbie waiting in the kitchen. He made breakfast, oatmeal with chopped pecans and wild blueberry syrup, and stayed to eat with her. There was no milk, but when she asked, he brought some thick, sweet cream to the table. "You have dairy cows, but you have no milk?" she asked, intrigued.

"It all goes to my great-aunt's cheese operation. We're not big on milk. It gives most of us stomachaches." He shrugged. "We like butter, though. And cream." A spoonful of it swirled into the oatmeal was decadent.

After they ate, he took her to a large study off the dining room. It was paneled in the same pale silvery wood as the upstairs rooms, which she realized must be the valley's own aspen. It was a luxurious room, with a broad fireplace, a well-stocked bar, more bookshelves, and a large desk, busy but tidy. Reggie was there, the third man from the morning before. It turned out that he was Emma's husband, and he asked if she would sit with him and answer a few questions.

A few questions turned into two hours. Who she was. Where she came from. What she did for a living, where she'd gone to school, what she'd studied, who she knew. Friends and lovers. Her family, where they were from. What had brought her to Colorado, what had brought her to that particular stretch of road. He was a deft and considerate interviewer, and one might have easily mistaken what was happening for a pleasant and curious chat.

But Kate had some experience with debriefings, and a growing uncomfortable awareness of how isolated she was. So she went along, and as she answered all of his questions she tried to put some sort of pattern together. The questions about her work made her feel edgy and trapped; she snapped at Reggie the second time that he circled around to the subject. He was unperturbed, and rephrased the question.

"Are you this suspicious of everyone who comes through here?"

His eyes crinkled, amused. "Well, we're a dead end and pretty far off the beaten path, so... yes. People don't generally end up here by accident."

"I did."

A long silence, and then he nodded. "I believe you."

She frowned, and leaned forward, intent. "Well, then I suppose I should be grateful. But mostly, I'm wondering why you suddenly lost interest in how I found my way here, and started asking questions – questions you didn't already have planned out when we started here – about what I do for a living. You're good at this, but not so good that I didn't see you switching gears. What did I say that made you decide I'm more useful than dangerous?"

"I'm just trying to understand a different part of the same big picture."

"What do you see?"

"I see a smart and dedicated scientist who can't let go of a good puzzle when she's got her teeth into it."

"You people are a puzzle."

He laughed out loud then. "And you wonder why

you make us nervous."

She stared at him, warily. "What are you hiding?"

"We like our privacy."

"How did you find your way here?" she asked. "You said nobody does by accident."

"I grew up down in Chesterton. My dad had a vet practice; my brother and I spent a lot of time up here when we were kids. Emma's uncle gave me my first job the summer I turned fourteen. I went away just long enough to figure out I wanted to come back to stay."

"Military?"

"Navy. You?"

"No, but I've spent a lot of time in those circles. But you knew that." He just smiled. She stood, agitated. "I think I'm done."

"Of course." He walked around the desk to hold the door open for her. "Are you all right?"

"People keep asking me that."

She was unsettled by the gentleness in the look that he gave her. "Yeah."

* * *

She fled upstairs, back to the grandfather suite. Too drained to go back to the letters, confused and anxious, she found a collection of poetry on the library shelves. Frost's *Mountain Interval*. A ragged and ancient crow's feather served as a bookmark, and she turned to the place it marked. Bond and Free. *On snow and sand and turf, I see / Where Love has left a printed trace...*

Emma popped in an hour or so later, and invited her to eat lunch outside. They sat together on the big wraparound veranda, watching the farm activity below, making small talk about nothing of note. The morning had left her rattled, but she found this soothing, the pleasant company and the cool breeze off the cliff wall blowing across her shoulders.

I could be friends with this woman, Kate thought. *I could be friends with all of these people, if they would let their guard down. And of course, they won't.* No more than she could. The thought left her sad.

***

As they were finishing lunch, Jake stopped by and talked to Emma for a few minutes, again in that unfamiliar language. Kate wondered if it was the language of the old journals and the odd pieces of glass. After he left, Emma asked if her offer to help was serious. "Oh, please! I'd love something to do."

The peach harvest was coming in. So, for the rest of the day, she was in the kitchen, helping a group of women to blanch, skin, and chop the fragrant fruit. Most of the harvest, Emma explained, was going to farmers' markets nearby, or to the big industrial kitchen; this was the family portion. A few teenagers came in later in the afternoon, curious but shy. Emma's cousin Ilona eased the awkwardness by teaching Kate some old Latvian working songs.

They all sang as they worked, which saved them from having to find things to talk about, and the afternoon soon passed into night. A woman named Susan brought up a crockpot of soup for the workers from one of the other houses, and other people wandered in and out, asking

Emma questions, carrying messages or just chatting. By the time they had finished and cleaned up, it was nearing midnight, and she was tired enough to shower and stumble into bed.

* * *

On the third day, she woke late, her arms and back sore, but rested as she had not felt in a long time. No bad dreams; no dreams at all that she could remember.

There was a note on the desk, in a strong, feminine hand. Everyone was working, it said, but there was plenty of food if she cared to put some breakfast together for herself. *Don't forget to eat,* she could almost hear Emma chiding, and smiled. So she wandered down to the kitchen and puttered around for a bit, uncertain of what parts of the house she was welcome to explore. She took a cup of coffee out on the porch and sat where she and Emma had eaten lunch the day before, petting one of the big black-and-white dogs, who sprawled dozing under her hand. *I should have made Santa Fe last night,* she pondered, and then realized that she didn't care a bit about Santa Fe; she was content to stay right here. She poked around the edges of the lassitude, trying to puzzle it out, startled to realize it was neither fatigue nor fear.

It was an absence, she finally realized, of restlessness. Of anxiety. Something in her was settling.

Mid-morning, Robbie pulled up to the house in one of the trucks, and sauntered over to plop down on the porch next to her. "Mama sent me to check and see how you're doing."

"I'm fine. Just sitting here enjoying the view." He

nodded, stared out at the landscape, contentedly taciturn. That lasted for two or three minutes, and then Kate couldn't stand it anymore. "Robbie? Can I ask you a question?"

He looked at her, startled. "That's why I'm here."

"What is happening? Does anyone know anything about my car? Is anyone making any decisions? We sat in the study all morning yesterday and I answered every question you people had, and not a word since." Her voice rose sharply at the end, and she caught her breath.

"You want to go home?"

She shuddered. *No. I don't know.* "I want – something. To go home. To have something to do here to earn my keep. To know what's going on, at least. Something."

Robbie looked at her for a long time. "You were on vacation when you crashed, right?"

"Yes."

"My mother says that you look... more tired than anyone she's seen in a long time. She says you need to just be safe somewhere quiet for a while."

Kate felt a familiar tightness in her chest, a passing shadow. She pushed the feeling away, made an abrupt warding gesture with her hand. The dog sat up, alert, and she scratched his ears. "They put me to work yesterday. That was nice."

"That wasn't about you, uh, earning your keep, or anything." The idea seemed odd to him. "That was about letting the family see you, and getting you out of that stuffy old room for a while."

Letting the family see me? What the hell does that even mean? "You didn't answer my question."

"I really shouldn't speak for – look, I don't know what all is being discussed. Mama said there's going to be a family meeting tonight. Be patient a little longer?" Plaintive, worried. "Everybody likes you."

"I like everybody here too." Kate sighed. *I just wish I knew where I stand.*

* * *

She returned to the suite for the rest of the afternoon, immersing herself in the old ledgers. It seemed that the farm had been founded on some windfall, grown by investment in timbering, but every penny of that was poured back into the operation; it had been a hardscrabble subsistence deal until after the First World War. Up on the mountain, the family watched its first generation of children and orchards come of age, and brought in rugged mountain breeds of livestock from Europe.

After the war, they bought the first trucks and started shipping fresh fruit down into the rapidly-growing cities of the Front Range. The farm closed in on itself during the Great Depression, grew again during the forties and fifties, eased out of the timbering business, and then, somewhere along the line, it seemed it had grown enough. Diversification and the clearing of new land slowed, and their energies turned to infrastructure, equipment purchases, producing new streams of revenue from existing production, paying children's tuition. Kate had a sense of continuity; someone careful and thoughtful, with a long view, had overseen this property and community for many years. Kate wondered about the founder, when he'd passed on, and what his relationship was to the absent Goban.

She lost track of time, and was startled when Robbie popped his head in. "I'm to bring you down for dinner."

There were fifteen or so people in the big dining room. Kate started to make sense of the family tree, or at least a few near branches. Conrad and Emma were the second and fourth of four siblings; a sister worked in Denver, and their older brother was dead. Cousins gathered: Rita; Ilona and her brothers; Theo, whose wife, Susan, had brought dinner up the night before. Reggie, and Rita's wife, Marina. A few of the younger generation. There were too many names to remember, and the intensity of family resemblance among the entire clan was stunning, gathered together in one place: a sea of startling cat-green eyes in long pale faces, clouds of dark hair, and the occasional outsider spouse standing out. Kate felt as though she was being debuted. There was roast lamb and fried trout, mounds of potatoes and piles of grilled vegetables on the buffet, and bottles of mead and wine. She let the crowd swirl around her and tried to pluck out what observations she could.

The mix of languages was generational, she realized. Everyone was meticulous about speaking English to her – university-educated American English with a flat Rocky Mountain accent, the faint trace of an Eastern European cadence underlying it. Speaking amongst themselves, the younger people only occasionally threw in loan words, some Latvian and some in the other language she'd heard a few times. She had not begun to pick up either, but was starting to tell them apart.

But Emma's generation spoke a fluid blend of the three, sometimes switching from one to another in mid-sentence.

After a while, Conrad came and stood next to her, out of the way, his vigilant eyes scanning the crowd, observing. "Your family has an interesting post-immigrant thing going on," she said.

"It's useful sometimes," he replied curtly. "For privacy." And then he stalked off, asking his cousin Rita a question in the third language, underscoring the point. Kate sighed. Emma watched from across the room, and wandered over.

"I'm sorry my brother's a grouch," she said.

Kate shrugged. "He has a tough job."

"Right." Emma's look was appraising. "And I have business partners I've known for thirty years who are less... generous than you are. I know my family is odd, okay? You don't seem bothered by it, though."

"I try to judge people by their actions." Kate sipped her wine. "Not just by how hospitable you've been to me. You've built something pretty impressive here, and you didn't do that by being mean or self-centered. Or short-sighted. I'm intrigued."

The older woman didn't reply, but she looked thoughtful.

On some unspoken cue, people started drifting into the kitchen. Kate was wondering whether she should follow when Rita appeared next to her. "Kate, come have a nightcap with me," she said, with crisp authority. "Jake, join us."

Kate raised an eyebrow at Jake. He shrugged, his face bland. "Sure," she said, and followed the two of them into the big study.

"What would you like?"

"Oh, nothing, thanks." At the other woman's questioning glance, she added, "The wine was lovely and I think I've had enough. Also, I can read, *Kate, come talk with us somewhere away from where everyone else is talking about you,* just fine without the booze. But thank you, really."

Rita laughed out loud, delighted. "Oh, my cousins are right about you! You'll do fine." She took her time at the bar fixing herself a whiskey sour, and sat down on the settee by the big stone fireplace, tucking her slender legs under her, gesturing for Kate to sit.

She did, in the matching chair, uneasy. Toyed with the silver pendant she wore on a chain, rubbing it like a worry stone. "What are they talking about, exactly?"

Rita leaned forward. "I was noticing that earlier, may I see?" Her fingers brushed the linked polygons of the molecular model. "Serotonin! That's pretty. I thought it was an abstract shape, from a distance." She sat back and sipped her drink. "They're talking about whether to extend a more permanent invitation to you."

Kate's eyes widened. "I don't understand."

"Your car will be fixed soon. You've been here for three days, and at any time we could have taken you down to town and set you up in a hotel. Did you wonder why we didn't?"

A sharp laugh. "Yes. I have. I've also wondered what would happen if I straight-up asked."

Jake spoke up. "We'd have taken you. Of course. Someone, probably me, would have driven you to Chesterton, by a different road, and not one that would make it easy for you to find your way back here. But if you decide to stay, it would be as a hired hand, more or less. You'd be welcome to come and go as you please. You'd have access to some of the operational knowledge of the farm, things we don't share with outsiders. And the social support of the family. If you want to work, you'd sure be valued for your skills."

Rita picked up the thread. "You've been a considerate guest, and we've been unfair to you — confined to this house, with only a few people to talk to, without answers to your questions. It's not kind and we're not proud of the way we've treated you. We'd like to think we're better than that. If you're going to stay here any longer, it's not to be as a passing visitor."

Kate was stunned. "That's... unnecessary," she fumbled. "I'm grateful for your hospitality. I've enjoyed my time here quite a lot. But I –" *can't stay here? Can I?* The thought she had been edging around for days, carefully not opening up the cascade that lay behind it. She hesitated, tried again. "I've been here, eating your food, reading your precious books, taking up your time, and I don't know how I can say thank you. Contribute. I feel a little lost."

"Of course." Rita nodded. "We have some ideas about what that might look like." Jake's lips tightened; Rita met his eyes. Some tension rose between them and settled again just as quickly, an ongoing dialogue that Kate wasn't privy to. She continued smoothly. "But we can all see that you're recovering from something. If we can offer you a place to get yourself healthy again, then you'll give back in your own time. I have faith in that. We all know how important that is."

Vertigo washed over her. Was she that transparent to these strangers? She had thought she was doing better, these past few weeks of travel and solitude. Kate reminded herself to breathe; the desire to bolt abated. She absorbed the invitation to take time and sort out her troubled head in this serene place.

Despite all the weirdness, insularity, and uncertainty, for no reason she could articulate, she liked these people. She wanted to feel safe here.

A thought fell into place. She looked around. "What does Goban think? I haven't seen him since the first morning. Some of you must have spoken to him about this. Why isn't he here?"

"He's had a few rough days. This situation in stressing him – that's another reason we need to settle this. He likes you –"

"We had a five minute conversation."

"He's decisive." Rita was amused by that. "You made a good impression. He'd like for you to stay, if you want to."

"I think I need to hear that from him."

"Maybe in the morning. We'll see how he's doing."

The wine found its way home; Kate's head was

pounding. She stood up. "Well. You are both delightful and it's been a lovely evening, and I'm quite honored. But it's clear you're not all on the same page with this, and you have to talk with the others. So thank you, and good night, I think."

Jake stood quickly, shared some silent exchange with Rita. "I'll walk with her." She nodded.

On the stairs, Kate asked, "So what was that all about?"

Jake hesitated. "Rita and Tereza –" that was the absent aunt – "want to offer you a job. My mom thinks that it's not fair. That if you're going to be family, then we should be focusing on helping you with whatever you need to take care of yourself, not putting any kind of obligation on you."

If you're going to be family. Kate didn't know how to respond to that. "What do you think?"

"I'm not sure. I think it would be hard to know whether you want to stay without knowing more about the job. But I take my mom's point too. She knows what she's talking about."

"Jake... what job? I am a research biochemist. Why are you people so interested in my work? What are you messing around with here?" He just looked at her, steadfastly silent. "I – I left home to think, because I was having issues with my work, the ethics of the work I was doing. The time I've spent here just reinforces that. I'm not sure I even want to be in research anymore."

"You didn't tell my dad that yesterday." He had striking eyes, intense sea-green, and that appraising gaze

left her feeling both unsettled and reassured, a prickle at
the back of the neck that skirted the edge of familiarity.

*Your dad wasn't the one who pulled me in from
the rain. Why do I feel like I know you?* Her throat closed
over the words; she felt panic rising again. "Things have
changed since yesterday morning."

"Yes, they have." He shook his head. "The vote
hasn't been cast yet. I can't, okay?" They stood at the door
of the grandfather suite, facing each other for a moment.
His eyes were troubled; he seemed to want to say more
than he had. But he just pulled her into a rough, quick,
brotherly hug. "It'll all work out. Good night, Kate." And
he was gone, and she stood in the hall alone, still baffled.

* * *

CHAPTER THREE

Morning found Emma and Conrad in the kitchen at first light, for a few quiet moments before other people started drifting in. Upholding a long tradition.

She handed him a mug. "Are you all right?"

He laughed and shook his head. "I know when I've lost a fight."

"Viss būs labi," she murmured, smiling. *It will all be fine.*

"You think so? This isn't just a hire. Everything is changing, and I can't see where we'll end up."

"Everything was changing anyway. He's dying. Are you ready to face that? I'm not. We have a chance here. Maybe it's a long shot, but it's something, and I'll take it."

"Well, you're the bravest of us, you always have been. When did I get old and timid? That boy of yours — it's not going to be many more years before he's running this place. And I'm wondering when I quit being the man who would bring that poor girl in from the rain and damn the consequences. Maybe it's past time to let the kids take over."

That boy, she thought, looking at her brother, *turns forty at the new year, and that is just about the age that you were when you took the job. Maybe you're not wrong.* But she scoffed. "Hell, Conrad, you'd have done the same thing. You'd have groused about it, but you wouldn't have hesitated." She glanced away. "But, not for nothing, you could let him know that you approve of what he did." He gave her a sudden startled look of understanding, and started to speak, but then the back door banged and Irena came in with the eggs, and he just tossed back the rest of his coffee and headed out into the morning.

* * *

Kate found several other women in the kitchen just after sunrise. Emma and Irena were there, and Emma's cousin Paula, and Marina, but no Rita. Nor were any of the men anywhere to be seen. It was as though the previous night had never happened. There was small talk, oatcakes and thick slabs of heavily peppered bacon and fried potatoes, washing up. Irena was recently married, and pregnant, and anxious about it; the older women were amused, indulgent.

As Kate was about to give in and ask what had happened the night before, Marina glanced up at the clock, stood abruptly and left the room. A moment later she came back smiling. "You're wanted in the study."

So Kate followed the other woman through the dining room, to the door of the big study. It seemed to be the room where the important conversations in this house happened. Ruth was walking out; she caught Marina's hand, held on, then nodded at Kate, and gestured for her to go in alone. *Here we go.*

Goban was stretched out in the upholstered chair where Kate had sat the night before, by the dormant fireplace, head back and hands folded, his face gaunt and pale. Kate thought that he was asleep, but his eyes opened at the sound of the door. He smiled, the warmth of it enlivening his face, the fatigue falling away. He gestured to the chair next to him. "Please, come sit down. Rita said you wanted to talk to me."

"She also said you haven't been well." She sat, hesitant and edgy.

He made an offhand gesture. "Nothing new. So. The kids have decided to welcome you to our little refuge here."

Is that what happened last night after I left? "Evidently. I don't understand why." Also: *kids?*

"Because we like you. You're gracious and considerate. You inspire some trust, in these people who don't trust easily. That's a gift."

"I... don't know what to say." If she'd found it disconcerting, the ease with which she had begun to feel fondness for this place and its people, she found the news that the feeling went both ways even more startling. And yet...

He laid a hand over hers, and she felt the tremor in his cool fingers, and her nervous fidgeting stilled. "Say yes. Work out the details later." His grey-green eyes were luminous; the smallest hint of a smile tugged at the corner of his mouth. It would be so easy to let herself be enchanted, taken in by his charisma and warmth, to forget that roiling just below the facade of this idyllic village was barely-contained turmoil. That there was an edge of desperation in all of this, an uneasy feeling that they wanted her for something, and that she still didn't know who he was or how he fit in.

She disentangled herself, stood abruptly, pacing.

"What do you think?"

He glanced away, and for an instant she thought she saw uncertainty there. Vulnerability. When he looked back at her, it was gone. "It'd please me for you to feel like you could make a place for yourself here."

"Jake said something about a job. What is it that they want me to do?"

He seemed puzzled. "We're nowhere near that yet. Emmie was insistent that you've been through a rough time and need to rest and think."

That startled her. There was no duplicity in him that she could sense. *So what are they not telling you?*

Just then, Rita slipped back in and took in the scene: Kate pacing, Goban watching her, the fatigue and strain on his face. She nodded, as if settling some internal assessment. "How are you doing?"

"I'm fine. Quit fussing. Kate and I are having a nice chat." He smiled disarmingly up at her. She found herself smiling too, even as she shook her head. *A nice chat. Very revealing. No actual information exchanged.* "All right. I'll get out of your way. Get this settled, will you?" He stood, wincing, gathered up the papers spread out over the desk, stumbled, as Rita stepped in to support him, smooth and practiced. She took the bundle of papers, walked with him through the second door that Kate had not, till just now, noticed. He paused in the doorway, looked back at her and gave an oddly encouraging nod, and disappeared.

A moment later, Rita came out and sat on the edge of the desk. "He'll keep working for a bit and then sleep, I suppose."

"I'm sorry. I had no idea. Rita – what is wrong with him?"

Rita sighed. "If we knew that, Kate, I'd sleep a lot better myself." She was composed, her pale face glass-calm; but Kate realized, looking at her, how much tension was coiled in her body. "This has been going on for about eight years now, but there were traces of it long before that. It's autoimmune, both progressive and cyclic. It self-limits, or has in the past, but every cycle is a bit worse. I'm a clinician, not a researcher, and this is out of my field. I've been able to ease the symptoms some, that's all."

"Who else has he seen?"

Fear and frustration. Something Kate couldn't identify; she tried to puzzle out the emotions at play on the older woman's face. "It's complicated."

All at once, Reggie's questions made sense. "So this is what it's about? Nothing to do with the farm at all. Why me? What do you think I can do?"

"I have no idea, but I'd love to give you a chance to take a crack at it."

Kate walked to the window and stood there for a moment, looking up at the aspens and the cliff wall, and the blue sky beyond. "It's not like the movies. I can't set up a basement lab and whip something up. If he has some kind of metabolic imbalance or whatever, maybe – maybe – I can help identify it, but developing pharmaceuticals is multimillion dollar work for teams of people over years. I would absolutely do more harm than good. There are better ways to go about this."

Rita waited, quiet while Kate tried to sort out the

tangle of questions. To pick one and tug on it.

She turned around. "Also, who is he? I've trying to puzzle out how everybody is connected, and there's a big gaping hole around him."

"You've been reading the letters?"

"Is that a problem?"

"Oh, no." Rita smiled a little. "We more or less invited you to, didn't we? Have they clarified things for you?"

"No, they haven't. They've confused me more. There's a lot missing," Kate said. Rita raised an eyebrow, a trace of laughter around her mouth, and waited for Kate to continue. "Like... Emma talked about the sawmill shutting down when she was a girl, but I read the ledgers, and the records for the mill end in the late forties. Other things. It's like there's an entire generation just missing."

"No, that's right." The amusement deepened. "My cousins and I are the second generation born here; I am Arturs and Annika's daughter."

"That doesn't make any sense, Rita, you'd be, what —"

"I'm seventy-nine."

Kate scoffed. "That's ridiculous." The woman could not be more than fifty-five. Rita shrugged, spread her hands. Kate frowned.

Now Rita stood up and paced, unaccountably nervous. "I'm sorry," she said, and sat back down, composing herself. "It's been a long time since I had this conversation with someone." Any hint of humor was gone; her face was dangerously serious. "Kate, this is the threshold. Beyond this point, you're — *gatseptat.* Kindred." *Family*, Kate thought. There had been something lost in translation, talking with Jake in the hallway last night. More to this than she understood. "I'm here to answer whatever questions you care to ask, but if you choose to go down that road, then you have a responsibility to the people here. It's important."

The older woman was really afraid, Kate realized. She felt her own agitation drain away. "Rita, I've worked in classified research for a long time. I'm not unaccustomed to privileged information."

"Oh, I know. That was one of the factors that came up when we talked about bringing you in."

"Bring me in to what? Can we quit dancing around it?"

"Sure." Some uncertainty within Rita seemed to settle. "You asked who Goban is. You'll hear people call him Tēvs sometimes; it means Father. He's father to all of us. He founded this valley."

Kate stared at her, confused, unbelieving. "That's impossible. He'd have to be, what, a hundred and fifty years old?"

"About that, yes. A hundred and sixty. We think. We're not sure how old he was when he came here."

Kate blinked, frowned. "Came here... from where?"

Rita sat, tense and silent, waiting for it to connect, and then it did. Kate considered, for a fleeting instant, the possibility that it was a joke, or an elaborate test before Rita gave her the real story, but then all the puzzle pieces slid into place; strange as it was, it made sense.

He was not a cousin.

It was his bed she'd been sleeping in — his old room, his desk, his letters to Amalija.

His diaries, the text in the center of his tattoo, in some strange language — some alien language. His old flight suit. His pressed-flower mementos of another world.

She felt weak in the knees. "How many people know?"

Rita guided her to a chair, a gentle hand supporting her. "The grandchildren, my cousins and I, our spouses, and our children. A very few select employees and friends over the years. You, now." She waited, gave Kate a minute to get her head around it.

"You understand — what's wrong with him — it might be environmental, it might be genetic. It might be the cumulative effect of decades on a world that rejects him, or something missing from his diet. He might really just be sick. I mean, he might have gotten sick if he'd never come here at all. We just don't know." Her despair was palpable. "My fear — on one hand, I'm afraid that the flare-ups are going to continue to get worse, and closer together, and one of these times, he won't come back. The fever will kill him, or do damage he can't recover from. On the other hand, I'm afraid that it won't. That he'll go on like this, outliving us all, suffering. He's our grandfather, Kate, and he's suffering."

"Wow." Kate was subdued, thoughtful. She looked at the closed door to the bedroom suite, deeply disturbed. But the panic of the day before, she realized, was absolutely gone.

She had been drowning, for a long time now. Pulled under, crushed. These weeks away had been a joy, but the passing of the days had been on her mind, inescapable. She had been bracing herself to go back, to the nightmares, to the morning panic attacks and evening drinking, from the day she left.

Never go back. Stay here. Fix something instead of breaking things. The lightness of that release was a physical sensation; her skin tingled and her heart was racing. If for nothing else but blessed relief, she said, "Of course I'll help." And immediately thought, *what have I gotten myself into?*

They talked for a long time, after that. Rita shared what she knew of her grandfather's early history. It wasn't much. He had been living alone on the mountain for perhaps a year, unaware of the frontier towns on the other side of the massif, when a group of homesteaders passed through in 1890. The family knew almost nothing about his home world; the computers were destroyed in the crash, all of the navigational data lost, and he didn't like to talk about it.

He was on the high side of middle age. They thought his normal lifespan might be another half-century, but they had no idea what impact the disease was having. His descendants lived a long time, but not as long as he would. The first generation had all died in their eleventh decade, and Rita's generation was just now settling into their middle years, in their late seventies and early eighties. Kate gasped, understanding a little more of the complex landscape of emotion that animated those thoughtful features. She pushed that away; too much to process right now.

She marveled at their trust and thought, *they must not feel they had any choice at all.* Poor Rita, working alone against insurmountable odds, all those years; then Kate and her medical research background showed up on the doorstep out of the blue. That sense of desperation made sense, now. *I can't let them down,* she thought, surprising herself with the unbidden thought. She had no idea how to begin. But she was in the thick of it now.

The door opened and Irena peeked in. "How is it going?"

Kate smiled up at her. "Rita and I have been having — a good talk. I understand better what my place could be here. I think I'll stay on, at least for a while."

The younger woman's face lit up. "Oh, that's great! That's wonderful news." She glanced at Rita. "Does he need lunch? Do you two?"

"I think we're about done here. I've overloaded poor Kate, I think. Go ahead and check on him."

Irena passed through, into the inner room, and came back in less than a minute. "He's up and about. I'll be right back." She looked at Kate. "He asked about you." And she was gone.

Kate looked at Rita, who gave a little encouraging smile, gestured toward the room. "You're one of the inner circle now."

She pushed on the door, tentatively, and entered the inner room. He was sitting at a secretary desk, working on a spreadsheet on a laptop. He looked up and saw her, desperate relief and fierce vindication playing across his face, but it did not diminish the strain lines around his eyes. She walked over and rested a tentative hand on his shoulder. "Rita and I talked. About everything. I understand what you meant now, the gift of trust."

* * *

The next days were a whirlwind. There was so much territory to cover — a more thorough orientation on the farm, more family to meet, legal paperwork, and all of it during the early days of the harvest. She worked, and paid attention, and learned.

Jake's cousin Valerija brought her a laptop. There was wi-fi only in parts of the first floor, Val apologized, and directed her to a smaller study-library off the parlor. Kate accepted what she was offered with gratitude. Checked her email, which was thankfully sparse.

She looked at a map app and found the valley, studied the satellite photos. Tried to make sense of how she had gotten turned around, and where she had found herself. A fork in the road, a bend off to the left where she should have taken a right, an easy mistake to make in the dark and the storm.

Hanging in the dining room was a framed reproduction of a hand-drawn map: *Ghost Towns of the San Juan Range*. A few inches from the top edge, a dot marked "Darzins' Mill." Reggie laughed aloud when he saw her looking at it one morning. "They sell copies of this at the historical society down in Telluride. Makes Conrad crazy. Every summer there are a few tourists ringing at the gate, looking for the 'ghost town.'"

In the evenings, she spent hours with the letters and ledgers stored in the old suite, making sense of the timeline and the breadth of the family history. She joined Goban in the study twice, once for dinner, and then, a few nights later, for evening drinks along with Emma and Reg. He was quiet, and clearly in great pain, but insisted that he welcomed the company.

On the eighth morning, she woke and thought about home. Lying in the big bed in the cool shade of the great stone wall, without tightness in her chest for the first time in months, she decided it was time to check in. After breakfast, she hiked down to the ridge just past the property line, on the road they'd driven in on the first night, and called her mother.

"Where are you? Are you all right? You were supposed to be home yesterday. Katie, I called the police, I didn't know what to do."

"You — what?" *Oh, no, no, no. Oh no.*

"We were worried. You on the road alone."

Kate rubbed her forehead and sighed. *You complain that I never call or visit, and then you do things like this.* "Mother. I'm a mature woman. I can take a road trip without checking in every day." Then it sank in. "We... who?"

"Craig called me the day before yesterday. He said he hadn't heard from you in a week."

Kate's brow furrowed. "Craig? He had no business calling and worrying you. We do not have... that kind of relationship."

"Well, that's changed, hasn't it?"

"Mom, I have no idea what you're talking about."

Hesitation. "Oh... I've spoiled the surprise."

Confusion blossomed into horror. This was the kind of thing her mother did: the innocent game, the comments dropped in passing to throw one off balance, the guilt trip, the undermining gossip. Kate had come to terms with it years ago, but hung on out of some vague sense of duty.

And her mother had found a kindred spirit. *Damn him. Just assumed, and told her it was a done deal. I might have even said yes, too. Before everything changed. Oh no.*

"No, Mom, you've armed me for a difficult conversation. We are not engaged. We're not going to be." She took a deep breath. "I am perfectly fine, I am having a lovely time, and I'm extending my vacation a little. I... have found a nice little retreat in Colorado. I'm doing some thinking." Not quite a lie, but close enough to come back to bite her, she was sure. "It's a bit of a hike to get a cell phone signal, so I'm probably not going to call again until I get on the road, okay?" She made some more small talk before promising to email and ending the call.

She was dialing the lab when a sedan came over the ridge, pulled over. A tall, striking woman stepped out. Luxuriant salt-and-pepper curls tumbled around her pale face, which put Conrad's glower to shame. "What are you doing?"

Kate met the glare, unflinching. "You must be Tereza. Hi. I'm Kate. I just called my mother to let her know that I am not dead in a ditch on the side of Highway

50. Now I'm calling my boss to say I won't be in to work tomorrow."

"I know who you are. You should have talked to Conrad first."

"Oh, I intend to, as soon as I get back to the house." Watching the other woman's face, she finished dialing. Navigated the directory and got the lab director on the line. Chatted for a few minutes about nothing in particular, and then took a deep breath and settled down to business.

"See, here's the thing. I've stumbled into an opportunity. I've been offered a job, and I'm going to stay on down here. But it'll take me a little time to get back there to wrap things up and I don't want to take any grief about it."

David snorted. "What? You're giving me notice over the phone? And you want me to lie to your mother about it?"

The incredulity made her laugh. He'd been her boss for a long time; he knew the score. "Just don't tell her I've quit, if she calls. Tell her I extended my vacation, and didn't give a return date."

"Well, true enough. I can cover you for a few more weeks. What's this great opportunity?"

Steady. "It's... a conservancy."

"I didn't know that was your thing."

"Neither did I, until I spent some time in the place. I'll be doing analysis, supporting fieldwork. Running my own lab." It was not an actual lie. As such. "The guy who runs the place is amazing. I want to stay here awhile and learn from him." *Shut up, shut up.* Tereza looked like she might make a grab for the phone at any moment.

"Well, I'm sorry to hear it, but you sound excited. You know you have to come in to debrief. Should I send your personal things to your apartment?"

"That's... fine, that's great. I'll let you know when I'm back in town. Thank you."

"Good luck. Thirty days, Kate. I cannot give you more than that."

The drive through the orchard and the lower valley was silent, frigid. Tereza pulled into the motor pool, turned off the engine, took a deep breath. "What were you thinking?"

"I was thinking that people might worry. I was right. My mother called the police. Between GPS" — Kate held up her phone — "and the credit card activity that stops cold in Crested Butte, and the VIN number on my car, which, by the way, was delivered by your brother-in-law and your nephew to a shop fifteen miles from here, where it's still sitting right now, if someone decided to put some effort into looking for me, they would trace me here. Now they won't. I was looking out for the family, okay?"

Tereza's lips tightened; she did not look at Kate. "You really are sitting there and talking to me about looking out for this family. You don't know anything. You've been here for a week."

The hostility was shocking; Kate had not encountered anything like it, even during those first few wary days. "I thought you wanted me here. You and Rita."

"I wanted to hire you to do some consulting.

Strictly short term, strictly need to know. That's what we do with outsiders, we conduct business. Not — what's happened."

Kate stared at her. *Do you not understand anything about how research works?* She barely held back from blurting that thought out. "You wanted me to do analysis without any direction? Any information about where the material came from, or the problem you're trying to solve? That's completely ridiculous. That wouldn't have been of any benefit at all. Rita figured that out right away."

"Rita and I disagreed."

Kate stared out the window, down the valley toward the vineyards and orchards, trying to decide what to say. She needed time, to tease out the underlying tensions, map the fault lines. This woman was key to a part of the story Kate didn't yet understand, but wanted to, if she could avoid making an enemy right now.

The silence settled. She realized Tereza was studying her, as if seeing her for the first time. "You thought the vote was unanimous."

"I... thought it had to be."

A short, humorless laugh. "Not hardly. It was a majority, barely. This is a benign dictatorship passing for a family business; when my grandfather sets his mind to something, it happens. The family will abide, but we're not all happy about it." Tereza met her eyes, briefly, the hostility softening, then glanced up at the house. "Oh, well. Come on, then. Let's go talk to my brother."

* * *

CHAPTER FOUR

"Why didn't you let someone know you needed to make calls? One of the boys could have run you down to where you could find a signal. Or you could have used one of the house phones." The hunch of Conrad's shoulders, his wary frown, belied the nonchalance of his tone. Trying to keep it light, and failing.

Yes, that was just what she wanted, Kate thought, indignant, still chafing. Someone hanging around monitoring her. She hadn't realized how much a source of contention her presence here still was, how fragile the mutual trust. *Step carefully,* she thought. She'd taken the leap, she reminded herself, signed up for this of her own free will. *So play by their rules.* She sighed, made a conciliatory noise, and relayed the substance of the calls.

He made a phone call of his own, nodded at her as he hung up. "You did fine. One of my boys is a deputy down in town. He'll keep an eye on the chatter, see if anyone comes around asking any questions. And your car will be done by noon, so someone will bring it up later today. No need for it to sit in the shop and start people wondering when you're going to turn up asking for it."

"That's good. I am going to have to go back at some point. For a few days, fairly soon. Close things up."

"Whenever you need to do."

This conversation was making her dizzy. Conrad's unexpected decency after Tereza's hostility, and the sudden uncomfortable awareness of how complacent she'd gotten here, how quickly, without knowing much of anything at all about these people who treated her with suspicion while they shared their secrets with her. Some of their secrets, anyway. One. *The important one.*

* * *

Kate was agitated for the rest of the day. The phone calls, and the emails that she sent after, had stirred up all of the anxiety over going home that she thought she'd gotten past. Tereza's hostility left her with fresh uncertainty about staying. She doubted her own judgment; the emotional rollercoaster left her tired.

She went for a long walk above the hydro dam. The valley narrowed as it sloped upward, the cliff walls only two hundred or so feet high up here, but not more than two dozen yards apart. Even now, in the heat of the afternoon and almost August, it was cool and damp and green, and the creek sounds soothed her. Among the alders and aspens, she saw a doe with a half-grown fawn, birds, an enormous blood-red dragonfly. In the beauty and the solitude, she breathed the humid, fragrant air, slow and deep, until the knots in her stomach and between her shoulders eased. Found her composure again. It was going to take time; these people were adjusting too.

But they offered, she thought, *they invited me.* And then she was embarrassed by her own petulance.

In the lengthening twilight, she had a desperate craving for a reality check, for the company of the one person whose forthrightness she was confident of, so she found her way back down to the house. No one in the kitchen, no one around. The quiet bothered her; in the stillness, she heard muffled voices drifting out from the study.

Emma, Reggie, and Tereza were gathered in there, talking, intense and worried. They all stopped and looked at her when she walked in.

Kate looked to Emma for some direction. The older woman shook her head slightly. Not a good time.

The days of isolation and polite compliance, the morning's weirdness, came over Kate like a wave, crested and broke. *What's wrong? And what happens if I go off script?* She strode past the little group, who — to her surprise, perhaps on account of theirs — made no move to stop her, and into the inner room.

Goban was a big man, but he looked small and lost on the antique bed, drenched in sweat, tossing. Irena was there, caring for an IV, changing an empty fluids bag out for a fresh one. She turned. "Oh."

"What's happening? How long has he been like this?" Kate stared down at him.

"Yesterday and today. The fever came on night before last. This — this is what a really bad day looks like, Kate. This is not the first time." There was a shadow of worry around her eyes, but her face was calm and professional.

"How long will it last?"

"Tonight, maybe sometime tomorrow. Then he'll sleep, and then he'll be better for a while."

Rita had mentioned a recurring fever. She watched his lips move, a stream of subvocalization, too soft and slurred to make out. "Is he hallucinating?"

"Probably. We don't know. He never remembers."

Kate reached out, brushed a wet lock of his dark hair away from his forehead. Her fingertips connected with his skin. So hot.

She looked up at Irena, saw how tired the younger woman looked. "I'll stay with him for a while," she said. "That's what I'm here for, right? To help figure this out."

Hesitation, then Irena nodded. "Thank you."

His eyes opened, a sudden moment of clarity, and he reached for her hand, startling her with the strength of his grip. He seemed to focus on her, but then he was gone again, into the fever dream. So she sat on the edge of the bed, watching him, just holding on, helping Irena with ice packs and whatever she needed.

After a while, she pulled the chair over from the desk to sit at the bedside, and tried to make sense of what she was seeing. More than a century on an alien world — what did that do to a body? He didn't look like an alien; he looked perfectly ordinary. No, not ordinary. He must have been so strong before the disease wore him down. Robust, charismatic, and handsome: he would have been an unstoppable force. And his family, all from the same mold.

His family, who shouldn't exist. *Who are you? What are you? How are you even possible?* She could feel her world upending in the face of this mystery; it was the challenge of a lifetime, and although she knew that she would almost certainly fail, the fascination was in the attempt.

He seemed unaware of her presence, but touch calmed him, so she kept a hand lightly on his arm, even as she dozed off and on herself. Just oxytocin at work, or was he conscious of her on some other level? He slept fitfully, and the night wore on.

Autoimmune, cyclic, progressive, Rita had said. Getting worse. This was not, she had a gut certainty, a chronic infection. This was a metabolic imbalance, something happening within his body chemistry. What had triggered it in the beginning? What continued to trigger it? Maybe a poison, or was some fundamental, needed nutrient missing? These were things she could study, a familiar landscape.

What a really bad day looks like. Kate had watched him get sicker over the last eight days, and this, she fervently hoped, was the worst of it. She needed to understand the structure of the cycle. As she drifted in and out of sleep, a testing and analysis protocol started to take shape in her mind. In the early hours of the morning, she rummaged around the desk for pen and paper to make some notes, and that was what she was doing when Rita came in, as the sky was beginning to lighten. They talked, quietly, for a while.

The fever broke a little after noon and he slept like a ragdoll, clinging to her hand. Gingerly, she pulled her fingers out of his still-tight fist, and stumbled upstairs, and slept , all afternoon and on through the night.

* * *

On the tenth morning, she woke to soft predawn light and the sound of voices and laughter tumbling through the big house. Following the noise out into the hall, she met up with Jake at the top of the stairs. He was grinning broadly. "You're going to see something you haven't seen before today."

A cluster of people gathered in the kitchen, all talking very loud and fast, and in the middle towered a flushed and laughing Goban. He met her eyes as she came in, sketched a wave. "Kate! Beautiful girl. Join us! Robbie, get this woman some coffee." She walked over and hugged him wordlessly, and he draped his arm around her shoulders and squeezed tight.

He leaned down and whispered in her ear. "Thank you." She looked up at him, startled, wondering what he really remembered of that long fraught night. He grinned. "Do you ride?"

"Horses? Um. Not in twenty-five years."

"You never forget. Jake! We're going riding today. You kids haven't shown Kate the whole farm, I bet."

She pulled back and eyed him, doubtful. "Are you sure?"

A dark shadow crossed his smiling face. "There are only so many good days," he said in a low voice. "Not so many as there used to be. We make the most of them." And then he was being pulled into some other conversation, and Robbie handed her a mug; Jake was on the phone to the stable, and Kate was helping Emma dish up eggs. "Is he always like this after a fever?" she asked, her voice pitched for Emma's ears only.

"For a week or so. Then he'll go downhill, bit by bit, and it will be like when you met him, and he'll stay that way for a while."

Emma's green eyes were shining as she watched her grandfather move about the room, laughing, carrying on three conversations at once, cheerfully devouring a mountain of food. "This is how he was all the time. Before. He has always had the energy of ten men. Built this place with his bare hands, mostly before we were born. Him and my uncles. Just look at him." She touched Kate's hand, a fleeting gesture full of hope and faith. "We want him back like this. All the time."

"Me too." *Oh, me too.*

* * *

Someone scrounged up some riding boots in her size — Tereza's old boots, as it happened, well-made and worn. The mare they brought was petite and gentle but lively. Kate had an uneasy sense of being *handled*, like a valuable and fragile package. She wasn't happy about the feeling. But it fell away once she and Goban were mounted and off, away from the house.

They took the road down the length the valley, past the millpond and beehives, over the ridgeline and down into rolling foothills, between the apple and peach orchards and as far as the gate, then followed the fence line to the creek that marked the western edge of the fruit orchards. He'd said she hadn't seen the whole farm, and he was right; she had the idea that the valley was it, more or less. They rode upstream through the pecan orchard, along the moss-verdant bank trail to the place where the cliff wall rose up out of the foothills, and then left the creek behind to follow the top of the cliff toward the line of big wind turbines on the rim. A vast high meadow spread out to the west, several times larger than the valley, with two big barns and a stock pond down near the fence, and a huge flock of sheep grazing above. There were a few men and a truck far on the other side of the meadow; they waved, but did not come over. Three of the big black-and-white dogs patrolled the flock. One of them broke off and came up alongside his horse; he reached down and scratched her ears and made soft, loving noises at her. "This is Jauka," he said. "She's my special girl."

They were Mollos dogs, Goban said, a Balkan breed as old as Western civilization. He had come across them while he was looking for hardy mountain sheep breeds in Europe in the 1920s. "They're gentle and sweet with people, but I've seen two of them kill a grizzly bear. Seen them gather around a ewe with an early lamb and keep it alive with their own body heat in a spring blizzard. Best dogs in the world."

He gestured out over the valley, the farm below, the eastern wall beyond. "The other meadow's half again the size of this one. We own the rim, but the rest of it is government land; we lease it and run the dairy herd and the horses over there." The property, he told her, was surrounded by national forest on three sides, the northwestern terminus of a broad band of unbroken wilderness that stretched all the way to Taos, two hundred miles away.

At the top of the big meadow, just below where it narrowed to a sharp ridge, there was a small octagonal building with a domed roof. "Is that an observatory?" Kate asked.

"Yes, it was Julia's. Conrad's wife." Old grief crossed his face, regret, and something like homesickness.

"We built it many years ago. Every so often one of her old friends passes through here, stays for a few days. Not so much in the last few years. It's a good telescope, but the computers aren't up to date anymore."

They passed the observatory, and followed the high ridge until it opened up on a sloped expanse, a few hundred feet wide and perhaps half a mile long, thinly wooded, carpeted with alpine wildflowers. They rode to the apex of this smaller meadow, where they had a superb view of the entire mountain range, a few miles to the south but seeming close enough to reach out and touch, lavender-grey and snow-draped above the tree line. He named the near peaks, east to west: Uncompahgre, Silver, Matterhorn, Wetterhorn, Coxcomb.

They rode back down a short distance, into a softly sloping bowl full of young aspens that they had skirted on the way up. Kate realized that she was looking at the crash crater, eroded and overgrown. Down near the ridgeline toward the big meadow, half-sheltered in the woods, was an odd little round cabin, walls sloping inward like a beehive. Long unoccupied and grey with age and weather, but lovingly maintained.

On the other side of the crater was a tiny graveyard, ringed by a low stone wall. She dismounted there, walked among the graves; there were twelve. She recognized the names. She felt as though she knew these people, from his letters. Five children, three children by marriage, an entire generation outlived; she could not imagine that heartache. Anna's husband, Kate knew, had died in England, and she'd come home afterwards to spend the last decade and a half of her life here. Mikels had never married. There were three from Emma's generation. Julia; the oldest brother, Henriks; the wife of one of the cousins. Fragments of stories that she had not yet begun to piece together.

Kate traced her fingers along the letters of the tall, simple headstone in the northwest corner. *Amalija Darzina, 1870-1899. Mīļotais – Beloved.*

All through that long ride, he talked, endlessly, as though the talking had been pent up during the interminable weeks of wretched pain and fatigue. *That's probably true,* she thought, thinking back to the reserved man she'd met in the kitchen that first morning, and shared evenings with in the quiet study. She mostly just listened, tossing in a question from time to time. He was a solid field guide; he knew every plant, every wildlife track, every stone and distant peak.

"I have never gotten used to internal combustion engines. I don't like them. We use electrics a fair bit around the farm, but whenever I can, I ride. You can see, smell, feel your surroundings. So can the horse, and he'll tell you things if you know how to listen. Horses and dogs have saved my life more than once.

"My youngest son went to fight in the revolution — the Latvian Independence; do you know anything about that history? Nineteen years old, and he was just a baby when his mother died. He had no memory of her. But he went to fight, to help toss the Bolsheviks out, and when it was over, he wrote and asked if I would come to help with the rebuilding. So that was how I saw my wife's country for the first time.

"I used to do a fair bit of traveling, but I would always wake up one day in some strange place and find that the fascination's worn off, and all I could think about was coming home. This world taken whole will seduce you and then break your heart, but a small piece to come home to will heal you. I know these mountains like I know my own skin.

"Up here, everything's a little harder, but it's worth the effort. With our hard winters and rocky soil, none of our crops return the kinds of yields you get down in the lowlands, but what does grow is magnificent. It's true everywhere that you have these hardy little mountain farms; I grew up in country like this. The river valley down there is more like the country that Amja knew, and we talked about setting our stake farther down, but we had come to love it up here, the valley, the cliffs. I wouldn't choose anything else.

"Things have changed, these last thirty years. We were so isolated up here for so long. You could go months at a time without going into town, without any visitors from off the farm at all. But it's harder to make an outfit this size blend in to the countryside, anymore. We had to put the gate in when we started getting a lot of campers headed for the national forest wandering in by mistake. And we've started to participate more. Tereza did a stint as a county commissioner a few years ago, and we have a few kids living down in town now.

"The internet changed everything about the way we do business, but it's not the first time. We've reinvented ourselves half a dozen times, building on whatever we were doing before. Mining, then milling, then fruit and wine, then sheep, then dairy cattle, now this luxury goods internet business. You can try to limit change, or at least make it on your own terms, but in the end, you adapt or you die. Another generation, and the life we knew in the early days will be gone, but the farm and the family will still be here."

Resting on the ridgeline, looking out at the great jagged peaks, she asked, "What brought you here? How did you end up here, originally?" *From... wherever it is you come from.*

A sharp look, a slow smile. "I was a geological survey engineer. I was running a survey when I crashed."

She stared at him. "Into the Colorado backcountry, at the end of the gold rush. My God. You must have made a killing."

"Oh, yes. That's where the early capital came from." An old sorrow darkened his face, but did not take away his smile. "Amja was the brains of the outfit. I didn't know anything about how things worked here then; I just knew how to find the gold. She took it into Denver, came back with whatever we needed to build the farm. Set up the investments. Figured out when the mines were drawing too much attention and got us out of that business. The valley was always her vision, and every day that it lives on is a gift."

She must have thought you were an angel from heaven come to save her. Kate had learned pieces of the story from Emma. Amalija was sixteen years old when she left home for Daugavpils and teachers' college, barely nineteen when she arrived in Philadelphia with a new husband and his relatives. Headed west, toward the promise of a farm and a schoolhouse of her own, she found herself violently widowed instead. Nowhere to go but forward. Riding out of Ouray looking for a stake, when the stranger stumbled out of the woods, not speaking any language they knew; but then again, almost no one in this hinterland spoke her language. So she stayed on with him, in his tiny hand-hewn cabin up on the meadow, and they taught each other everything they knew, and built the pretty little house, built onto it later. Ten years, three miscarriages, five babies, and an unstoppable hemorrhage with the birth of the last one. Then all those years of letters. *She saved you too.*

"Have you ever tried to go home? Or to reach out?"

He stared out over the broken, undulating country, the starkness of it reflected in his face. "I've spent most of my life not more than five miles from this spot right here. The better part of a hundred and thirty years, Kate. Can you imagine? My wife and children are buried here, and I will be too. This is my home. No, those people hold nothing for me."

"Not even the chance of a cure?"

"At what cost? The turmoil it would cause for two worlds? I'm not that selfish. I'll take my chances with Rita. And with you, now."

Kate frowned at that; it seemed a bad bet. She wanted to argue. But his expression was resolute. *There's a lot you still don't know,* she told herself.

"What are they like?"

"Like people here, more or less. A few good people trying to make sense and beauty out of the chaos. A few real bastards. Mostly people muddling along, not thinking about much but how to scramble to stay in the same place. I guess I worked for some of the bastards, although I didn't know or care at the time. The crash was the best thing that ever happened to me."

* * *

In an office in a low stone building, built into a bluff on the forest edge of a medium-sized city, a maps archivist was metadata-tagging new downloads when a clerk from another department stopped in, packet of documents in hand.

"Survey 99502-778-98. I don't know this one."

"It went down in the field some years ago. Review seems to think that the driver went down soft, went renegade, set up his own little pirate operation out there somewhere."

"Pirates," the archivist scoffed. "Who believes those stories?"

The clerk shrugged. "Someone higher up, it seems. If he's still alive, he'd be middle-aged now. He's got to be tired of the frontier life, ready to come in from the cold. Development wants to offer him amnesty in exchange for turning over whatever he might have found – if it's valuable enough."

"So they want him tracked down."

"That's the idea."

"The time they must have on their hands at Review, to dredge up this shit. And it's my time that's wasted, like I'm not already overburdened. What if there's nothing there? Not a squeak from this fellow in –" the archivist flipped open the file – "eighty-seven years. He's probably rust on the side of a mountain on some rock that's not even on a map yet."

"Then you get the closure bonus anyway. So have fun with it." A wink, a nod, and the clerk was on his way. The archivist sighed and tossed the packet onto the growing stack.

* * *

CHAPTER FIVE

The kitchen, formerly so quiet in the mornings after everyone went off to work, became the hub of activity. Goban holding court, one of the young cousins keeping the coffee and food flowing, a constant parade of people and papers and discussions. Tereza figured prominently in these. "When our grandfather is well enough to work, by God, we *work*, and it keeps our heads above water through the next downturn."

Harvest season was nearly in full swing; right behind the peaches came potatoes, and then, Emma told Kate, shearing and apples and grapes and nuts, and finally the fall slaughter. Fourteen-hour days from the first of August right on through the end of October, and those who worked on the business side were not spared, because contracts needed to be negotiated, deadlines and deliveries met.

Left largely on her own, Kate spent most days in the small but well-outfitted clinic, where Rita worked with Irena and the other nurse, Sylvia, and which did, indeed, have a very serviceable basement lab. None of the equipment was cutting-edge, but it was all of good quality and well-maintained. She became immersed in old files, reams of bloodwork reports and clinic logs, the meticulous records that Rita had kept over the years, trying to puzzle out a place to start, any loose thread to pull on.

* * *

Tereza pushed open the study door, late in the evening, after helping with the washing up, when everyone was settling in for the night. The desk lamp was on, but her grandfather was sitting in the big chair, watching a fire. He looked up and smiled.

"Can we talk?" she asked.

"Of course. Come in. Would you like a drink?" He started to rise, but she waved him off.

"I'll fix one." She went over to the bar, poured a glass of port, came over to the fireplace. "I haven't had a chance to just sit and talk with you since I got home. You're always surrounded by people." He had a glass in his hand too, whiskey from the look of it, and an old photograph. She looked over his shoulder in passing as she sat down, and caught her breath. "Oh, Māmiṇa."

He handed her the photograph, and she studied it more closely. A formal portrait, taken in the smaller study, in the old part of the house. A statuesque blonde, fashionably dressed in a fine silk jacket and skirt, standing, with her hands on the shoulders of a small serious-faced boy. The tall young man next to her, dark-haired and light-eyed, his hands on her waist, looked at her with naked adoration. "Look at that smile," Tereza said softly. "You never see people smile in these old photos."

"You couldn't get her to stop smiling for anything. We were so happy. Our whole lives ahead of us." He looked at her. "I look at you kids and all I see is worried faces all the time."

"We have a lot to worry about." She rested her head against the brick of the hearth, studied him through half-lidded eyes. Let the acid-honey warmth of the port roll over her tongue. "This young woman. Do you really think she has a shot at finding out what's happening to you? Do you think she's reliable?"

"Rita thinks so." He shrugged. "It's worth a try, isn't it? And — you know, little bug, I've had a good long run. I've built something here to be proud of. I've long since handed over the real work to you kids, and I'm tired. If I can see the end from here, I'm content with that."

"I'm not," Tereza said, bitterly. "None of us are. And it frightens Emma when you talk like that, so stop it." She looked at the photograph in her hand again, at the grandmother she had never known. *You've just been alone for too long,* she thought. She knew a little about that. No attachments, no loyalties except to the family. The land. The secret.

She felt his gaze on her, looked up. "Don't you feel it?" he asked. "The end of everything we know is coming. I have lived much of my life in fear, and just as long in denial. But I'm ready. I'm tired of secrets, lies, and loneliness." She started to protest again. He waved her quiet. "I'm not talking about death. I'm talking about *change.* Are you ready?"

* * *

"So, what we already know," Kate explained to Emma and Tereza over lunch one afternoon, "is that Goban is not, um, an *alien* alien, okay? He's fundamentally human. Within the normal genetic and biochemical range of human, anyway. There are some interesting differences, and I'm poking at those."

"But –" Tereza looked skeptical. "We know otherwise. Kate, we know. He came here on a survey ship built by an alien civilization, from another planet, in another solar system. He crashed here. I've seen pieces of the ship with my own eyes."

"Right. He came here, where he met and married a human woman and had babies. Your mother, and her brothers and sister. Um, naturally, without medical intervention." Not without blood and heartache. "There's no way that he is the product of some other entire evolutionary history. It's not possible. Has Rita not explained this to you before?"

"So, what does that mean? He's from some mythical lost colony, or...?"

Kate shrugged. "Or the reverse? There are a lot of stories — both in science fiction and in old folklore — about beings from, I don't know, other worlds I guess, coming here, tinkering with our ancestors' biology. Australopithecines or whatever. There's no way for us to know, without talking to them, getting into their scientific knowledge base, and he's made it clear that's not on the table. The point is, this changes everything. It's a much less enormous, terrifyingly daunting job than I thought I was getting into at the start." Not impossible, just the next thing to it.

Emma looked hopeful. "So you can cure him? Or at least diagnose him?"

God save me from non-scientists. She chose her words with care, not wanting to lead them on. "I have a much better shot than I thought I did at being able to explain some of the processes underlying what is happening to him. Some of those findings might suggest a direction for

Rita to look for some useful therapies. No promises."

The sisters looked at each other. Tereza nodded. "Well, that's something."

"I know we got off to a rocky start –" Kate said, but Tereza made a dismissive gesture.

"What's done is done. Look, whatever gets our grandfather healthy, right?"

Kate stared at her, and sighed.

* * *

"Every day?" Goban frowned.

"We're going to start doing bloodwork every day. I need the whole baseline to study."

"Rita has done a lot of bloodwork, at every stage of the cycle. Don't you have access to those samples?"

"Oh, sure. But they've been taken at different times, and...." Kate shrugged. "Rita has approached the problem as a clinician, trying to figure out what factors she can introduce or withhold, drugs or nutrition or whatever, to disrupt the cycle, affect the symptom presentation. I'm approaching the problem as a biochemist, trying to create a conceptual model to explain why it's happening in the first place. I need to analyze changes from day to day as the cycle develops, document the process. Consistency is important."

So Irena started bringing her a blood sample every day. She stared at readouts, ran tests, searched for changes that might represent a buildup of some toxin, depletion of some nutrient, anything. Marina was her occasional lab partner, doing some kind of work involving the dairy herd. The company was pleasant, but she missed having a team.

She took to riding the little mare up in the backcountry in the evenings, to clear her head, following the creek up past the powerhouse, into the steep, winding canyon, or down through the orchards and into the foothills. By the low light of the old lamps, late at night, she read stacks of letters, trying to build a deep medical history, hoping for a clue from another direction.

One night, her fingertips brushed the false bottom of the old trunk. She gasped. *Oh, my. These pieces... have been here all along. How did I miss this?*

The clinic was still and dark. In the basement lab, she laid one of the pressed-flower plates on the bench, slid a scalpel between the two panes, held her breath as it popped open. Prepared a tiny sample, and fed it into the DNA sequencer. Then she put a second sample in one tube of solvent, and threads from the old uniform in another.

She sat at the lab bench, put her head down. She had no idea what she thought she was going to get out of cutting into those treasures. There had to be something. Clues in anything. She had been working for a month, and she was nowhere.

She left the big machine running, closed up the building, and walked up the hill again. It was clear and chilly, colder at the top of the valley than it was down at the clinic. A snow-laden wind funneled down from the mountaintop, through the canyon. In the lowlands it was barely coming into autumn, but up here, winter was just around the corner.

That thought stopped her, right there in the road. She had put off thinking about it, but her thirty days was almost up. Going away was the last thing she wanted to do, but she needed to do it, so she could come back to the work.

She told Goban over coffee, the next morning.

"We were wondering. How long will you be gone?"

"I don't know. A week or two. I want to get back here before winter settles in. I have a question for you." She had wrapped the pressed-flower plate in a linen handkerchief; she unfolded it and showed it to him. "I need to know — is this from your home world, or from one of the worlds you surveyed?"

His fingers brushed the imprinted text, his face a complicated terrain of memory and wonder. "I put these away a long time ago."

"I thought so. I found them in the bottom of a trunk in the old bedroom."

He looked up, furrowed his brow. "You are stirring up things better left alone." He caressed the pressed-flower plate again. "Yes. This is from... home." She wondered how long it had been since he'd looked at these precious objects, if he'd half-forgotten they existed at all.

You are skirting the edge of a mess you can't get away from, I think, from too many years of leaving things alone. The foreboding overwhelmed her again, and she could not put words to it.

She left that afternoon, before she could change her mind. The sun was setting as she crossed into Utah, and she caught a few hours of sleep at a rest stop outside of Provo. She drove west with the sun, watched it set again over the Columbia River from a little park on the side of the highway, and pushed through the last few hours in the gathering darkness. The city lights were jarring, but the sea scent was on the wind, and she was so tired. And then her own well-lit street, the apartment complex driveway, the familiar parking spot outside her door, the stairs, the key, and she was home, home, as if it had all been a dream.

* * *

She wandered the city adrift, that first day. Remembering what it was like to go to a coffee shop, check the mail, rent a storage locker, as if she had been on the mountain for years instead of five weeks. She let friends take her out to lunch, let her mother take her home and cook her dinner, and then broke the news, and it was both worse than she thought possible and not nearly as bad as she expected.

She listened to all of their chatter and caught up on their lives. She didn't talk much. What was there to say? That she'd found peace in her own company again; that she hadn't known how deeply she'd craved silence. That when she closed her eyes, all she could see was the swallows against the sunlit granite wall, the green dark shadows of the vineyards against the edge of the orchard, and the shimmering light in the aspens. That she woke before dawn now, and cried herself to sleep at night, missing the smells of apples and horses and old books; but when she did sleep, it was without nightmares.

* * *

She checked in with the apartment manager. David, bless him, true to his word, had seen to having her few personal things packed up neatly and mailed; the box was waiting for her in the office. One less chore to deal with. She put in notice and set up a PO box for the apartment deposit and paperwork, and then called a moving service and made an appointment. It took half a day to sort through and pack the things she wanted to take back to the farm with her — books, a few clothes, fewer mementos. She went shopping for jeans and good boots.

On the third morning, she went to work to process out. She went through the motions numb, almost disembodied, as if it were someone else making small talk and signing papers, sitting through the excruciating debriefing, answering questions. The guard walked her to the door at two o'clock, and she sat in her car and stared for a while at the bland steel-and-glass building. She'd been happy here, a long time ago; thinking back, she could not remember where she'd gone off course. She had lost her perspective, lost her nerve. Stayed far longer on a bad road than she should have, out of a sense of duty, or because she didn't have any idea what else to do, despite knowing where it led, if she had cared to stop and think. *I am never,* she thought, *never going to let things get that bad ever again.*

That made her cry, finally, and then she found a fast food restaurant to wash her face and pick up some lunch. She drove down past Tacoma to the botanical gardens, spent the afternoon walking among autumn's remnants of the summer's glory, and watched the sun set over the water at Chambers Bay.

On the fourth morning, it was raining. She bought

a coffee and a pastry on the way out of town and headed north on the coast highway, composing a story that covered the necessary details and avoided outright lies. There was only one person whose good opinion mattered all that much to Kate, and so she was sitting in line at the border crossing before she swallowed her anxiousness and called.

In downtown Vancouver, she worked her way through lunchtime snarls of traffic, and then there was the big red brick facade of Waterfront Station rising up, with the water and mountains beyond. She found a parking spot and walked the few blocks to the cafe, right on the water. The rain was letting up and the patio was empty, except for a blonde in a black-and-red floral print dress.

The smile that broke over her face left Kate breathless, and when she leaned over the low decorative fence for a hug, there was desperation in the embrace. "Katie! I'm so glad you're here! I have been hearing some weird shit about you."

Kate grinned. With both feet: that was Gretchen. "I'm glad I'm here too. What kind of weird shit?"

"You had a nervous breakdown, quit your job, skipped town. People keep asking me what's going on. I tried to call a couple of times."

Kate laughed, came through the gate and sat down. "No, that's it more or less, just... not quite in that order. I have been in the land of no cell service. Wow, you look fantastic."

Gretchen dimpled. "So do you. So much better than when I saw you last, so you have to tell me, what is going on with you?" Her blue eyes went wide. "Oh, you really did it. You finally quit that awful job."

Careful, careful. This is why we've stayed friends for so long. Because she reads me like an open book. "There was nothing wrong with that job; I just wasn't cut out for it."

A sour face. "You're the only person who believes that. So, you did it! Vacations work! That's wonderful. Do you have something new lined up?"

"Yes." Kate smiled. "Vacations work. I spent a lot of time thinking, and I stumbled into, um, it's a long story, and I'll tell it to you sometime, just not — yes, I quit. I've been offered a new job, in Colorado, and I like it a lot, and I'm moving down there. I'm just back to close up my place."

Gretchen took a deep breath. "Wow, Katie. Just like that. Colorado. Wow. What kind of work?"

"So, this is the other reason I'm here. I have a project for you, if you're interested." She pulled a sample tube from her bag and passed it to Gretchen.

"What is this?"

"It's a sample of fabric, from a flight suit, from a crash. The aircraft was experimental. The pilot survived. It was... many years ago, and now he's an older guy, right, and he's having some bizarre health problems, and I'm working with the family on that. I have a couple of different theories, and one of them is that he was exposed to something nasty in the crash. And he has no access to that information. So that's what I want you to do — run a full analysis on it and see if there are any unknown toxins, or anything weird, or whatever. The lab I have isn't set up for this type of stuff. I'm working the problem from the metabolic side."

"Huh. I assume the family's run an FOIA request?"

Kate gulped the water the waitress brought, grateful for the hesitation. "Uh, it was not an American aircraft."

"Oh. That makes it more complicated. Not impossible, though; you should look into that. Any volatiles will be long gone, but I'll see what I can do with it." She turned the sample over, stared at it, thinking. "How long are you in town?"

"The movers are coming to pack up my place on Tuesday."

"I should have something for you before then. You don't get to leave without letting me come down and see you. We'll make it memorable." Gretchen grinned. "You like the work?"

"I love the work. It's important, and I think I can help these people. It matters to me. And it's the most beautiful place you can imagine. I... miss it terribly already."

"And? Someone interesting?"

Karen smiled a little. "There is nobody, Gretchen, just the work."

"You keep telling yourself that."

"Really."

"Okay." Smirk. "Let's order."

They ate trendy sandwiches and gourmet soda, and talked about anything else for a while, and then Gretchen was running out of time. They walked together, back to the station. "I'll call you; we'll get together before I leave," Kate promised.

They hugged, and held on. "I hope this job is everything for you, and I mean everything, because it's too damn far away and I'll miss you so much."

"It is everything. I love you."

"Love you too."

* * *

On the fifth day, she agreed to meet Craig for lunch, against her better judgment. They hadn't spoken since she left; she had sent one furious email, after that disastrous conversation with her mother, and ignored the replies. But she felt a lingering guilt.

"I broke up with you," she said as she sat down. Just to get that out of the way.

"You broke up with me in an email. People do crazy things on vacation. I don't accept the premise."

Kate frowned at him. Had she found him charming, before, or just convenient? "I don't really think you've got a choice."

"After two years, Katie, I think I deserve more than that. We're not twenty; we both have something invested in this." He leaned forward. "I wanted this to be different, but I'm not walking away without making a point." He opened his fist, revealed a small jewelry box. *Oh no.*

She shook her head, pulled back. "No. Don't do this. It's just uncomfortable for both of us."

He left the box on the table, a silent challenge.

"There has to be a reason."

"Okay, here's a reason. My new job is a room-and-board gig. I'm moving to a ranch on the side of a mountain. The nearest town is fifteen miles away. There is no place for you."

"So I'll move to a town fifteen miles away. I can work from anywhere, Katie. It's not about the job."

"No. No, it isn't. I don't want to be mean, Craig, but I don't want to be here. Doing this. With you."

"You wanted it enough when you left," he sneered, crude and vindictive. She flinched. *I didn't. I just didn't know any better.*

Kate looked away. "I was so miserable. So miserable. I needed to make a change." She surprised herself with that; she hadn't known it until she spoke the words. She had been working so hard on convincing herself and everyone else that she was fine, that everything was just fine. She'd had nothing left to put into taking a good hard look at what was wrong and what she needed to do. The farm had changed that.

"You don't just dump a perfectly good life. People don't do that."

She snorted. "People do that all the time."

"Responsible adults don't."

"Responsible adults *do*, most of all. You take care of yourself when you have to."

"This isn't what taking care of yourself looks like, Katie. You're acting like a child. I'm not going to let you do this."

She stared at him. *Who are you?* "You really don't

have a choice," she repeated.

"Do you think I won't follow you?"

She looked at him with horror. The cheerful, easygoing guy she'd dated all these months, the outrageous flirt of the grand romantic gesture, was gone. Had never existed at all, she suddenly realized; it had been a performance in service of a goal. The man across the table from her, she felt certain, would cut her to pieces for spite, and not just her, anymore. Rita's voice in the back of her mind: *you have a responsibility to these people.* "You are delusional."

"I am determined. I liked what we had, Katherine. I'll fight for it."

She shook her head. "This is why I broke up with you! I didn't know it at the time, so thanks for making it clear."

"What?" He seemed genuinely puzzled. She had him off-balance, for the first time. A calm fury overran the rising panic, overwhelmed it.

"You asked me to lunch, which I wasn't crazy about, but whatever, I thought, we can have a civil conversation, close this door, you might even show some *interest* in me, in my new job, which, by the way, thank you for asking, I am enjoying ever so much more than my old job. But no, you had to do *that* instead, and I'm sitting here thinking, wow, *Katie, look at you, dodging that bullet.* We are done. Stay away from me. Stay away from my mother. Stay away from my friends." She shoved the ring at him roughly, grabbed her bag, headed for the door.

"You've never had a problem being a bitch, Katie."

She froze, turned. "Well, you never called me a bitch until I dumped you." She walked out of the restaurant, left her car behind, boarded the first bus she saw without looking to see where it was going, and fell into an empty seat, shaking.

Kate rode the bus for an hour, ended up downtown, circled back and collected her car. She went to her mother's house for the night, and early the next morning she cruised around until she found a tiny used car lot, traded her car and two hundred dollars in cash for a battered little yellow Nissan pickup truck. She was already waiting when the DMV opened, left with new tags in hand and drove straight back to her apartment, loaded her few boxes, and drove north to Vancouver. She hadn't expected leaving to be so easy.

* * *

CHAPTER SIX

The road trip was Gretchen's idea. "I'll take a couple of days off, fly back home from Calgary. It'll be fun. I haven't been to Banff in years. Have you ever seen Banff? The mountains go straight up. It's barely September, if we're lucky we won't hit a snowstorm. It gets you away from here, away from that creep, before you cross the border."

"It'll add, what, ten, twelve hours to the drive."

"But it will be ten hours with me." A wide smile. "We can talk about your guy."

Kate laughed. "Gretchen, there is no guy!"

"Your aging flyboy, goof. I may have found something for you."

So they headed east in the little yellow truck at dawn on a Sunday morning, loaded up on road snacks, singing along to the radio, retelling stories they both knew, falling into the easy rhythm that had carried them through college, grad school, moves, jobs, heartbreaks, distance, and all the years. The miles fell away behind them as they climbed into the mountains, with autumn all around and winter coming on fast.

Kate told Gretchen what she dared about the farm, glossing over the wary insularity, talking at length about the natural beauty of the place and the friendships she'd formed.

"In back-of-nowhere Colorado?"

"It's not what you'd expect. You'd love it."

They stopped for lunch in a resort town at the top of a long, dazzling lake. Sat in a park on the edge of the water with overpriced takeout, and got down to business.

The sample itself, Gretchen told her, was some kind of polyester, but not of a process she was familiar with. "The thing is, it's older than you said, a lot older, or has been exposed to some degradation process, or both. And yes, it was saturated with a slurry of several chemicals, heavily, for a long time, probably days. If he was wearing the suit, he was definitely exposed, and some of them are weird, and probably pretty toxic. Problem is, of course, it's been laundered more than once, and the traces are so faint I can't do much with them. Can you get a better sample?"

"I cut that one off the garment. The whole thing must be in about the same shape."

"Hm. I might be able to separate them out, produce some testing samples, but it will take time, and a lot more material. And then figuring out what this junk does to a body is your show."

Kate rubbed her forehead. "I told the family it's not like the movies."

"That is the damn truth."

* * *

It always started with the little pains, easy to brush off. A hand cramp after too much writing, a dull ache on a cool autumn morning. A little breathlessness, walking up the long hill after a day down in the orchards. Nothing that would slow down a robust person, except that he had felt it before and he knew what would follow.

Soon, there would be evening headaches, a creeping

cough, a deep chill that neither whiskey nor the fireside would ease. He would try to ignore it for a while, and when it couldn't be ignored anymore, to hide it. When he couldn't suppress the tremor anymore, when it hurt too much to stand unaided, when it started to eat into his clarity of mind, he knew, he would draw on anger for strength, push himself harder.

And they would be attentive, worried. Gentle. He couldn't fault them for that, but he couldn't bear it either, so he would close in on himself. Pull away. He would start taking meals alone, sleeping more. Quit fighting altogether, in the end; give in to the exhaustion, the rage, and the haze, and grimly wait out the worst. Same old story again.

* * *

The packet sat, forgotten for a season, before the archivist strolled in one morning to find a terse message from two levels up. "99502-778-98. Development is harassing me so I'm passing it on to you. Deliver a status report before the end of the day." He had to go look up the file number, to remember what it was about.

This was how it went. A project was nothing until it was everything. The archivist sighed and got to work.

The final reports from the missing survey ship had it headed out into an area known as the Island: a sparsely populated bubble on the edge of the galactic arm, gateway to the greater void of the dark nebula beyond, plagued by ancient superstition and bad luck. Nobody went in there; there was nothing worth the trouble. Puzzled, the archivist plotted a most-likely course out into the black beyond. "What did you find out there?" he mused, drumming his fingers on the console, waiting for the plot to return visuals.

There were seven systems within the most-likely plot; this wouldn't take long. The first two were well mapped. If there was anything there, it would have already turned up. He put in a stored-records request on anything the company had on the remaining five, and waited.

* * *

They said goodbye at the airport, the mountains behind them like a low curtain across the sky, clinging to each other as if their lives depended on it. "Are you going to be okay? I don't want to just leave you here."

"My flight is in a few hours. I'll buy a trashy paperback. You go. Go do your good work. I'll keep working on what I've got, so send me more if you can." Gretchen sniffled. "If you need anything, you call me. If you need me to come, I'll be on a plane. They do have planes that go to where you are, don't they?"

Kate laughed. "How do you feel about puddle jumpers? There's a tiny airport in Gunnison. An hour away, I guess."

"I want the whole story sometime."

"You got it."

* * *

It was a main-sequence star of middling size and middling age – nothing much. An asteroid belt and a few gas giants that might have useful moons. Probably not worth a close review from a manned craft, but it was within the plot, so he reviewed the archive. You never knew with these geologic surveyors; they were an odd, solitary, gut-driven lot, and the hunches they chased often made no sense. And yet, they paid off, often enough to make the manned flights worth the incredible cost.

He almost missed it. It wasn't in any of the remote survey data, but in a deep-sky astronomy study from four hundred years earlier, before the first manned flights that far into the frontier. They had recorded trillions of terabits of data back in those days, but only had enough personnel and budget hours to index it. His must be the first living set of eyes to open this report and look at it, because if anyone else had come before him, they would have seen it too. The distinctive spectral signature of chlorophyll.

He ran the ancient report through every filter he could think of, not daring to request an updated scan from the orbital observatory, not daring to speak to anybody at all.

The results were fuzzy, but unmistakable. The chlorophyll was present on the small third planet. There was a lot of it, and a lot of nitrogen, and a lot of water.

"You beautiful poor lost bastard," he breathed, in awe. "You found a habitable."

* * *

The Canadian prairie belonged to Kate, and she flew through the night. Montana, Idaho, Utah. She found herself at the same rest stop on the outskirts of Provo, nine days almost to the hour after she'd left. Slept for a few hours, and then drove into the rising sun.

It was midday when she pulled up and rang from the phone box by the gate. It had begun to snow a few miles east of Montrose, swirls of tiny dry flakes at first, thicker and faster as she climbed. Conrad's son Leo was in the gatehouse when she pulled up; he took in the truck, the boxes in the bed, the impatient drumming of her hands on the steering wheel. "Go on up," he said. "I'll call ahead for someone to bring your things in. You don't want them to get soaked."

"Thank you," she said, fervently. It was all she could do to contain her speed, up the ring road. *I'm here, I'm home.*

There were people converging on the big house from all over, and Emma reached her first, pulling her into a fierce hug, and the boys were there, and Rita and Marina too, and she was passed from embrace to embrace. Her face was wet, with snowflakes, with tears. *This is what home feels like,* she thought, with wonder. *I never really knew.* And then she looked up and there was Goban, looking over the little truck with an odd half-smile on his face, and when she met his eyes, he just said, "You came back."

"Did you have any doubt?" she asked, and was startled by the flash of uncertainty – there and gone, almost too fast to see.

But he said, deliberately, "Not for a minute," and then the smile broke across his face and he pulled her close for a hug too, and then they were all moving toward the house.

The inevitable flurry of things to do followed. Robbie and two of his cousins unloaded her boxes, disappearing into the house with them under Emma's direction, moving her back into Irena's old room. Irena and another cousin were making coffee and soup. Rita took her coat and her keys, sat her down in the kitchen, sent one of the boys to take the truck down to the motor pool. *A beehive designed by Swiss watchmakers*, Kate thought, amused and awed by the practiced efficiency.

In a quiet moment, she pulled Conrad into the study. "It's probably nothing," she started.

"'Probably nothing' has a bad habit of turning into something." He waited.

"Right." She fidgeted. "So, when I first came here, I told you I had been dating a guy and it wasn't serious or important. He evidently thought it was more serious than I did, and he proposed to me, and I turned him down flat. He got a little weird about it, made some threats. I thought you should know."

"Hm." Conrad drummed his fingers on the desk. "What did you tell him?"

"Nothing. I mean, I wouldn't have anyway, but" — a bitter laugh — "I didn't even have a chance. He wasn't interested in me at all, just in a, a — suburban middle-class status symbol."

"You have a name and a picture?"

"Sure."

"Well." He paced, looked out the window. "We can only hope he gets the point and leaves it alone. If not, we'll deal with him." Decisively. "Thank you. You did the right thing, letting me know right away. You know, Kate — I didn't know what to think of you when you first came here. It's my job to worry about what can go wrong, and things out of place set me on edge. You sure did. But I've come to have some respect for you."

"Thank you, Conrad. That means a lot." She met his eyes, looked away. *I wonder what he'd say if he knew about Gretchen.* That would come back around, too, she knew. Entanglements. Complexities. The unpredictable actions of others. Keeping the outside world at arms' reach seemed so much simpler.

The snow continued to fall, and the walls of the valley closed in.

* * *

CHAPTER SEVEN

"I thought farms were quiet during the winter," Kate said to Rita, while swabbing dirt and snow out of the skinned cheek of a ranch hand's redheaded daughter.

That first storm had melted off by midmorning the next day, and had been followed by three weeks of magnificent weather, clear crisp nights, golden aspens, and cloudless skies. Then the second storm had come, three weeks ago, and autumn was over, just like that. As Kate's work in the lab settled into a routine, the larger pattern of the farm's days were shifting to a winter footing. The usual winter infections were starting to go around, and a rise of minor injuries among the restless, snowbound villagers. Very pregnant Irena had been pulled off of clinic duty, so Kate was pressed into service as lab tech, orderly, and runner.

"Oh, I don't know, probably some are. The kind of big Midwestern outfits that grow one crop and sell it all at harvest time and are done. We're year-round. There's so much work that gets shunted aside in the spring and summer and then caught up on at this time of year, building up for holiday sales. Off you go –" this to the girl's companion, a young grandniece, poking at the fine line of fresh stitches on her shoulder. "If you don't show your tails in here again, I won't tell your dad how fast you girls were driving that snowmobile." She watched the girls go, shaking her head and laughing.

"So how is your work going? You've been quiet about it since you came back from Seattle."

"Yeah. Well. I have a couple of theories, and I'm still building the baseline data, but I'm not zeroing in on anything yet. It's tedious work. Running the same tests over and over, looking for patterns. Digging into the historical data. I'm finding hints that this has been going on a very long time, Rita. He just ignored it until it got out of hand."

"Yes, I suspected as much."

"It's not that — in a way, I'm relieved that he hasn't had another flare-up, you know? The first one was horrifying. But at the same time, I'm holding my breath waiting. And the last week or so... let's get it over with. It hurts to watch."

"I know. It's worse in winter, with the normal aches and twinges that anybody would have, compounded."

"I'm running some computer models on common anti-inflammatories, trying to see where they break. If I can pin down why basic things don't work as well for him, maybe I can find a simple modification and have something that will help make the day to day less awful. Tylenol Max for Aliens." *So weird. All still so weird. You live with it day to day, but nobody ever talks about it out loud.* "I miss my team. I'm not asking," she clarified hastily. "But I'm so out of my depth. The solitary work is different from a group lab where each teammate has a different specialty."

Rita grimaced, wry and sympathetic. "Well. I wish I could make that team happen for you, but you knew what you were signing on for. Let's lock up here and go up to dinner."

Kate thought back to her latest phone call to Gretchen, up on the ridge with the little mare a few nights before. Talking around the edges of the things she couldn't talk about. *You've traded one set of secrets for another,* Gretchen had said, accusingly, worry masquerading as reproach. *Is it worth it? Is it beautiful?*

It is so beautiful, Kate had replied, *like something out of an Albert Bierstadt painting.*

* * *

The investigator was on his way home from an easy job. An automated mining station had quit communicating in a nearby system: go out, run diagnostics, schedule a repair crew, report in. Six days, out and home.

But at Nagoroneva Station, he was met by company guards and escorted to a transient flat, and briefed by a very senior administrator. They were sending him right back out, and this was not a short run; he was heading into the void, in search of a long-missing surveyor.

"What about the rest of the team?" he asked. "The oversight officer?"

"No oversight," he was told. "You're going alone. There have been rumors of something strange out on the fringe for years, but somehow, nothing ever turns up. It might not have anything to do with the fact that there's a Sanctuary Guard oversight officer on every search and recovery flight, but then again, it might. So you're gone before the day is over." Before the daily docking logs transmitted downside.

After the briefing he was allowed a short nap, and the guards escorted him back to his freshly stocked and

serviced ship. There would be plenty of time to read the
background reports on the transit.

* * *

"What was it like for you?" Kate asked, on a late
October afternoon. She was waiting for a report to run;
Marina was washing glassware.

The other woman turned around, dried her hands.
"Coming here, you mean?"

"Yeah."

Marina thought about it. "Well. I met Jake first.
He was just a young kid, right out of high school, and he
had some big ideas. You know they've always used horses a
lot here. Goban is very attached to them, and they buy and
sell stock locally. They know what they like, and they have
quality animals. But they had never done any real
professional herd management like they've done with the
other stock, or thought about breeding as a revenue stream.

"So Jake had this idea that that's what he wanted
to do — really work on this herd, maybe develop a breed
from the stock here. He begged some working capital from
his mom and went to this breeders' conference in
Kentucky, and that's where we met up. I'd been working
in racing for a few years and was making pretty good
money, but I just hated it. The money, the way people
tend to act around a lot of money, the... frivolousness of it.
And yet also dead seriousness and high stakes. I was pissed
off all the time. So we hit it off, and he offered me a six-
month assessment gig, and I jumped at it.

She smiled, remembering. "I came out here and was
just enchanted — with the place, and with Rita. We were

close friends pretty quickly, but I was trying to keep it professional, and she didn't catch on right away that I was interested. So. My six months were up, I was getting ready to leave, and she said to me that she wanted more time to figure out where we were going.

"And I said, 'Rita, it doesn't take any time at all to figure that out.' And I kissed her." Marina grinned. "We had a nice little family wedding a month later. Couple of years ago, we went up to Boulder for our twentieth, and made it legal.

"The way this family works — you go out and see the world, meet people, sleep around, have some fun. But you don't bring someone back here unless it's for life. And a lot of the time, the people who marry in have another connection, to the farm itself, aside from the person they fall in love with. Reg was an employee first too, he and Frank both." Kate had known that. Reggie and his brother had married cousins. Frank was the other veterinarian, an old-school cow-and-sheep man, more or less retired now. "It's not just about romance, or even partnership with one person; it's about shared values, and commitment to the bigger idea. It's about... choosing love, choosing to be all in. If you come here, as I did, it's with that understanding."

Marina came over, perched on the counter across from Kate. "Your first few weeks here must have been so hard. The suspicion and weirdness and all the questions. There were a few people who were pretty sure you weren't coming back from Seattle, and I'm not sure anyone would have thought worse of you if you hadn't.

"I think I had it easier, and harder, in some ways. It

took Conrad another year to treat me like anything but an employee." She laughed. "And he and Rita had some throw-downs over it. But she is just his baby cousin; he would never dare cross Goban that way. You have had to find your feet here much faster than I did." Marina's face went serious and thoughtful.

"Kate, Amalija's been gone a long time. There's no one left who remembers her – except him, of course. She is a legend. I think everyone thought he would be alone forever, which would be a shame, because he's a good person, and has had so much sorrow in his life, and he deserves to be happy. He seems very happy since you came here." Kate went still. She felt lightheaded, gripped the counter and hoped that her churning emotions were not parading across her face. "And there isn't any doubt about the quality of your character. You don't have to worry about being accepted, is what I'm saying. If you were worried."

Kate reflected on the small courtesies and gestures of welcome, the evening cocktails and conversations in the study, the horseback rides. The courting. She wondered, not for the first time, whose decision it had been to give her the old upstairs suite, to let her immerse herself in all that family history.

Say yes... work out the details later. Oh, Katie, you are old enough to know better. She closed her eyes, toyed with her pendant, and reached for some thought, some mental picture to soothe her. The image that came to her was firelight reflected in cat-green eyes, catching and illuminating flecks of grey and hazel, casting contrast on deepening laugh lines. How those eyes widened just a bit, and those lines deepened around the corners of his mouth, every time she walked in the room, as though her presence was a delightful surprise anew. How her spirit lifted at the sight of that small smile, every time. *Oh.*

Marina's brow furrowed a little, reading her expression. "I'm sorry. I wouldn't have — I thought that's why you asked."

A sudden fatigue washed over Kate; she was overwhelmed by a sort of paralyzing confusion. She needed a safe, quiet place to think.

A safe, quiet place. Emma had said that, at the beginning. Kate had run away to find a safe, quiet place. This was what she'd found, and this was where she'd chosen to stay, and had left and come back, had found a cause and committed to it.

The occasional feeling of being delicately handled, she realized, was in fact something else altogether. Having accepted her as one of their own, they closed ranks around her, an act as reflexive as breathing for these private people. They sheltered her in the way that they had always sheltered each other, from a hostile outside world, from whatever ugliness might follow on her heels. Defending that safe, quiet place, letting her take her time, to think and learn and settle in, in her own way. To choose, for herself.

* * *

Later that night, Kate curled up on the settee in the big study, drinking wine, watching the fireplace, writing up lab notes, one of the farm cats nestled at her feet. Emma and Goban were bent over the desk together, working on some kind of accounting. She was overcome with a feeling of perfect, pure peace. There was a routine here, a more sedate pace, a sense of purpose. Nothing out of place. Real, hard work, but also time for rest and conversation, or companionable silence. No busywork, no waste.

So why does it feel like the calm before the storm? Can I not just be content?

Goban came over and sat down next to her, stretched, rubbed his ashen face. "It looks like we've had a good year. We'll know more after the holidays. Held our ground, for sure. We'll be able to put some money into improving the dairy herd in the spring. These kids know what they're doing. They barely need me anymore."

Emma looked up sharply. "Don't you believe it for a minute."

"Maybe I'm just tired, Emmie." He looked it; he put his head back and closed his eyes. The little calico jumped up onto his lap; he flinched. Kate reached over to push the cat away, and brushed his hand.

"Oh! You're burning up." She set her laptop aside, pressed her hand against his forehead. "Do you feel it?"

"I was sitting too close to the fire."

"You weren't." Kate frowned. He wasn't sweating. "You don't feel that? Really?" Emma was already calling Rita. "Tell her to bring a bloodwork kit." She checked his pulse; it was thready, racing. "Okay, you're going to bed right now."

"Yes. That's a good idea." He looked at her, but his eyes weren't focusing on her face. He stood too fast, stumbled, sat back down. "I'll just... stay here for a minute."

"Nope, up with you." Slower this time, with Kate and Emma supporting him. *So fast, it came on so fast.* They didn't dare wait. They half-carried him into the inner suite, laid him down. He immediately struggled to sit up. "Okay, okay." She sat on the edge of the bed, supporting him, rubbing his shoulders. "You should lie down."

He shook his head. "Not ready. I don't... want to go."

"You're not going anywhere. You're right here. I'll be right here with you."

He closed his eyes, rested his cheek on her shoulder. "Tired."

"I know."

Rita came in and got to work; Kate pitched in to get him undressed and settled. He fought, but as the night wore on and his fever climbed, he settled into a restless sleep.

Rita nudged her arm, and she realized she had dozed off sitting up. "Sweetie, go to bed. There's nothing else for you to do here. Sylvia is coming to take over, and I'm going too."

"Um. I said I'd stay. What if he wakes up?"

"He's delirious. If he wakes up, he won't know who you are anyway. Do you want to sleep in the study so you're close?"

"Good idea." Kate yawned. "Even better, let's move the settee in here."

Rita shook her head and smiled, and helped her

move the settee.

She dozed, woke from time to time to help Sylvia change ice packs and bedding. Toward dawn, his temperature came down, and he woke, shivering and disoriented, trying to get up. She sat with him, rubbed his shoulders, and kept up a running stream of low soothing chatter.

He muttered something in his own language. She stroked his sweat-soaked hair. "I don't know what that means." But the fever was starting to spike again, and he slipped away.

It went on that way, through that day and into the night. They struggled to manage the fever, and waited it out. He slept off and on, hallucinated at times, carried on agitated conversations, tossed and turned, and slept again. At times, he seemed to surface for a moment, and at those times he clung to her. She slept when he did, stretched and moved around when she could, drank water and juice when Sylvia and Irena brought it, helped change fluid bags when they decided it was time to put him on an IV. The fever spiked, and broke, and spiked and broke again, and finally, did not return.

Sometime during the second night, she woke alone. Irena heard her stirring and came in, arms full of fresh bedding. "Oh, hey, give me a hand?"

Kate rubbed her eyes. "Where did he go?" she asked sleepily, then came wide awake. "What's wrong?"

"Nothing. It's over. He woke up clear-headed and went to take a shower. He's pretty wrung out. He's going to come back and sleep, so –" Irena held up the bundle of sheets. So Kate shook herself awake and they worked briskly together, making up the bed and tidying the room. She took the soiled bedding from Irena and headed for the laundry room.

As she was loading the washer, she had a sudden thought, and ran back toward the study. She met Rita in the dining room. "How many blood samples have you pulled?"

"One a day, like we have been. Um. Each evening. Last one was four or five hours ago."

"Go ahead and take another one *right now*."

Rita looked at her, questioning, and then her eyes widened in understanding. "Right. Come on."

Goban looked up when they opened the door, stood unsteadily, smiled. "Hey."

"Hey." Kate crossed the room and wrapped an arm around him. He leaned into her. "How are you doing?"

"Better. You stayed with me." He sounded sleepy, but his eyes were sharp and clear, and she thought of sunlight dancing on tidal pools.

"I said I would."

"All right, Tēvi, give me the arm," Rita said. At the face he made, she added, "She said so," smirking, nodding at Kate.

"It's true. I'm sorry. I need a fresh sample as fast as possible."

"Well, then. For you." He sat back down and held out his arm, yawned.

Kate felt a wave of unbearable exhaustion in sympathy. She swayed on her feet. *What time is it?* She had no sense of the hour at all. "Okay. I am going to stagger off to my own bed now. I have work to do in the morning."

He clasped her hand, suddenly vulnerable. "Don't."

She turned and looked at him, uncertain. Looked at Rita, who shook her head, smiling. Rita touched her grandfather on the shoulder, a little half-hug, picked up her bloodwork kit, and slipped out.

The two of them were alone, and Kate was still holding his hand. She sat down next to him on the edge of the bed, put her head on his shoulder, and just sat like that for a moment. "I am so glad that's over." She sighed, yawned again. "Are you sure? You don't want me to get out of here, let you sleep?"

"Oh...no, I do not want you to do that." He shook his head, as though trying to nudge himself awake. "Let me sleep, yes." So she turned out the light, and he was already out by the time she crossed the room and laid down on top of the coverlet, to settle into the warm hollow along his body.

* * *

In the predawn light, she woke up in the circle of his arms, rolled over, and studied the planes and creases of his face. Felt his forehead. His skin was healthy warm, without fever. His eyes opened, clear and bright, and he smiled. She shifted closer, kissed him tentatively, and then again with more vigor, wrapping a hand around the back of his neck. His hair still held a trace of damp, and he smelled like soap, and she liked his lips.

He stretched, groaned. "Ohhh. I feel like myself."

A deep, satisfied sigh.

"Mm." Kate smiled too, sleepy and content. Then the realization hit, and she sat up abruptly, swung her feet over the edge of the bed. "Let's keep it that way." *I have the whole cycle. I have the whole cycle! I have to get to the lab!*

He rolled over, wrapped an arm around her waist, rested his head against the small of her back. *No hurry*, the gesture said, and oh, it would be so nice to just lie back down and spend the morning right here. She turned and looked at him, sorting out her complicated tangle of emotions. She brushed his face with her fingertips, and tried to find words. "I think... that I am crazy about you, but I don't know that this is the right time. I need to understand this. I need to focus on the work that I'm doing. To get you healthy. So that I can just... be with you.

"Right now, I have so much work to do, and you have this farm to run. And your family needs to see you. So let's get up and have a cup of coffee and celebrate the good days."

* * *

CHAPTER EIGHT

Kate gathered up the blood samples from the medical refrigerator concealed behind the creamy aspen paneling, grabbed her coat and keys, and slipped out the front door without seeing anyone.

She blew out a little puff of breath, watched it dissipate. The air was crisp and dry, the valley still in shadow. A frozen fog hugged the vineyard and the houses lower down, thinning out to nothing up here; the rim of the cliff was drenched in golden light. The farm was waking up. There were shadowy, fog-wrapped figures moving in one of the corrals, and distant truck noises. She stood still for a moment, taking it in, and then headed down the hill. Jauka, sleepy and warm from the horse barn, padded out and kept pace with her, down to the clinic door.

It took less than half an hour to fire up the big automatic analyzer, set up samples, and start the samples processing. The sun was up by the time she came out of the clinic; the fog seemed to glow from within, embracing her in a strange, platinum, ghost-lit world.

The fog muffled the morning sounds of the valley; the crunch of her boots on the hoary snow was the only thing she could hear. She took it slow, grasping for time to think. Was she in love with him? Did she want to be? He was a mystery and a fascination to her, with his long life, stories about travel and family, and the implacable silence about what had come before. She'd abandoned all pretense of objectivity some time back. Kate accepted that. She felt unreasonably protective toward her subjects and that was always a problem for her. But he was special by any measure. Anyone would be moved by the depth of pain and heartache in him, and his buoyant optimism and humor in the face of it. Anyone would.

But it was more than that. She found solace in his stillness, the balance between the quiet façade and the intensity underneath. She found herself gravitating toward his company, craving it. And she had never been with anyone — since Gretchen, *and that was such a long time ago*, she thought — who just seemed to like her for herself, in whose company she felt so unguarded, and so comfortable. She had never wanted to be. Maybe she was finally old enough to take that leap of faith.

She loved this place, though, she knew that for sure; she felt a responsibility to these strange, close-knit, private people. She felt at home here. She could imagine herself making a life here, if there was a place for her. After the work. There would be an *after the work*, she thought. There had to be.

But she could not shake the inchoate fear that had been hovering over her for weeks. Whenever a quiet moment left her free to think, she turned it over in her mind, prodding at it, trying to make sense of it.

Things out of place. A fragile balance. They had worked so hard to build this little self-contained world. To insulate themselves, limit the intrusion of the outside, keep things on their own terms. To maintain control. And yet everything could change in a space of minutes. Here she was, proving that by existing. You couldn't see the change coming until it was right on top of you.

It started snowing midmorning, laying fresh light powder down over the encrusted layers of old snow, and when it cleared in the early afternoon, she took a long, hard ride up past the old observatory to the little meadow. The wind up here left a thin crust of snow, sculpted into ridges and drifts, piled up deeper in the crater and along the edge of the woods and up against the gravestones. She laid some dried flowers on Amalija's grave, and talked for a long time. Gretchen was right; she needed someone that she could talk to.

Then she went to the lab and processed the morning's data.

* * *

Kate left the lab as the sun was setting. Walking up the ring road, she heard shouting and laughter beyond the horse barn. As she rounded the corner of the building, someone shouted, "Duck, Kate!" and then something hit her shoulder and she was blinded, for just a moment, by a glittering spray of snow. A hand grabbed her and pulled her down behind the corral fence; it was Conrad's middle son, Nick, and he was laughing. She collapsed in the snow and dirt as Nick's oldest boy jumped up and lobbed a volley of snowballs over the fence. There were half a dozen younger kids holed up behind the fence, shaping more balls, passing them up to the teenagers for throwing.

"What's going on?"

"Well, Robbie and Stefan started it, and then these two rascals got in the middle of it" — ruffling the younger boy's hair — "and they took Stefan's side, so then Jake got involved. And Tēvs and Tēvocis Brencis were coming out of the garage and Stefan tagged Brencis, so those two jumped in, and it just grew from there. So now it's all the kids against the old guys with Jake and Robbie, and my dad decided that wasn't fair, so he's taken the side of the kids."

"Wait – what? Your dad's out there?" Several thumps against the fence, and one of the teenagers squealed. "I've got to see this."

"He's on the other side of the barn, engineering a fort."

"Of course he is." She scrambled up and peeked over the fence, and saw Jake, and he saw her and grinned.

"Kate! Come over, join our side!"

"Don't let her, kids! Get her!" Conrad's voice floated from the other side of the barn, and she ran, and two of the little kids grabbed her knees and she went down, but bounced right up again and made for the corner of the corral, rounded it before the kids could catch her, sped through a long straight stretch out in the open, and she was hit four times before she made it to cover on the other side. She fell down behind the shelter of the fence, laughing, brushing snow out of her hair and eyes, and lay sprawled there for a minute, looking up at the orange-streaked sky between the cliffs, gasping. Goban crouched next to her, grinning furiously, shaping snowballs and stacking them in a pile.

She laughed at him. "Hitting little kids with snowballs?"

"Hey, those kids outnumber us three to one, and some of them aren't so little. And they have Conrad and

Nick." Beyond him, Jake bounced up, tossed a series of well-aimed shots, and from the grunts and squeals across the corral, connected a couple of times. Kate sat up, looked over the edge of the fence, ducked when four of the kids let loose, then peeked again.

Five older kids, ranging from twelve to seventeen, were spread six feet or so apart, enjoying the shelter between the fence and the barn. The younger children were well protected, and out of sight. Off to the right, a zigzag of low walls of snow, a few feet apart, crept forward along the east line of the fence. Conrad had been methodically building up one wall from the protection of the one behind it, working his way south, and he was nearing the corner. "I think you're in trouble, there," she said, pointing.

"Hah. Yes, he's been plugging away at that for an hour." Goban stood to lob a few snowballs over the fence, hesitated — on purpose, she realized, when the volley of return fire hit his chest, five or six all at once, and he theatrically flailed, and there was a great deal of squealing and shouting from the other side, and then he tumbled slowly backwards, and the kids hushed, watching in awe as he vanished from their view. For just a moment, silence descended, and he rolled up into a crouch, graceful as a cat, held a hand up as Robbie and Jake and Brencis watched. Made a fist. Held up three fingers.

Kate gathered up half a dozen snowballs, handed one to him. *Two.* She was almost holding her breath. *One.* Looked around, made sure everyone had ammunition in hand. *Zero.* He shouted, "Go!" and all four men were flinging snowballs as fast as they could, and she laughed to realize that only Nick and the oldest of the children were getting hit. Most of the snowballs hit high up on the side of the barn, exploding, showering the little kids with snow, and they squealed and giggled.

Then Kate saw Conrad pop up, glancing back at his charges, and she couldn't resist lobbing one at him. He turned when it connected with his ribs, looked across the open space at her, shook his head warningly and grinned. Turned around. "Okay, kids," he shouted, "follow me!" And the whole lot of them were pouring around the east side of the fence, weaving through the protective walls, and Kate's group was running away, around the west side of the fence by the road, between the north side and the barn, and they grabbed as many as they could of the already-shaped snowballs that the children had abandoned, and turned around and ran back the way they had come, and the two groups collided in the road, and there was flying snow everywhere and everybody was falling down, and she was at the bottom of the pile, with two little girls flopped on top of her, giggling.

Several of the smaller boys, the ones who hadn't gotten to throw any snowballs earlier, were pelting the group of men, and then Goban threw his hands over his eyes, laughing. "Okay, kids, you win, we surrender! Surrender, boys!" The others shouted their agreement, and the little ones gave up and collapsed, and he gathered several of them up in his arms, great-grandchildren and great-great-grandchildren, and Kate had never in her life seen anything quite like the light of joy on all their faces.

* * *

The next morning found her back in the lab. The data processing on the samples taken during and after the flare-up was all done, and Kate had a long, dull couple of hours of slogging through reports.

Huh. She pushed her chair back abruptly.

"Marina... why don't you go get Rita?" The other woman's eyes went wide, and she nodded and headed upstairs.

Kate leaned forward again, tapped the back key a couple of times. Stared at the screen.

She heard steps behind her, looked up.

"What have you got?" Rita asked.

"Okay. So." Kate took a deep breath. "You know I've been taking daily samples, and running the same series of tests against them, looking for changes over the progression of the cycle, right? Looking for changes that might signal an underlying cause. So look at this."

She tapped the arrow keys, paged back to the beginning of the set of screens. Each chart looked like a watercolor painting of an abacus: lines of blue stains in vertical rows, like strings of beads. "This is a chart showing a variety of different proteins and their proportions in the sample. See this blot here? Watch." Forward. Forward. Forward.

"Okay, the one that's diminishing?"

"Yes. Watch." Forward. "This is the evening the flare-up started." Forward.

"What..."

"Yes." Forward. Forward. "This is early yesterday morning, the first sample after he came out of the flare-up." Forward. "This is yesterday evening."

"Ai, look at that!" Rita leaned over her shoulder, paged back and forth a couple of times, fast and then slowly. "What is this chemical? What is happening here?"

Kate shook her head. "This is a regulatory hormone of some kind. It's not on the standard charts, and it seems to have an impact on a huge range of metabolic functions. So when the level is... oh, middle-high, he's at his peak. I'll have to isolate and identify it to find out more.

"But some process is suppressing the production of this hormone. When it's low, he has pain, fatigue, circulatory problems... and depressed liver and kidney function, which leads to other issues. Everything we've been seeing. Depression, difficulty concentrating. Poor thermoregulation. Fever. Something's happening during the fever that resets that process, and the hormone level bounces way back up, and we see hyperactivity, euphoria. Appetite changes. When it settles down a little, he's at the top of the cycle, and it stays that way until his body's production of the hormone can't keep up with the depletion." Kate tapped a pen on the edge of the desk, staring at the screen. This was familiar. Why?

Marina frowned. "I've seen something like this in racehorses that have been doped. The drugs override their natural processes of regulation. It stresses their ability to regulate cortisol and other steroids, and you get these crazy up-and-down metabolic swings."

Kate nodded. "So it could be environmental, which

is what I've suspected all along. So. Rita, if I can synthesize this hormone – if we can figure out where he should be – is that a treatment?"

Rita was staring at Marina, stricken. "Cortisol. The flare-ups look a lot like an Addison's crisis. I... recognized this but I couldn't put my finger on it. It's the IV solution we give him to keep him hydrated that brings it under control."

"What does that do? What's in the IV?"

"Just saline and some glucose. Keeps blood pressure up, keeps the patient from going into shock, stabilizes the system. We'd supplement the deficient hormone at that point too, if we knew what it was, if we had a synthetic..." She shook her head. "Yes. It's worth a shot. Do you think you can do that?"

"I'm sure going to try."

"But what's causing the deficiency?" Rita straightened, an anxious, unsettled movement, and began to pace.

Marina stopped her, gripping her wrists gently. Met her eyes. "So Kate figures out how to produce it. That will take time, and give you a chance to figure out a safe test protocol. Address the symptoms, and then keep working on the cause. One step at a time." Kate was struck, again, by how difficult these years must have been for Rita, fighting a one-woman war against the disease, without help or much hope.

"Right." Rita nodded, relaxed and suddenly smiled, squeezed her wife's hands in silent gratitude. "This is a huge breakthrough."

"It really is." Kate sighed. *So why am I so worried?* The job ahead was daunting, but the path was clear.

She was still thinking about what Marina had said, about doped horses. Environmental damage. Where was Gretchen on the uniform samples? She had to find time to call and ask. Autoimmune damage could take years to manifest. This many years? It was a lead. It was a chance.

There was something else, needling at the back of her mind, just out of reach.

* * *

CHAPTER NINE

Irena took the call. "Mama," she said, her voice strained. "Company. Leo said Air Force. Three men."

"Not Army?" Emma asked.

"No. He asked if it was about Paul, and they said no." She looked scared, though. "They asked for Tante Tereza."

"Okay." Emma took a deep breath. "Irena, please go sit with Tēvs." The girl nodded and left. "Kate, did anyone ever explain to you what a blowup it caused when our grandfather introduced himself to you? That first morning?"

"I had that impression, but I never got the whole story."

"Even then, he was thinking about bringing you in. And we didn't know anything about you at all. It stirred people up." *I'll bet it did.* "You know that his legal name is Henriks, right? That's what most people know him by, really."

Kate nodded. "Conrad and I talked about that." Henriks. Amalija's first husband.

"I hope it won't matter. We're going to keep his name out of this altogether if we can."

A few minutes later, a dark blue sedan rolled slowly through the village and parked outside the big house. Three uniformed men got out. The two women looked at each other, the air heavy with fear. They were through the parlor and at the rarely-used front door by the time the strangers knocked. The oldest of the three, wearing major's leaves, held up an ID. "Good morning, ladies. We'd like to speak to Tereza Darzins."

"Tereza is at her office in Denver for the week. I'm her sister, Emma Darzins-Kelley." Her voice was light and pleasant, her face composed. "Won't you gentleman come in?"

Kate followed Emma's cue. Perfect, practiced hospitality. They led the uniformed men to the kitchen, sat them down, started more coffee. Smiled disarmingly, made small talk. "What in the world brings you fellows up here?" she asked, her tone cheerful, curious.

The major frowned. "And who are you?"

"Kate Hutchins. I'm a hired hand, of sorts. Doing some consulting work."

"Hm." He looked at Emma, laid his ID down on the table. "Mrs. Darzins-Kelley, I'm Major Louis Farris, and this is Lt. Khouri, and Sgt. James. We came up from Peterson, down in Colorado Springs." He watched for a reaction, found none he could parse. "We, ah, have some questions."

"I cannot imagine what about." Emma fingered the ID, feigning half-interest. She looked up; exasperation crossed her face and vanished again, beneath a disciplined façade. "Oh. Hello, Henry." Goban was standing in the doorway, Irena behind him, making a helpless gesture.

He nodded to Emma in unspoken reassurance, and shook the major's hand. "You fellows are some way from home."

"Not all that far. The mountains sure are beautiful this time of year." Farris glanced toward the window, back to Goban, realizing he was less in charge than he had been, and unhappy about it. "See, the reason we're here – "

"We should wait for Conrad. I wouldn't want you to have to repeat yourselves."

"Calling in the whole crew?"

"Just... one more." A slow smile. "We can wait. Shouldn't be long."

So they waited. The major frowned. The younger men watched him for some kind of cue, gratefully accepted the cups Irena offered. Emma made another pot. Kate sat, still and watchful, enjoying Goban's cool, effortless command of the scene.

The door clattered open, and Conrad barreled in, stopped short, took in the scene. The uniformed men drinking coffee. The coiled tension of the women. Goban smiled. "Good. Conrad, sit down. We can start."

The strangers introduced themselves again. He shook all of their hands, warily. "Conrad Darzins. Operations manager here. You boys lost?"

The major looked Conrad over, a long, careful, assessing stare. The animal dominance in it made Kate nervous; if he couldn't get Goban off balance, he was going for the next best target. Trying to regain control. It was working.

Satisfied, Farris got down to business. "Not long ago, Lt. Khouri's unit began monitoring some unusual microwave signals originating from this mountain. We're here to locate and retrieve the source of the signal."

"What does it say? The message?" Goban smiled a little, sipping his coffee.

"Well, it's encrypted," Farris said, carefully. "We're working on that; we're not there yet."

"So it's not yours. You haven't misplaced a drone or..."

"You see our problem."

"I do. It's automated, I assume? I can certainly tell you there's not some... secret hidey-hole of drug dealers or terrorists or whatever operating out of our back forty."

"You sure of that? Lot of old mines in these mountains."

"I know where all the old mines are." Goban was barely restraining himself from laughing, now. Kate could see that; she had learned to read the nuances of his reserve well enough by now. The strangers, perhaps, could not. Emma could not seem to stop herself from puttering; it was better than fretting. Conrad just sat, arms crossed, silent and suspicious, watching his grandfather.

Farris grimaced. "Yes, it's automated. It repeats. The current theory is that it's some kind of locating beacon. Maybe a downed drone or satellite. As you say, not one of ours." He looked around, studied each face, looking for something. "You folks know anything that might help us out? Any, ah, meteors last summer? Unexplained fires? Find anything... strange in the woods? Do you have any objection to us looking around?"

It was painfully obvious what he wasn't saying. *They think we're some backwoods farmers who might have seen a UFO crash.* And every bit of the major's body language said how much he wanted nothing to do with this particular duty. *We can still contain this.* She felt her nails digging into the palms of her hands, hidden under the table.

Lt. Khouri looked up from the tablet he'd been working on, spoke for the first time. "Sir. It's broadcasting. Fourteen hundred meters away." He nodded down toward the valley. "The outbuildings we passed on the way up."

Farris looked at Conrad, at Goban. "Anything you want to tell me before we go look?"

Goban shook his head, unperturbed. "I'm curious myself."

"Let's go, then. James, you stay here. You came up in a truck?" This to Conrad, who nodded. "Good. Khouri will ride with you." He included Emma in the gesture. "You and you" — to Goban and Kate — "you're with me." *Shit. They're not going to give us a chance to talk, are they?*

So they all drove down the ring road in the two vehicles, Khouri in the bed of the truck tinkering with his tablet, making gestures and giving Conrad instructions through the window, until they came to a stop next to the horse barn. Everybody trooped inside.

The lieutenant steered straight to the storeroom, rummaged around under a pile of empty feed bags and old leather scraps untouched for years, and came up, triumphant, with a small, squared-off, corroded cylinder in his hand. It was no larger than a car battery.

Farris took it, turned it over, and ran his hand over it. Took in its age and wear, the caked clay and the pitted, dented surface. He laughed to himself, a low, humorless chuckle. "Anything you want to tell me now?"

* * *

The Air Force men set up a working space in Kate's little study. The major was busy on the phone while the young sergeant took pictures of the barn and the cylinder, and wrote up a report. *Cooperate*, Goban instructed Emma and Conrad quietly, and they got the word out.

Work on the farm continued more or less as normal, disrupted as various members of the family were brought in, one at a time. There wasn't much to do except wait. It was mid-afternoon when Kate's turn came around.

Farris gestured her to sit, continued to type for a minute. Closed his laptop. Sat back and regarded her.

"So. Katherine Hutchins. Until recently, of Seattle and Alcon Biotech. What did you do there? And what are you doing out here in the middle of nowhere?"

She eyed him suspiciously. "Let's not play stupid, okay? You already know that my work at Alcon was DOD contract work, and I'm sure you've already gotten the clearance and the details. I wasn't a good fit. I was falling apart. I started having panic attacks. I went on a road trip to sort out my head, and," she spat the words as someone who was absolutely sick to death of repeating the same story, which was not far from the truth, "*honest to God*, I was driving through the backcountry and I took a wrong turn in a rainstorm and crashed my car into a cattle gate. The gate you came through this morning. I stayed with these folks while my car was in the shop. They offered me a job. It really is that simple."

"What kind of job?"

There was nothing better than the unelaborated truth. "There's an undocumented disease in this family. They offered me a chance to work on identifying it, helping the family doctors to work on it. It seemed interesting, and different from what I've been doing. And I like it here, I like these people. So I stayed on."

The major puttered around for a moment, tapped a pen. Shuffled the papers around on the desk. He looked up and met her eye. "Miss Hutchins, I think you're full of shit."

"Excuse me?" Her voice was sharp, defensive. She took a slow breath, cooled the nervous edge.

He leaned forward.

"No, let's not play stupid. You are a bioweapons specialist, working off the grid in a remote, undocumented laboratory, for a man who doesn't exist, supposedly sick with a disease that doesn't exist either, although he looks pretty healthy to me, surrounded by people who are not what they claim to be, and who have operational security that makes the Russian Mafia look slack. But there are some loose strings, and I'm tugging on them.

"They claim to have been here for a hundred and thirty years, and the buildings and financial paper trail match up with that, so where's grandma? There is no one here older than our friends Frank and Reggie, the Kelley brothers, who were born in the town down there; both went away for a few years and came back, no living immediate family – how convenient. But the story is different on paper. Conrad? He doesn't exist in the public record before a marriage license filed in Gunnison in 1961."

Enunciated the date, for emphasis. "Does he look eighty to you? The others are the same. Sparse public records, most of them held in these small towns that haven't been e-archived yet, so it's impossible to verify them without going around to every little courthouse and town hall, and what little there is does not line up with the situation on the ground.

"But they slip up with the service records. That woman cannot be the same Rita Darzins who was discharged from the Army in '72, which makes me wonder if she's really a doctor either. And cousin Henry? There have been at least two, maybe three men with that name, all dead, and none of them the right age to be him. The youngest of those was Major Henriks Darzins, shot down over the Vietnam highlands in 1969.

"Who are these people, really? If I call the FBI to bring in a forensic team, are they going to find the real Darzins family in a mass grave in the woods?" *Oh, Amalija.* Kate had a vivid, horrible vision of the little family graveyard on the high meadow, all torn open. She was icy fear, and rage, all knotted up. "What the hell are you people cooking up out here? And who is going to answer that beacon?"

What would Tereza do? An anxious laugh rose in her throat; she clamped it down, took a slow, deep breath and stared at him, trying to sort out what to say, what to avoid. She wondered if he had even spoken to any of Nikolajs' and Anna's branches of the family. Maybe he didn't know. With all of the first generation now passed on — all of them having been born on the farm and married on the farm or overseas, leaving sparse public record behind, and with the property ownership concentrated among Eleonora's children — it was possible that he didn't realize how far the ties of blood and marriage spread through the residents of the valley. This was Conrad's territory, and she had a sudden new appreciation for him. She needed to keep her mouth shut until she had a chance to talk to him. "You're all wrong about them," she said with a sigh, not knowing what else to say.

"Why are you so protective of them?"

"Why wouldn't I be?" She made an exasperated gesture. "They have never been anything but straightforward and hospitable with me. I enjoy my work here, and I *like them*. They're private, self-sufficient people, and I have respect for that. I don't know you at all, Major, and you haven't given me any reason to trust you or give a damn about your agenda. Congratulations, you've cleverly sussed out my loyalties. I'm astonished that you expected anything different." She stood, ending the interview. "There's got to be a record of my car repairs in July. I honestly don't know which shop, but I'm sure Emma can dig up a receipt for you.

"It's a healthy lifestyle. I feel ten years younger since I've been here. Stick around; you'll feel ten years younger too." She smiled brightly.

The major's face was sour. "This place is weird and you people creep me out. I don't want to stay on this mountain one damn minute longer than I have to." *Good. Go away.* "But I will stay as long as it takes to figure out the story with this beacon."

* * *

Lt. Khouri was the good cop. Kate was sitting on the front porch with a glass of mead that night, wrapped against the November chill in one of Amalija's antique handwoven coverlets, watching the valley under the narrow ribbon of stars between the cliffs, when he came out and sat down next to her.

They just sat like that for a few minutes, not speaking; and then, not looking at her, so quiet that she was startled to realize he'd spoken, "Miss Hutchins, are they keeping you a prisoner here?"

"What? No!"

"We can help you. If you want to leave."

She pulled the coverlet tighter around her shoulders. "I don't want to leave. I'm happier here than I've ever been, anywhere." A short, sharp laugh. "I want you people to leave. No offense."

"Not used to strangers here?" He glanced, sidewise, at her. "Not so long ago, you were a stranger. You've fit in."

"Well, I didn't come here digging up the property and making accusations and — and invading their privacy."

The rebuke seemed to sting him. "We just came looking for the beacon! It was after we got here that things seemed strange." He was studying her, now. "Nobody seems to want to talk about the beacon. If something like that turned up in my backyard, I'd be curious."

"Oh, we're curious, but I don't know what there is to say. Nobody knows! Nobody knows where it was before it was in the barn, or how long it's been there." She shook her head and made an impatient gesture. "Maybe the kids found it in the woods. Maybe it got dug up during some construction. Maybe somebody will remember; that would be helpful. It doesn't look like much, does it? Just a piece of mechanical junk. We would have never known it was anything important if you hadn't traced the signal. I guess... everyone assumes that you're going to take it to your labs, take it apart, figure it out. Come back here in the spring and look for a crater or whatever. You know more about it than we do, at this point."

"The major isn't certain of that at all."

"The major strikes me as the kind of guy who kicks over anthills for fun." Turn the good cop act around on him. "You... don't. Tell me, what do *you* think is really going on here?"

He hesitated, seeming to consider the possibility that he shouldn't be the one doing the talking. But forged forward anyway. "All right. I believe that nobody knows what's going on with the beacon. I have no reason to think you people are lying. About that. But you're hiding something, that's for sure. Everyone's too sharp and, uh, prepared for every question."

"You're complaining because these backcountry people are better educated than you expected them to be?" She laughed harshly. "Has that inconvenienced you?"

He looked insulted. Not a good idea to antagonize these people, she reminded herself. "I'm *interested*, because everyone's story is exactly the same. Almost rehearsed. Nobody makes a mistake. No operation runs this tight for

no reason. It feels like a cover. For what, I don't know."
They had saved Goban's interview until near the end,
hours after her own, and she would have loved to have
listened in on that; clearly, they hadn't gotten whatever
they had hoped for from it.

She sipped the mead, lingering on the taste of
honey, gathering her thoughts. Offered him the glass.
"Have you ever had mead? They make wine here, too.
They grow the grapes right down over there. Colorado's
Western Slope is going to be the next Napa Valley. But
they only make mead for the family."

"Ma'am, I am on duty, for as long as we're here."

"Your loss."

"Are you? A cover? You left a good job to come
here. Do you know what the work you're doing is really
being used for?"

She shook her head, bitterly amused. Such a good
job that she'd started wrecking cars to get away from it.
"See, here's the thing. The work I'm doing is not
compartmentalized, because there *are no compartments.*
There's just me, doing independent research. Nobody's
telling me what to do. I run my own show here. I report to
Rita from time to time, but really, I haven't even been
working long enough to have much to report. There's not
any possibility that I'm being manipulated, because there is
no agenda. It's very refreshing, after defense contract work,
let me tell you." That was more spiteful than it needed to
be.

"They're letting you come and go as you please?"

"I came back from Seattle about eight weeks ago. I

went to close up my apartment and see some friends. My personal truck is down in the motor pool. You want to go see?"

"And if we look into your financials, will we find that they're paying you a fair salary? Everything legit?"

Kate went cold and still for a moment. Then she remembered all the paperwork she'd signed, the morning after the first family meeting, another round of it when Tereza had come home a few days later. Nondisclosure documents. Powers of attorney. Direct deposit forms. A consulting contract. A tiny smile tugged at the corner of her mouth. *Emma, bless your level MBA head, and bless your paranoid, hyper-prepared, security freak siblings.* Of course there would be someone making sure that the paperwork was straight.

They left in the morning, having found only dead ends to every question they could think of. They took the strange cylinder, and the feed bags that had been tossed on top of it, and soil samples from the barn and several places around the property. Major Farris watched from the kitchen window as Khouri and James loaded their papers and equipment into the car. "We're not done here. Don't be surprised if you see aircraft in the area." He walked out, Conrad following to open the gate, and several of the younger men watched the two vehicles driving down the hill.

"Has anyone seen Tēvs this morning?" Emma asked, suddenly.

Jake turned from the window. "I saw him riding out toward the west meadow before dawn."

His cousin Leo stared at him, and then stalked out the back door. Kate looked at Emma, who shrugged, and got up to follow.

She caught up with him at by the main corral. They walked silently down the hill, watching the big farm truck just disappearing over the ridge, the sedan following behind.

Leo started to speak a couple of times. Didn't know where to start, it seemed. "There's a lot of history here that you don't know." He was headed somewhere, but not in a hurry, hands thrust deep in his pockets, trudging along, brow furrowed. Thinking.

"Tell me," she said.

"Tēvs and my mother were very close – "

"The alien who doesn't want to be found, and the astronomer looking for his home world."

That stopped him in his tracks. "How did you know that?"

She shrugged, with a wry smile. "It's what I'd do."

He laughed, shook his head. "You're a lot like her, you know? That's why you make my dad edgy. He feels very protective of you, and he doesn't know what to do with that."

"I did eventually figure that out."

"Anyway, yes. Tēvs had a lot of respect for her, because she did the work even though it frightened him. While he was building that observatory for her, he told my dad that he was afraid what she learned there might be the ruin of us. But he built it anyway."

"You think he's up there looking through her

notes?"

"Maybe. I'm going to go find out." They reached the garage; he stopped, hand on the door. "She said to me once, not long before she died, that we would never see them coming."

* * *

The investigator was relieved; his long, solitary, tedious trip was coming to an end. Within a few days, his ship would cross the heliopause of the little yellow star and drop to sub-light speeds. After that, it would only take another day to decelerate in. He was eager to get to work.

He had spent much of the trip reading up on the missing surveyor and his unknown final mission. There was a substantial file. The man was a solid engineer with good instincts, good attention to detail. He'd brought in a lot of finds, made a lot of money. But he never seemed interested in spending it; he'd report in, spend a day or two carousing, a few days camping in the wilderness, and then he'd be out again. Resistant to engagement, said the profile. Asocial tendencies. High potential for risk-taking behavior. Atheist – that was unsurprising. Some of the old beliefs had fallen away with the rise of industry, but the fear of that part of the sky was not something that was easy for a believer to shake off.

And he had survival skills, having been a skilled and active outdoorsman since childhood, raised in the rugged mountain country around Bva'tat.

"I like my own company," the surveyor had said, in one evaluation recording, with a small smirk, a middle-distance stare. "I'm good at my job. But I don't want to do

it forever. I'm working hard for a few years and saving up, that's all."

The investigator had realized, with a jolt, that he knew the man — or had, many years before, in school. They had run in the same circles for a few years, had gone their separate ways and lost touch after finishing. It had been a long time, but what he recalled agreed with the evaluations. Solitary and driven, charming when he wanted to be but not very active on the social scene, a talented student who didn't seem to have to put much effort into consistently landing at the top of the class, and didn't much seem to care.

Yes, he seemed like the type who might go rogue.

The mission prep report suggested that he was heading into the dark nebula in search of mature, metal-rich planetary systems. He'd reported in a few times. His last contact was thoroughly routine, even bored. "Nothing worth pursuing here. Full report attached. Outbound to my next target." And then — nothing, for all these years, until they pointed a query pulse toward the unmapped star system and got a prompt reply from an automated recovery beacon.

Why hadn't he reported in as soon as he bounced? Had he run into trouble out on the system fringe? If so, how had the beacon ended up all the way in the inner system - on a planet with water and life? Had he picked up those traces as soon as he bounced in, decided to go investigate first? Or had he stumbled across that ancient report? Had he already known what to expect? Did he land? Did he crash? If he survived, why didn't he trigger *the beacon right away?*

Was this a planned desertion the whole time?

* * *

Thanksgiving on the farm was uncomplicated: a big midday dinner, followed by a business meeting. "Christmas is more festive," Emma explained, a little apologetically.

"Do you think there will be a discussion about our visitors?" Kate asked, sitting at the big table, peeling and cutting up squash.

"I think there has to be. People are nervous." Flannel shirt and jeans, up to her elbows in goose guts, was a different look for Tereza, Kate thought, amused. "I wish I'd been here."

"Farris asked a question... it was a good question, it made me furious, and part of what made me so mad was that I didn't have an answer."

"Who's going to answer the beacon?" Tereza grimaced sourly. "He asked everyone that. And then he called me at the office and asked me too. Nobody knows, of course, and Tēvs is not talking."

"He's going to have to talk eventually, don't you think? Just pretending that it doesn't matter isn't working anymore."

Tereza shook her head, laughing. She passed the cleaned bird to her sister, washed and dried her hands. "Dear girl, you have just not been here long enough to understand that if there's a thing my grandfather doesn't want to talk about, there is no force in heaven or on earth that will get him talking. He's stubborn as hell, and he is sharper than any of us." She leaned her hip against the counter, crossed her arms, regarded Kate. "But you get under his skin."

"Sis –"

"No, Em, I'm not being mean. In sixty years of needling him, I haven't been able to get a straight story. Poor Major Farris was just outclassed. But Kate's not wrong. There should be some answers, amongst us. These people are not just going to go away, and we need to know what to expect." She looked at Kate. "Let's not tiptoe around it. You have an in that the rest of us don't have, that no one has had since our grandmother died. Really, maybe he will open up to you."

"Tereza, I'm no Amalija. I have no illusions about that."

Emma cut in. "Don't sell yourself short, Kate. In all these years — well, he has had a few affairs. But not often, and never for long. *Never* anyone he ever showed any interest in bringing home. You're different."

I guess it doesn't much matter that I'm not actually sleeping with him, does it? It had become clear that everyone assumed she was. After the night they'd spent together, she'd expected some pushback and gotten rather the opposite; the family had been warm and cheerful, the whole lot of them riding on the crest of his post-fever gregariousness, and any lingering hesitation over her welcome had evaporated. Just as Marina had said.

As it turned out, she never had a chance to talk to him. Two generations of cousins converged on the kitchen not long after that, and the serious talk fell away in favor of more general chatter and kitchen work. The afternoon passed with laughter and camaraderie, and then Emma was directing the setup of the buffet, and everyone was gathering.

* * *

Bouncing in was like stepping out of a quiet building onto a loud, busy square in a bustling city at midday. Incoming-signal alerts came in so fast they layered over each other in a nonstop frantic clatter, until the investigator scrambled to turn them off. He pulled up visuals on the communications panel, and stared openmouthed at the results.

His craft was swimming in a churning bath of electromagnetic signals. Microwave, radio, visible spectrum. And yet, none of those signals tunneled into transit. None except for the steady, strong, heartbeat-like pulse of the emergency beacon's carrier signal, overlaying all the noise.

He plotted the sources. There were a tiny handful of outliers: point sources in the outer system, a few on the surfaces of, or in orbit around, various planets and moons, or traveling between one and another. But not many. By far, most of the signals originated on or very near the little blue planet, lighting it up. A festival house in the darkness, full of noise and life.

He fired up the transit broadcaster and composed an urgent message for home. His hand hovered over the send button for a moment, and then he saved it, unsent, waiting. Aware, in the back of his head, that he might just be recreating the same chain of events set in motion by the missing surveyor, he hesitated anyway.

He started working through the checklist for the long deceleration.

* * *

CHAPTER TEN

After the financial reports, the planning discussions, and the reading of letters from the members of Robbie's and Irena's generation off at school, the younger family members headed off, either to clean up the kitchen or go to their own houses. The core group left in the big study was, Kate realized, much the same as the one at the gathering where her status had been voted on, months ago. Ten grandchildren, six spouses, and the great-grandchildren who held key positions in the farm business. And her.

There was good Spanish brandy, sent home by Rita and Marina's younger daughter, spending her gap year apprenticing as a winemaker. There were vintage gilt crystal glasses.

"These glasses belonged to my youngest daughter," Goban said — telling a story that, Kate was sure, everyone else already knew. But the recollection seemed to soothe his nerves, as he paced up and down the room. "She bought them when she was living in Riga, just a few years before the Soviets closed the border. It was a long time before any of us saw that country again." He nodded to Anna's children: solitary Pete, the sheep man and retired teacher; Ilona, the weaver; Brencis, the mechanical engineer, born during the long, fraught spring that Anna and her husband had fled from the imminent invasion; Sofie, the master cheesemaker, married to Emma's brother-in-law. A branch of the family Kate hadn't had much chance to get to know.

"I always regretted that I never found the time to

visit Anna during those years, and even more, that I never had a chance to take my wife home when she was alive. She came to this country as very young woman, believing that she would make the journey back someday, and died with that hope unrealized.

"We built a home here, though, a refuge. I saw my children born and buried here, saw another generation raised in you, and now your children and grandchildren are out there creating the future every day. I am grateful for those of you" — he raised his glass to each of the spouses in turn, and then to Kate, brushing her hand in passing — "who have come from other places and other families to make your home here among us, a blessed burden in the service of someone else's dream, taken on faith, for love.

"What we have here is my heart's desire; I have never wanted any more than this." He raised his glass. "To home."

"Priekā" The answering murmur ran through the room. *Cheers.* The brandy was golden on Kate's tongue. "To home."

"But we do not always get what we want. Our mistakes catch up with us. My mistakes caught up with all of us last week."

He sipped the brandy, savored it for a moment. Set his glass down. "When our visitors asked where the beacon came from, several of you said the same thing — that it must have been dug up by children playing in the woods. In your ignorance you hit on the very truth. That's an ignorance I cultivated, because I knew that someday the questions would come, and I wanted you to be able to speak truth with sincerity. You all handled yourselves with grace, and I'm proud." He shook his head, as if realizing he was starting to ramble, and backtracked.

"The reason I know, as I'm sure you realize, is that I put it there. When I first came here, I didn't have the equipment to destroy it, so I buried it in the woods. And I just... flat-out forgot about it. I got comfortable and complacent, and I quit looking over my shoulder.

"I should have dug it up and destroyed it years ago. I am so terribly sorry for dragging you all into this mess with my carelessness."

Rita shook her head. "How could you know that the beacon would go off after all that time?"

"I never had any doubt of it. I had no idea when, but I have always known that it had to happen, because ships and personnel are expensive, and the day must come sooner or later when some relentless, soulless *accountant*, hunting for a stone to squeeze blood from, will go looking for the missing. You just do not get to fall through the cracks."

The room was dead silent, processing this. Kate closed her eyes and shivered. The storm she had felt coming was breaking over them.

It was Reggie who broke the silence, Conrad's ever-practical right-hand man. "So what happens now? Who will they send? When? And what do we need to do to get ready?"

Goban nodded, approving of the decisiveness. "You know I have never had a way to correlate our increments of time here to those... back home, but I think the transit time is two, three months. Something close to that, anyway. The Air Force men didn't say exactly when the beacon went off. But I think that it could be any day now."

He took another sip of brandy, cleared his throat. "It will be an assessment and retrieval team — a small craft at first, a team of five or less. They'll think they're looking for a downed craft and a dead pilot, or a small renegade mining operation. They will not expect anything like what they will find here. And they'll be agitated.

"The Air Force team did us a great favor by taking the beacon away from the farm. They'll aim for wherever it is; they have no reason to come here. But the Air Force does know about us, and the answers to their questions will fall into place when the retrieval ship turns up on their doorstep. To somehow keep them from talking to each other, that would be for the best, but I don't how to do that, or if it's even possible."

* * *

In Pasadena and Boulder, in the Arizona desert near Tucson, in Darmstadt and San Jose, on Maui, and in Colorado Springs, mission control centers received signals from their charges, radar and optical observatories lit up, alarms went off, and telephones rang. At Edwards and Hickam and Peterson, families were left alone at their Thanksgiving dinners as recall orders went out.

Something had crossed into the solar system with a brief but enormous flash. Hours later, the aging Cassini spacecraft ceased broadcasting, and then sputtered back to life. Something small and very fast had passed near Saturn, spiraling in toward the inner solar system.

There was no keeping it a secret; there were too many telescopes, too many people who had seen the flash. Contingency plans, both civilian and military, were activated. By telephone and email and social media, the data circled the globe in the space of a few hours. As the F-15s scrambled to meet the incoming craft over the Pacific, the world was watching.

* * *

"What's the goal?" Tereza asked. "What can we hope for?"

Goban's face was bleak. "I am not getting out of this. They are going to take me back. Fighting that will make things go badly for the rest of you. My hope is to insulate you here, until things blow over.

"More Semhet will come. Bigger ships, more personnel. Not an invasion force, but a diplomatic one, and, ah, a commercial one. Once they understand what they're dealing with here, their goal will be trade, economic exploitation. There's no keeping this quiet: Earth is about to meet the neighbors.

"Over time, the situation will stabilize. You can come forward. No reason to keep the secret anymore. I have faith in you all to decide when, and how. Maybe — if I'm lucky, if I cooperate — they'll let me come home. Eventually."

Tereza set down her glass and stood. She was a tight coil of rage. "Who the hell are you, and what have you done with our grandfather? I have never in all my life seen anyone who could budge you an inch on something you didn't want to do. What hold do these people have over you that you would just roll over and give up? I can't believe you. No, of course we're going to fight. Of course we are. *You* are going to go somewhere safe, and I am going to go deal with this. What did you think the Stanford tuition was *for*? No," she repeated, when he started to interject, "I'm not arguing with you, Tēvi. This is my job."

"All right." He smiled despite himself; his voice was patient. "Where should I go?"

"Out of the U.S., for sure. Quickly and quietly. You still have contacts in Europe, don't you? Can you go stay with the Bartulis cousins in London? Alicia in Spain?"

Kate sighed. *Here we go.* The moment she had been dreading was here, and she wasn't as nervous as she thought she'd be. She took a sip of brandy and a deep breath. "I have another idea," she said. "Closer. Easier, faster. Maybe more discreet."

"I'm listening," Tereza said, with a wary frown, a raised eyebrow.

"I have a friend in Vancouver. We've never worked together, haven't lived together since college; you'd have to go a long way back to find a connection to me, on paper." *There's no particular reason to tell the rest. Except that it will come out, and it will be worse if it comes out later.* "When I was in Seattle in September, I took some samples to her and asked her to run some tests for me. We've talked a few times since I came back. I... did not tell her the whole story, and she's never asked, okay? She's absolutely reliable. If I call her, she'll answer. She'll do whatever I ask her to do and not ask any questions."

Everyone was staring at her, and the silence stretched out.

Conrad finally spoke. "Kate, why in the hell did you do that?"

His wounded disappointment chilled her; she wondered if Conrad, or any of them, would ever trust her again. Whether she would get a chance to try to win that back. But she met his eyes, stood her ground. "Why do you think? It was in the beginning. I had no idea what I was looking for; I was looking for — anything. She's a materials chemist. I had her working the problem from another angle. I didn't tell her the truth," she repeated, despairingly. *I lied to my best friend for you people.*

"What did you tell her?"

She lifted her chin. "That it was an experimental aircraft, and we didn't have any more information than that."

Tereza started to say something, stopped. She looked at Conrad; he was rubbing his forehead, at a loss.

Goban held up his hands. "Everybody take a moment. Kate and I are going to step out."

She followed him out into the dining room. He didn't look angry; he didn't reveal any emotion at all. She bit her lip. "I'm sorry. I should have…"

"Doesn't matter. It's done." He sighed. "Do you trust her?"

"With my life."

"With mine?"

"If I had to trust someone with your life, she would be the one."

He considered her for a long moment, and then nodded. "Well. You'd better go call her, then."

* * *

Sitting in the truck waiting for the call, the pilots did not speak. They were thinking about the briefing. The real deal: not something unidentified, not a foreign experimental craft, but a confirmed extraterrestrial. "If the spacecraft breaks orbit over Asia or the western Pacific," the briefing officer said, "you will attempt to intercept it and escort it to a handoff point, where aircraft from Edwards Air Force Base in California will meet you to escort it the rest of the way in."

If the spacecraft breaks orbit. It was the sort of thing that you couldn't think too closely about; you focused on the job at hand.

Then the call came, and everything happened very quickly. The walk-around, the startup checklist, the crew chief disconnecting the starter unit, clearance from the tower, and the big fighter was moving, accelerating, seeming almost a living thing, eager. There were a handful of heartbeats, between the forward movement and the upward arc, for him to think to himself, don't screw this up — and then up over the mountains, out over the blue.

Three hundred miles northeast of the islands, they found the thing. Grey on grey, still glowing from re-entry.

He expected something bigger, and weirder; he couldn't have said how exactly, but an alien ship should not look like something that had come out of one of the secret R&D shops in the California desert. It unsettled him. *Physics,* he thought, with a mental shrug. *Airfoils were airfoils in anybody's atmosphere.*

It was bleeding speed fast, glow fading.

The aircraft took up formation as the pilot hoped like hell that the alien would understand what they were trying to do, and cooperate, because they didn't have many options. But the ship, compliant, matched speed and trajectory to theirs, and they headed for the distant California coast.

It was only after the handoff, after the F-15s turned around and headed back towards the islands, that the pilot let himself think about what had just happened. The rest of it — however it turned out — he would watch on the news like everyone else, but that terrifying and hopeful moment of first contact belonged to him.

* * *

They continued to talk through the night, arguing, kicking plans back and forth, making phone calls. The storm over Kate's sharing of the samples had blown over blessedly quickly. It might have been different had it not been just one thread of a much bigger tangle to sort out, had Gretchen herself not stepped up, without a moment's hesitation, to be part of the solution.

As the clock chimed two, Kate swam up to consciousness to realize she'd been dozing on the settee for a while. Goban was sitting next to her, having shifted her feet to find a place, contemplating the last of his brandy. She stretched, shifted, and rested her head on his shoulder. It was nice; she sighed, enjoying the sleep haze.

Tereza had been the last to leave, gone to her own

house down the hill to pack an emergency bag. It had been decided; she would go, when the word came, to wherever the ship landed, to negotiate. If she couldn't prevent the meeting, she could at least hope to take control of it. Goban and Kate would leave first thing in the morning for Vancouver, hoping to be over the border before anyone came looking.

"So, that... went well," she murmured.

He buried his face in her hair. "It's late. Everyone else has gone to bed. You should too."

Kate had never been don't-want-to-be-alone-tonight girl. She'd kicked plenty of lovers out of her place because she was tired, wanted to think, wanted her space to herself. But she had a little sympathy for the sentiment, right now. Everything was spinning apart, and the stable center was coming undone. He was warm, and his bed was only a few feet away; hers, up a floor and down a hallway, seemed like the other end of the world.

But she was too sleepy and brandy-sodden to think the question through, and unwilling to let herself be tossed by circumstance, like some small winged thing in a storm. And so, by long habit more than anything else, she gave him a lingering kiss and stumbled out, up the stairs, alone.

Less than three hours later, Jake came around pounding on doors. His cousin, Tommy, the sheriff's deputy, had called up from town. It was on the radio; it was on the news, everywhere.

* * *

CHAPTER ELEVEN

Kate turned the key in the little Nissan as the first pale glow appeared over the eastern ridge of the valley, pulled up the ring road and past the gate, waved at Reggie on her way past the gatehouse. "Be safe!" He shouted. "Don't call!" She grinned and gave a thumbs-up. It was a quiet drive, both of them still sleep-fogged and lost in their own thoughts, and the big lake was still and beautiful, ice-rimmed. Kate had not traveled this road since that first night.

They pulled through the gate of the tiny Gunnison airport as the sun crested the mountains. The charter pilot was there waiting for them — a stocky blonde woman, a few years younger than Kate, athletic, wiry, and deeply tanned. "Chris Carver," she introduced herself with a firm handshake. "My daddy started flying for the Darzins in the sixties, and I've been tagging along since I was thirteen."

"You're a bit taller than back then," Goban said, with a wink, and the pilot laughed.

"Not that much. And you have not changed a bit, sir. Some people have all the good genes." She gestured toward the runway. "Preflight's done, we can be rolling in ten minutes. No Tereza today? Mostly what I do is shuttle her back and forth to Denver —" this last was an aside to Kate. She kept up a steady stream of small talk as they loaded the luggage and climbed the ladder. "Bellingham's a pretty far haul and we're not going to be in any kind of hurry today. Flight time's just about three hours, over some pretty scenery. You got coffee here, you got soda and sandwiches, you got the satphone right here, you got TV – have you seen the news this morning? It's crazy. I'll be up here, don't hesitate to pop your head in if you've got questions. You ever flown in a small jet like this?"

"Um, no," Kate replied, bemused by the woman's exuberant energy. *Colorado is full of morning people.*

"There's going to be more turbulence than you're used to feeling in an airliner. It's normal, don't worry; if it's time to worry, you'll hear it from me first. I don't anticipate that."

"Got it." It was a beautiful day, winter-crisp and clear. Kate laid her hand against the cold glass of the tiny window and took a deep breath. She felt an impulse to dash outside, breathe in the mountain air, take one last good look around. But the door was already winding closed, and Chris was in the cockpit, and then they were rolling, and the faint lurch in her belly told her they were off the ground before it started to fall away.

Sometime later, she opened her eyes, shifted, made a sleepy, surprised noise. "Oh, I dozed off." *Master of the obvious, there, Katie.*

"Not a lot of sleep for anyone last night." He was watching her, his face thoughtful.

"Last night..." she started to say, but he held up his hand.

"You were right. There are so many things pulling on both of us, right now, and we have responsibilities. We're neither of us adolescents. We can take our time figuring it out." He smiled a little. *I took the wrong turn, last night,* she thought. *Missed the sign and flew right on by. How can I get back? Where will we be when all of this is over?*

He fixed her a coffee, settled in, and watched her watch the grey-green folds of southwestern Wyoming pass beneath them. She wondered at his stillness. *How can he be so calm?* Did that self-assurance come with time? It was sometimes easy to forget how much time he had been in the world, until she was struck anew by some gesture, some old-fashioned turn of phrase, or that intense, quiet patience.

What she felt was something else, uncertainty bordering on inarticulate terror. Everything she thought she knew, everything that she had tossed her old life away for, seemed to be slipping through her fingers.

"So. What do you want talk about?" She turned away from the window, looked at him, sleepy and uncertain. He shrugged. "We have a couple of hours. Just the two of us, this quiet," — *before the storm,* he did not say, but it was there — "and nothing to do but talk. I know... you have questions. So ask away. Anything you'd like to ask."

The last tendrils of sleepiness evaporated. She sipped her coffee, watching his face warily, looking for clues, scrambling at scattering thoughts. *Oh, so many questions.* She thought about Tereza in the kitchen; was that only yesterday? It felt like last year. *Maybe he'll open up to you.*

"Tell me about the crash."

He glanced away for an instant, and there was a flash of old grief, and something else — you could miss it if you weren't looking for it — and she thought he was going to say, *anything else*. But he didn't.

* * *

"It's a solitary life. You spend months at a time out, alone, in something the size of a two-room cabin. I was young, fresh out of school, and brash, and very, very good at my job. I thought... I could spend a few years working hard, gamble hard, make a lot of money, and get out. That it wouldn't change me.

"You don't think about how isolated you really are; you'd go crazy. People did, especially in the early days of manned survey. Just stepped outside and took off their helmets, or flew into a star. There were safeguards against that kind of thing, by the time I contracted, both in the profiling of recruits and in the ship systems. The kind of crazy you're more likely to see anymore is a kind of – arrogant asociality. You get it into your head that other people are a waste of your time, that the only thing that matters is the next transit, the next score. You come home long enough to get drunk, get some fresh air in your lungs, and then get back out there.

"You start to hold back a little on your reports, because you don't want to let slip what you're thinking, the leads that you're always chasing down that might lead to the next big score. Maybe you don't report in as soon as you bounce into a new system; you wait for the first scans to come back, until you have an idea of what you're dealing with. It's not like there's anything out there that you can't handle anyway. It's sloppy and dangerous, but everybody knows that it happens.

"So there I am, this hotshot kid, sitting out on the edge of the system, and the reports are coming in, and I'm thinking I've just put a good two years' base pay in the bank, because there are petrochemicals, there are rare metals — it's a good score. A nice stable star, a complex system. Gas giants with geologically active moons, a lot of small rock bodies. And then the console lights up with chlorophyll sign.

"This is a really big deal. We've only found a few planets with life, and none of them have worked out for large-scale colonization, for various reasons. Creating a new Sanctuary is at the core of the Semhet religious idea of destiny, and one of the driving forces behind interstellar spaceflight. So this changes everything. I ignore the rest of the reports and head straight for the green.

"And the Earth... was so beautiful, Kate. So beautiful. So warm, and blue, and so vast, rising out of the darkness like some beckoning light. And remember, as far as I knew, uninhabited. This was just a few years before Marconi's first radio broadcast.

"There were two thoughts in my head. The first was the *absolutely inconceivable* amount of money that they were going to pay me when I got home. I was done; it was the mother score. I was set for life.

"The second was that I just wanted to enjoy it a little. I'd always been a backcountry enthusiast. I spent a lot of time hiking and camping as a kid, and that was my touchstone when I came back from the field — I'd go out for a few days in the roughest country I could find and let it try to kill me. So this, this untouched paradise made my head swim. It was like a hallucination, the idea of being a solitary lord of creation over this glory. For just a little while. No one would know, and it wouldn't do any harm. I think I lost my mind a bit.

"I don't remember the crash itself. I remember realizing that I was coming in too fast into too dense an atmosphere, and then..." He shook his head. "Rita tells me that it's not uncommon for trauma amnesia to affect a span of time before the blow. Failure of short-term memory to convert, or something. There are probably a couple of hours missing. I don't know if something malfunctioned, but I've always thought that I was not thinking straight, not paying attention, and botched the descent. The inevitable outcome of the reckless road I'd been traveling for a while.

"I remember waking up in the crash cage, half buried, with the burning fragments of my shattered ship all around and behind me, drenched in every kind of mechanical fluid imaginable, stinking, and mad as hell. I'd inhaled some of that stuff and my lungs hurt, and when I look back on it, I think I had a cracked collarbone and a concussion. I was bruised up good, but more or less okay.

"At first I was just angry. I was lying there, fuming, dripping, kicking myself, raging at the universe, ashamed at the thought of firing off the emergency beacon and waiting for somebody to come collect me, angry that there was no... *dignity* in my victory. And then I guess the concussion took over, or exhaustion, and my mad wore off, and I realized that I was going to have to survive until someone came, that it would be months, and I still had that time to explore this astonishing place. And I thought, *I'll fire off the beacon tomorrow, after I build a shelter*, and I slept there in that mess.

"And tomorrow and tomorrow. There was so much to do, and every day there were more questions I wanted to answer. I built a tiny cabin. There's nothing as tedious as felling and trimming trees with a little handheld laser meant for cutting rock samples, so then I had the idea to build a smelter and forge, and then I made some tools and weapons, and started hunting. I used every scrap of textile I could salvage to make packs and tool belts, and then I figured out how to tan hides – not very well. I loved every minute of it. It was the hardest work I'd ever done, just staying alive from day to day, but it was *mine*. No reports to file, no questions, nobody bothering me.

"I was stupid lucky, understand. I was young and fit and an experienced camper, and I came down in late spring, early summer sometime. It would have gone much worse for me otherwise. Even then, I came pretty close to dying that first winter. I spent a lot of time sleeping, ate nothing but meat. I was, I'm sure, badly malnourished. I froze, and I breathed in wood smoke, I half suffocated. I don't remember very much of it. I do remember spring, and staggering out of my cabin one day and seeing clear patches of ground, and green. I don't think I'd been out of the cabin for days; I'd forgotten that I could. Like being back on the ship.

"I'm not religious, but that winter... well. Cold, dark, starving, choking, and alone is a near perfect picture of hell. Semhet hell, anyway. I was weak and not at all rational, and it crossed my mind more than once that I was being punished for my pride and carelessness. So I more or less decided, in those last few weeks of winter, that I needed to head to the low country and fire off the beacon, and wait for pickup.

"As soon as I could, I gathered up some of my tools and what was left of my food, what I could carry, and headed down into the canyon. I came out into the valley, right above where the hydro pond is now, and almost stumbled into their camp. Amalija and her brother-in-law and father-in-law. They were headed north from Ouray, looking for a stake. They had run into some kind of trouble there — she never told me the whole story — and her husband was killed. So they were wary, and I was... I don't even know. Seeing people was disorienting. But they had food, and clean clothes, and even a tiny bit of civilization was very attractive. So I took a gamble and laid all of my food down at their feet, and they seemed to understand what I was trying to say, and they let me stay. Like a stray dog. Not wanted, but not kicked either.

"She helped me get cleaned up. They wouldn't let me touch the weapons, so I stayed around the camp and helped her with whatever I could – building, hauling. We communicated by hand signs, and got by. Bit by bit, I came back to my right mind, and started wondering who they were and how they'd come to be there, and we started teaching each other our languages.

"I was pretty sick later that spring. Something with a rash and a fever. I think probably it was some children's thing that they carried with them, but of course, I'd never been exposed to any of the diseases here. Chicken pox, measles — who knows? It was bad, and I don't know if it was fear or just self-interest, but they decided to leave me to die." A grim set of the lips, a whitening of the knuckles. "Amja wouldn't, so they left her too. That's not something I've ever told anyone, by the way.

"And then it was just the two of us, and you know the story after that. Mikels was born not quite a year later, and that's when I went and buried the beacon in the woods, between the house and the top of the valley. Then we built the hydro dam, and the pond filled in right over that spot. I can't imagine how it turned up."

Kate did not speak for a long time. Then, quietly, she said, "I'd imagined it must have been... difficult, but I really had no idea. I am so sorry you had to live through that."

"I'm not." He shrugged. "I survived, and it changed everything. You learn something about humanity, living like an animal. I had no place in my life for love. Or family, home, duty. Before. There's a reason, Kate, that I have always said that the person I was died in that crash. I can't imagine going back. I can barely remember that world."

"You told me that, that first week. The first time we went riding."

"Yes." He sighed. "I wish Tereza the best of luck. But I don't have much hope."

* * *

CHAPTER TWELVE

"It's kind of a jurisdictional nightmare. Technically, he's, ah, an unidentified foreign national, so both State and Homeland Security want a piece of it. Other governments, of course. The civilian scientists – the SETI Institute has sent a team down from San Jose, NASA's sending people, ESA, the UN. Everybody. But we have nine-tenths. For now, anyway. The contingency plans only go so far – there's some making it up as we go along."

"So that's why I'm here?" Lou Farris had flown out of Colorado Springs at dawn. When the C-38 touched down at Edwards, a car was waiting right on the runway; the driver was a staffer from the wing commander's office.

"Yes, sir. The 412th Test Wing has a huge range of technological assessment capabilities, and the equipment and personnel for containment and evaluation, so we have operational command. But the intel wing at Peterson wanted someone here to represent the work they'd already done on the communications, and you've been right in the middle of that. Ah, here we are." The driver pulled up and parked next to the gatehouse separating the main base from the separate, secret research base far out on the ancient lakebed.

He could see the runway and the blocky grey craft. They were waved through, and walked the rest of the way. Not a long walk; he had thought the craft was both bigger and farther away than it actually was. "It looks like a space shuttle." He was surprised by that. Even smaller. A hundred and fifty feet long, maybe, with a fat body and stubby small upturned wings. Interstellar travel in that tiny thing was hard to believe.

"Yes, it's definitely a transatmospheric vehicle. We haven't had a look inside yet. He came out pretty quickly after he set down, and the SPs hustled him right into the quarantine tent."

Under a protective shade canopy, the mobile isolation unit was a small, rigid, transparent tent, domed to fit inside an aircraft. It had been stripped of all of its equipment except for a cot and an environmental monitor.

The stranger was pacing the length of the tent. He looked perfectly ordinary. Human.

He stopped from time to time to stare at the guards, to drum his hands on the cot or the plastic walls. Made it as obvious as he could that he understood the purpose of the space he had been put into, and he didn't like it. He saw the two new arrivals watching him, stopped in front of the door, putting his hands flat against the plastic, and ranted at length. He walked away, then came back. There was no nervousness in his movements, only frustrated purpose.

The driver looked amused. "You get the impression he thinks he's the one in charge, don't you?"

Farris shook his head. "I'm not sure I'd want to be the one who has to tell him otherwise." He'd known guys like this: arrogant, tightly in control, accustomed to getting what they wanted. That, he thought, was the best thing that the team had going for them right now. He wanted something, clearly, and he would negotiate in order to get it, or get closer to it. If they could figure out what he was saying.

The stranger pulled a piece of some flimsy, paper-like material out of a pocket in his trousers, unfolded it with deliberation. He slapped it up against the plastic door. "*Nhoresh Goban,*" he shouted through the plastic, enunciating as if speaking to children. "*Garan'cha Nhoresh Goban? Garanda cha ve?*"

Farris blinked and stepped backwards, stunned. The driver looked at him, curious. "Familiar?"

The photograph was old, but it was crisp, and there wasn't any question in his mind that the smiling, young, uniformed man was Henry Darzins.

* * *

Face pressed up against the window like a kid on the approach to Bellingham, Kate saw the tiny blue Mustang in the charter lot. A blonde figure was leaning against the hood in a long coat and sunglasses, like a sixties movie star, watching the jet set down. She made a small, involuntary noise of happiness. A few minutes later, she was stepping off the plane under the steel-grey Pacific Northwest winter sky, inhaling the familiar scent of ocean and pines, feeling the gut-punch of the sudden change of place. Gretchen was striding across the tarmac, and Kate broke into a run, embraced her, felt tears well up.

Gretchen pulled back, hands on her shoulders. "Hey, Katie." She brushed the rush of tears from Kate's face, glanced toward the little jet. "What kind of trouble are you in?" she asked, softly.

Kate shook her head. "No, it's just — it's been an overwhelming couple of days." She gathered her bravado, smiled. "Remember when you said you wanted the whole story?" Goban was just catching up to them, and she reached out, entangled her fingers in his.

Gretchen saw that, and raised an eyebrow, with a small smile tugging the side of her mouth. She met Kate's eyes, and the smile spread. She held out her hand to Goban. "I can't wait. Hi. Gretchen Willoughby."

He grinned broadly, took her hand, and dipped his head in a half-nod, half-bow. Bringing on the cowboy charm. "Yes, Kate speaks so highly of you. Delighted to meet you. Thank you for being here."

"Of course. Anything for Katie. We've been friends for a long time." There was an unsubtle, territorial emphasis on that. *A lot longer than you've been around, and don't you forget it.*

Kate pulled away, anxious to break the tension. "Okay, I'm going to go get the car. I'll be right back. I have some errands to run," she added, seeing Gretchen's look. "I'm going to follow you two up tonight."

"I'll walk with you," Gretchen said. Goban caught the *just the two of us* message, nodded to Kate. He headed back toward the jet, where Chris was unloading the luggage, as the women walked toward the terminal.

"Okay, *what is going on?*" Gretchen hissed.

"He has to get across the border. Soon. This morning."

"You told me that last night. Are you in some kind of legal trouble?"

"No. I don't know. It could turn into that, I guess." There was no way to make that sound less awful. Kate stopped, turned to face her friend. It seemed better to take the plunge now than to wait until they could all get out of the airport and sit down at breakfast. No sense letting Gretchen get any more wound up than she already was. "You've seen the news? The thing that landed in California this morning?"

"God, everyone has. It's bonkers." Gretchen's eyes widened. "Kate…" The pieces fell into place. She stared at the small, distant figure on the tarmac. "How long has he been here?"

"A long time." Relief flooded through Kate. If Gretchen was going to be okay, then everything might be okay after all. "A long time, and no one has ever come looking for him before, but now they have, and the military's involved, and I don't know if it even matters, but putting a border between him and… whatever is happening in California, might afford him a little extra protection. Buy some time."

"Sure."

"I'm sorry. I couldn't tell you—"

"No, I get it." They were at the rental car counter now; Gretchen looked around, dropped her voice. "If I were in his shoes, I wouldn't want just any stranger knowing that about me, you know? It's okay." She squeezed Kate's hand, and stepped aside while Kate ran through the car paperwork and got the keys. She didn't speak again until they were well out of the building, walking toward the rental lot. "This explains a lot. It puts some things into context."

"Doesn't it just?" Kate fidgeted, watched

Gretchen's face out of the corner of her eye, still worried. She shrugged. "We have no idea what's going to happen. His granddaughter is on her way down there now to negotiate."

A startled look. "His high-schooler granddaughter?"

That made Kate laugh out loud. "His terrifyingly competent lawyer granddaughter. He's older than he looks, which is something that he gets a lot, so don't be weird about it, all right?"

Kate and Goban, in the rental, followed Gretchen's Mustang to a chain coffeehouse a mile from the airport, where they had the patio to themselves under the threatening sky. Bouncing back and forth, they told her everything.

She was quiet for a long time, and Kate tried to imagine what was running through her mind. Finally she laughed a little, shook her head, stood up. "Okay, then, Canada or bust. Let's get on the road."

Kate stood up and embraced her. "Are you all right?"

"I am. It's a lot to take in, you know? I'm going to go... start the car." Gretchen winked and grinned. "Tonight, right? We have a lot to talk about."

"Tonight. Thanks for everything."

Gretchen walked away, around the side of the building. Kate put her arms around Goban, rested her forehead in the hollow of his shoulder. "Oh, don't go."

A small wry laugh. "I didn't even want to leave the farm. I think the whole thing is pointless. But Tereza is an unstoppable force. It's not worth it to argue with her."

Kate shook her head and smiled. "I wonder where she gets that." She looked up at him, went serious. "Are we okay?"

"Did you have any doubt?"

"I really did."

His eyes widened. "I'm sorry, I didn't realize. I should have made sure that was clear last night." He kissed her lightly. "You made a hard choice in good faith. I have perfect confidence in you."

She looked up at him. "Oh, that's good, because I want to say something to you, and I want you to just listen, okay?"

He raised his eyebrows, smirked. "I'm listening."

"Don't laugh."

"I'm not laughing." The smile deepened, lighting up something in his eyes. She felt a little dizzy.

"Okay." She hesitated, feeling hot tears burn at the corner of her eyes. "I love you. When this is over, I want to be your wife. What I need you to do right now is to take this seriously. Don't be stupid. Protect yourself. Stay off the radar. Let Gretchen help you, let Tereza do her job. *Come home.*"

The laughter vanished from his face. He kissed her then, for a long time, lifted her off her feet; her fingers were caught up in his hair, and when he set her down, she felt like she might fall right through the ground. "Go," she said, pushing on his chest. "Go, get safe. I'll see you tonight."

*　*　*

Tereza drove slowly through the massed crowds of vehicles outside the north gate of the base. Media, and spectators. She held her breath in awe. You had to see it in person.

A crisp young guard stepped into the path of the rental car, but it wasn't necessary; Tereza was entirely interested in making nice, and rolled to a stop well short of the gate. She passed her driver's license out the window to him and smiled widely. "Good morning. I am Nhoresh Goban's attorney, and you are going to let me see the visitor."

It was gutsy, and a long shot. The kid was too professional; of course he would be. His eyes widened a little, but he offered no further reaction. He handed the ID over to his partner, who took it into the gatehouse to check, and then waved him inside too. He came back several minutes later.

"Ma'am, I can't even start to tell you how over my head that is, but I think I can see that you get to talk to somebody. Please pull over right here and we'll be with you shortly."

* * *

Lunch with Kate's old boss was uncanny deja vu, intensified when she put the small refrigerated sample case on the table. "This is what I called about. I need to synthesize therapeutic quantities of this sample for medical testing, and with the equipment I have at my lab in Colorado, it's too slow. You have access to more powerful equipment, and it's important that I get this done."

He regarded the sample case, suspicious. "What is

it?"

"I... I've been working on the analysis, but I'm not there yet. I've been focused on trying to get enough of it to work with." She shrugged. "It's some kind of metabolic regulatory hormone."

"I'm not sure I should be doing any favors for you, Kate." His expression was closed, his arms crossed.

"Oh, it's not a favor. The family will pay very well." *They'll pay in their hearts' blood if you ask them to.* "I'm just trying to get this ball rolling. We may not have a lot of time. Think of this as a feasibility assessment."

He looked away, made some kind of face. She knew that face. He was softening. "No, I mean, I've been getting phone calls about you. An FBI agent called me this morning, right after you called, asked me to let them know if you had come around trying to get into your old research."

She stared at him. "Really?" Then she made the connection. *Oh, Farris. Rot in hell.* "I promise you, the last thing in the world that I'm interested in is my old research."

He sighed elaborately and accepted the sample case. "You have a vector, too?"

"It's in there."

"Easy job then. I'll have some numbers for you later – timeframes *and* cost. Have your contract people get in touch with the front office."

He texted her later. *Don't go anywhere. Will call first thing AM.* She called Gretchen to tell her she wouldn't be up to Vancouver until the morning, and then called her mother. "Hey, I'm in town, I'm unexpectedly free. Do you want to go to dinner?"

* * *

"Let me be perfectly clear," said Tereza. "My role here is narrow and specific and really has nothing to do with you people at all. I am here to negotiate with the visitor on Nhoresh Goban's behalf, and *if* I'm satisfied that there is no danger to his safety or freedom, then I may contact him and advise him to come in for further discussions."

They had given her a lanyard with a temporary ID, taken her overnight bag away, and delivered her to a low grey building across a well-kept lawn from the base hotel, to a lounge outside a bank of conference rooms. She struck up a conversation with the man also waiting; his name was Erik Jansen, and he had just arrived from the SETI Institute. He was cheerful and gregarious, and it was easy enough to let him do the talking until she was called in.

There were two other people in the room. The officer introduced himself; Tereza recognized the name of the man she'd spoken to on the phone a few weeks before, the one who had come to the farm. She was already on her guard, and that edged up her uneasiness another notch. The other person, a woman, wore an expensive, understated civilian suit. Smooth, dark complexion, age impossible to guess. She could be a decade either side of thirty-five. She was quiet and watchful and didn't introduce herself; her ID lanyard just read *Thorne, Leslie.*

Major Farris eyed Tereza, curiosity warring with suspicion on his face. "How are you going to communicate with him?"

"I speak his language." Almost nonchalantly, but watching their reactions. Neither seemed surprised, which fascinated her. The woman looked intensely interested, while Farris' suspicion deepened.

"And how is that?" he asked.

"Nhoresh Goban — you were introduced to him as Henriks Darzins — is my grandfather. He taught the Semhet global trade language to all of us. We all grew up speaking it."

Farris stared at her; she looked back coolly. She could see him filtering through the pieces he had at hand, trying to puzzle it all together. The beacon, her arrival, her mention of a name that had come to their attention only minutes before she pulled up to the front gate of the base. His uneasiness, and the sense of insularity about the farm. Whatever words he had exchanged with her grandfather behind closed doors. Oh, yes. He didn't trust her, but he believed her. She had command of the moment. *Dig in.*

She shrugged, broke the silence. "Put me out there. You'll see us start talking. That's what you want, right? To start talking to him?"

Thorne, Leslie, nodded. "Of course. But as you say, your agenda is specific. We want to achieve a more... well-rounded communication, as you can imagine."

"I'm not opposed to quid pro quo. You give me the questions you'd like asked, and give me access; I'll try to get you your answers. You're welcome to make a recording that you can use to start building a vocabulary to communicate with him independently. But for the time being, I'm what you've got."

Thorne looked at Farris, thoughtful. "Why not?"

He frowned. "We're in pretty unfamiliar territory here. Excuse me, Ms. Darzins, we don't know anything about you except that you have a connection to the beacon that brought this — visitor — here, a connection with the fugitive that he is evidently pursuing, and an ongoing agenda of concealing an alien presence on earth. And by the way, why is he running?"

"I'm sorry?"

He gave her an exasperated look. "Give us a little credit. *Henry Darzins* –" there was contempt in the emphasis – "crossed the Canadian border an hour and a half ago in the company of a woman whose connection to your family is not well established, but who does seem to have some history with our favorite bioweapons specialist, Kate Hutchins. You want to comment on that?"

Damn. Thanks for trying, Kate. It had been worth a shot; if only they'd had even twenty-four hours. It would have to be bravado, then.

"Wouldn't you go to ground, if it were you? Under these circumstances? He's not a criminal, Major." She had nothing but his word for that, in fact, and her own questions about his long silence, but who was going to contradict her? "My understanding is that this is a corporate humanitarian mission seeking to rescue a person they believe to be an employee in distress. He's not in distress and does not have any desire to be rescued, and I'm here to relay that, and to clarify his right to remain here. In the meantime, it seemed sensible for him to go someplace out of the way for a few days. Ms. Willoughby is a close friend of one of our most valued employees, and she graciously offered her hospitality. You have to really want to twist that to make it sound like anything other than what it is."

Farris looked at her with tired and hostile eyes, and she had an idea of what he was thinking. "I've never lied to you," she said, enunciating.

"Just stonewalled."

Shrug. "Well, as I say, wouldn't you?"

"I would expect cooperation when national security is at stake."

"How long have you been stationed in Colorado? Have you not run into that culture of self-sufficiency before? There's a common theme here. We don't like to be bothered."

"Why should we let you talk to him? Without any kind of meaningful supervision? We have operational security to maintain here."

Tereza laughed out loud, then. "Oh, Major. If your own history has not taught you anything, maybe you can learn something from my family's experience. Operational security is *bullshit*. You cannot control this, you cannot contain it. Have you seen outside the gate of this base? This thing is already spinning so far out of your hands that the only thing you can hope for is to be allowed to give a little bit of direction to it, for now. Watch and see how long that lasts."

The young woman stood up, left the room without a word. The Major shifted in his seat, not looking at her.

The uncomfortable silence dragged on until Thorne came back in, a few moments later. She nodded to Tereza. "You have your access."

Oh, interesting. "Who are you, exactly?"

"I'm sorry, I didn't say? I'm with the Vice President's advance team. Special advisory committee on technology." A small, tightly controlled half-smile. "He's following, of course; he'll be here in a few hours. The decision was made that it was more appropriate to send the head of the civilian space agency than the commander-in-chief."

"Oh, that's a nice sentiment. Is it actual agenda or just message control?"

Thorne's smile spread. "I think it's your job to help us figure that out, now."

* * *

CHAPTER THIRTEEN

It wasn't that simple. First, she had to be prepped by the SETI team, who provided her with a set of questions. The Air Force had their own set of questions, and met with her separately. Then a third group of stern-faced bureaucrats explained to her the protocols of contact. She was not to approach within arm's reach of the isolation unit's surface. She was absolutely not to make any attempt at physical contact or entry. She would be asked to change out of her clothes and into clothes they provided for her, and would be examined for weapons, sharp objects, or recording devices of any kind, including paper and pencil. She agreed to the search but balked at the change of clothes; how could she keep a high-status appearance, which she might need to convey a sense of authority in order to gain his cooperation? There was a delay, a flurry of conferencing, and the decision was made at some higher level to allow her to keep her clothes, but not her stiletto pumps. Some junior staffer was sent to the Base Exchange to find black flats in her size.

By then it was lunchtime, and they insisted on feeding her; she fretted and picked at the very nice lunch they brought over from the officers' club, anxious to get to work. Then the Vice President's flight was landing, and there was another discussion about whether to allow her to begin her interrogation before or after he did his review. She suggested he might find it interesting. Thorne was consulted. Further discussion. In the end, it was almost three in the afternoon before they drove her out to the runway on the dry lakebed, followed by the SETI people in a second truck with their monitoring and recording equipment on big steel carts.

She walked all the way around the mobile isolation unit, slowly, watching while he watched her back, his body language pure tightly self-contained aggression. She stopped at the door. Their eyes met. His were black — intense, angry eyes set in a narrow, finely-featured face. Shorter, but he had that same spare, bird-boned frame; and his hair, dark like her own, kept short, but just long enough that she could see where he was going grey. About the same age as her grandfather, she guessed; mature, but not old.

She keyed the radio. Without it, she could shout through the plastic, but the quarantine people didn't want her to get that close. With it, they told her, her voice would be amplified and broadcasted through speakers inside the tent.

"*Garan'cho ahel?*" What are you doing here? Who are you? Why are you here?

He started, stared at her. Took a fast step toward the plastic barrier, startling her. She resisted the impulse to jump back, and stared right back at him.

"*Ehve Semhet?*"

"*Otyo, sepden ghene va.*" No, I belong to this place. She repeated her first question.

He began to visibly uncoil. He sat down on the cot, stared at her, suspicious. She felt sorry for him, a little.

He spoke slowly, chose his words with care. "I... am investigating. One of our craft went missing a number of years ago, and its recovery beacon has been traced to this planet. I have been sent here to recover it and to recover its personnel if possible. I am looking for this man." Once again, he pressed the picture up against the plastic. "Nhoresh Goban. He is a geologic survey engineer. Where is he? What is his condition?"

She studied the stranger, studied the picture. Took her time; she had all the time in the world, and all the power. She wanted him to understand that. "What are your intentions toward him?" A collective, hierarchical *you, the-you-that-you-represent.*

"Only to recover. His assessment will be conducted by others."

His answer confirmed her first impression: he was just an agent, with no real authority or latitude. "I see." She looked away, considered. She nodded at Dr. Jansen, keeping his distance. He nodded back, watching her interact with the stranger. "What outcome of that assessment can reasonably be expected?"

"What is your interest?"

She echoed his slow, careful speech, hoping that she conveyed precision rather than the uncertainty she felt with the language. This was very different from the flowing colloquial polyglot chatter she spoke with her cousins. "I am here to advocate for Engineer Nhoresh. He is well and safe, elsewhere. He is concerned about the intentions of many toward his wellbeing. Yourself and the Semhet authorities you represent, first. This government, second. An agitated and confused public, third. You can understand."

"My captivity is inappropriate! You must release me and escort me to him."

She scoffed. "I have no authority to do so, and I have no reason to. Also, your arrival has created a disruption here. Your safety is in question. This *containment* is protective." Emphasis in the distinction.

"How do you know the language of Semhet people?"

"I was taught by Engineer Nhoresh."

He narrowed his eyes. Hesitated, gathered his thoughts. "How widespread is knowledge of Semhet people?"

She pushed down a smile. Oh, he was sharp. "Not widespread at all. He has assimilated and has been living in relative seclusion among the people of this world. Only a small number of close relatives know anything of his life before he crashed here. Perhaps fifteen people. Twenty at most."

"You are a descendant?"

She inclined her head in acknowledgment, declined to clarify.

"Then you are Semhet also."

"I don't –" Cultural identity was not a concept she knew how to express in this language. "I do not have that experience." This was getting too personal, too centered on her. Turn it back to him. "When you arrived, the worldwide scientific community became aware of people from other worlds. We had not previously had this awareness, in general. We know nothing more than what we have observed from your arrival and your short time here.

"You still have not answered my question. What outcome can Engineer Nhoresh expect, if he returns to Semhaata with you for assessment?"

"To speculate would be pointless."

"Then you and I have nothing further to discuss." Tereza turned her back on the stranger and walked away.

* * *

"Why did you cry off? He was cooperating!" There were half a dozen people in the room this time. Farris again, the SETI scientist she had met that morning and then again out by the isolation unit. Several local officers.

"Not for much longer." Tereza shook her head. "He's incredibly arrogant, and self-righteous. Mission-oriented. It's clear to me that he didn't expect — well, us. He's out of his depth, and pissed off about it. But he cannot imagine that, in the end, we'll do anything but defer to his authority, as he's deferred to the authority of whoever sent him here. I'll tell you what he's thinking right now: he's thinking that I'm in here convincing you he's here on legitimate business, acting within his rights, and we very shortly will just cut him loose to go collect my grandfather. Of course."

"So he's a bounty hunter?" Farris asked.

She frowned. She'd explained this already, and she didn't like the connotation that he kept trying to steer toward. "More like an insurance investigator, from what my grandfather said. Loss recovery. The concept doesn't map exactly, of course."

"But I don't understand. What else did he expect?"

Dr. Jansen was standing by the window, staring out at the open plain of the salt flat, the distant haze of low mountains beyond. Hands in his pockets, he spoke for the first time. "You know, SETI has had people working on this for... decades, completely in the dark, having no idea what shape the thing would take when it finally happened, but mapping out scenarios logically and trying to create a plan that would perform on the ground. It's an impossible problem, to predict what is by its essential nature unpredictable. But one thing the community has had consensus on for a while now — we always thought we'd have more time."

He went quiet for a minute before continuing. "We just... thought we'd have more time. We expected that we'd find a signal, analyze it and confirm its intelligent origins, and form international committees, and discuss it, and... and control the message as it reached the public. And that is exactly how it started; because although, yes, the San Jose team picked up that first ping, it wasn't immediately clear whether it was an intelligent signal or a natural phenomenon. If you Americans had cared to share the beacon signal," — looking balefully at the officers — "we would of course have had time to discuss and prepare. Weeks, months. But no, we were still analyzing the ping, arguing about it, when we picked up the flash. After that, we had seventeen hours." He paused to let that sink in.

"It is possible that our visitor is reeling from the same shock. He traveled here using some kind of faster-than-light drive. We don't know anything about how that technology works, or its limitations, but I can easily imagine that while in transit, he wasn't aware of our electromagnetic signals." He spread his hands. "I think it's possible — even likely — that his first indication that we were here came at the same moment that he revealed himself to us with a great flash at the threshold of our solar system."

Tereza agreed. "That aggression we've all seen is masking a great deal of anxiety. He's trying so hard to maintain the upper hand in the face of circumstances that must be very confusing to him. The way he fixed on me when I spoke his language — he thinks I'm his ticket out of here. You know, my feeling, unfortunately, is that if he decides I'm not getting him closer to what he wants, he's going to quit talking altogether and start planning an escape attempt." She looked around the room, gave them all a chance to think on that. "That's why I walked away, to regroup and buy time, and to share that."

* * *

"Will you consent to some medical tests?"

The visitor was lying down on the cot, his arm thrown across his eyes, exuding an air of unbearable boredom. Either his aggression was exhausted, or he was trying a new tactic.

"No."

"It would be helpful for us to understand more about you. Also, to assess how much risk it might be for you to be released from containment. That can only benefit your mission, am I right?"

That got his attention; he opened his eyes and sat up. "What is it that you want to understand?"

"Why you are so much like us."

"But you are Semhet."

She shook her head, unwilling to get into that again. "No, I mean why you, and I, are so much like these people." She gestured toward Dr. Jansen and his assistants, and the guards.

He frowned, genuinely confounded, spread his hands in a gesture of bafflement. "One assumes all intelligent life is alike."

She blinked. Stared at him. There was no sign he was mocking her. She thought for a moment. "We, ah, don't assume that at all. We have always thought that intelligent life on other worlds would be so..." she grasped for the right word, realized to her surprise that she knew of no Semhet concept for *alien*. "So different. Perhaps even too different... to encounter, for useful dialogue. You are quite a surprise to us."

For the first time, he was interested in something other than his mission. "Why would you assume that?"

Oh, we're on to something here. She started to say, because of evolution — and realized she didn't have a word for that either. "Because intelligent life would reflect the diversity of its world of origin, yes? Unique to... the biological heritage of earlier life forms from which they have diverged."

His eyes widened; he froze. "This is heresy. You are trying to confuse me." He turned away.

"Huh." She stood there for a minute, puzzled, then walked over to Jansen and his team, and relayed the substance of the conversation in a hushed voice.

Jansen looked from the isolation tent back to her. "Heresy," he repeated, pondering. "Well then."

She walked back, tried to engage the visitor. He steadfastly ignored her.

With nothing else to do, they packed up the equipment and headed inside to regroup. Tereza went out a few more times, over the course of the evening and into the night, and tried to get him talking again, to no avail. He even kept his back to her when she tried to instruct him in the meal packs that the medical team brought. "Starve, then," she muttered, and rubbed her eyes, and gave up.

* * *

Gretchen and Goban were sitting in her tiny apartment living room, eating lamb korma and samosas, and watching the news. The short video the Air Force had released of the alien craft on approach in California played over and over, interspersed with aerial shots of the masses outside the base gate, an endless cycle of fluff pieces to feed the clamoring audience. They treated it like a bad movie, scoffing and mocking, while he negotiated the plastic packaging and utensils.

"You don't eat much takeout, do you?" she asked, amused. She had been wary at first, but she'd decided that she liked this quiet guy, with his understated wry humor and slightly old-fashioned manner of speech and work-calloused hands. She liked him for Kate. But she was still uneasy.

"Well, it gets cold before you get to the top of the mountain." He laughed. "I haven't been off the farm much in a few years. I used to travel more."

"I hadn't heard." Her eyes crinkled.

"Hah! More recently than that, in fact." He shook his head, grinning. "So. You've been friends for a long time?"

"Oh, yes." A low, throaty laugh, full of nostalgia. "We were the only two science geek girls in Wallace Hall, which, at the time — this was the early nineties — was dominated by the English lit and poli-sci majors. We were not the cool kids. We've... looked out for each other, ever since."

"Gretchen. Kate and I had time to talk, some, on the plane." Serious, but still smiling. "Did you think we wouldn't?"

"I'm not sure what to think."

"Well, that's fair."

All right, she thought, *let's have this conversation. Clear the air.* "She lied to me for you."

"I know. I'm sorry." He looked at her, sincere and concerned, and she took a pull on her beer and wanted to believe him.

"I don't know what I'm seeing here," she said.

"Just an old farmer." She made a face at him; he laughed a little. "No, really. I used to be something else. Hasn't been relevant for a long time. Now, suddenly, it is. I'm dealing with that." He shrugged. "You were lovers. Is it relevant? Seems to me it informs your friendship now, and that's what that matters. Your loyalty. I'm grateful for that."

She breathed a sigh of relief. "So we're good."

That's up to you, his smirk and diffident gesture

seemed to say. "Why wouldn't we be? No, that's disingenuous, I'm sorry. You're right." He was laughing now. Then he said the last thing she would have expected. "What do you know about me? Amja and Kate. There's history you don't know, between and before."

She raised her eyebrows, startled. "You're bi?"

"I'm *not from here*, is what I am."

"You've been here a long time."

"I have. Long enough to learn all the words. What they mean. That they *matter* here. I understand that bisexual is a word that matters to Kate. I respect that. You are perhaps the most important person in her life, and I respect that too. So I'm interested." He smiled, seeming to want to put her at ease, and here she had been thinking that he would be the one who found this conversation awkward.

"No, wait, I want to know more about this," Gretchen said.

"It's not an anthropology lesson. I'm interested in you and Kate. Your friendship." He hesitated. "You're not still lovers, are you?"

She laughed out loud. "Not for many years." The tension broke; she was still grinning. "We were nineteen, okay? Like I said, two nerdy girls, absolutely mad in love. But we were also both pretty screwed-up kids; neither of us was ready for a relationship like that. But... a funny thing happened after we broke up." After she'd moved back home, all of two hundred kilometres, but Kate had taken the border between them as a personal betrayal. Or so it had seemed. Who knew? One awful fight about it, and then neither of them had ever brought it up again. She shrugged. "We both kept picking up the phone. Just couldn't stay away."

"You understood her."

"I'd like to think so. She doesn't have a lot of people who do. She's reserved."

"Easy," he said, "to cross the line from reserve to secrecy." He stared off into the middle distance, frowning, reflecting on that. "I think Kate is developing an aversion to secrets."

"Good." Vehemently. "They're not good for her. See, here's the thing about Katie," she said. "I trust her. I have confidence in her. You know? She'll tell me the truth when she can. For all that she was scared this morning, she's also happier, these last few months, than in all the time I've known her. She says she has a responsibility to you, so... here we are. Not that it isn't weird, let me tell you. Sitting here eating takeout with my best friend's alien lover." He started to say something, stopped, looked embarrassed. Gretchen almost choked on her samosa. "You're kidding. What in the hell have you been waiting for? You're obviously wild about each other." She studied him. "Oh, I get it. A little skittish, is she? A little hot and cold?"

She put her food down and took a swig of her beer. "Look. You're her boss, and also the direct subject of her research study, which is complicated, and either of those two things should make you off limits. But that's not all. You're a — *phenomenon.* You've had this amazing life, seen so much, you've traveled all over the world, you got to see the tail end of the Wild West, for God's sake. You have a formidable family, you're smart and attractive and accomplished, and I'm going to take a wild guess here and assume you're not exactly broke. Am I right?"

"We do all right." He was looking at her warily, trying to make sense of where she was headed.

"Has it even crossed your mind that she is maybe, just a teeny bit, intimidated? In awe of you? Have you even considered the possibility that she might wonder what you see in her?"

"Really? No." He frowned.

"You're not as smart as I thought." She eyed him. "I mean, you and I both get how great she is, but we all think of ourselves as pretty ordinary, right? But she looks at you and sees anything but ordinary. So she's got to wonder."

"She's kind." His face softened, thoughtful. "She was very kind to me, when I was ill and afraid, and she had no obligation to be. It reminded me of someone who did something similar, a long time ago. She's warm-hearted, and... hopeful, but not naïve. She is tough-minded and pragmatic, and as relentless as anyone I've ever met, and when you meet my family, you'll understand that that's saying something. It's a charming combination. It inspires faith."

Gretchen was quiet for a moment. "You've never told her that."

"Now I think I won't get the chance. I danced around it too long, and now we've missed our shot."

* * *

CHAPTER FOURTEEN

The investigator lay on the hard plastic cot, staring at the first wan stars on the darkening horizon, uncomfortable and irritated. Someone in some kind of biohazard suit had brought food and blankets, but the tent was cold, and this sky was so empty and dark. The edge of the void.

The intense frustration he'd felt, his first hours here, was giving way to other emotions. He was tired and confused, and felt exposed, watching the movements of the guards through the clear plastic, knowing they were watching him.

Posturing aside, he did understand the isolation and the questions. Of course. If strangers from another world had come to Semhaata like this, his people would do the same thing: force the strangers down in some isolated desert place and study them. It was necessary, and inevitable, and he could only cooperate and hope to wait it out, hope they would let him get on with his work.

But the work was suddenly, impossibly complicated.

He rubbed his face, tried to think through the problem.

First: his captivity, separated from his ship, surrounded by armed guards, unable to communicate with anyone except the strange woman. Or not allowed? She seemed sincere enough, but he had no way to validate anything she said.

She herself was the second problem. If she was telling the truth, then she controlled everything: access to the target, access to information, any means of negotiating a release from here. Controlled the access of the security officials to him, too, he realized; they couldn't talk to him without her cooperation, and she could be telling them anything at all, whatever furthered her own mission. To protect Nhoresh.

Nhoresh, damn him. She was his advocate, she'd said. That could mean... almost anything. The renegade had been here all this time, living among these people. It was obvious now that he'd never intended to set the beacon off at all, but he also hadn't destroyed it, which was puzzling. A mistake? Had it been confiscated?

He reflected on the offhand comments she'd made, her references to disruption, confusion. Were these people unsettled enough by his presence that they might be willing to sacrifice Nhoresh to get rid of him? That could be useful.

The woman was the key. All of the pieces locked together, and he couldn't get any of them to move without her help.

He kept going back to her last words, turning them over. Why would she say that? What kind of people were these?

If he had seen nothing except this place, the security base they'd guided his ship to and the bleak cold desert around it, he might easily enough believe that this planet was Hell. But he had seen, in the few hours of his initial orbit and descent, orbital tech, cities lighting up the night side, vast oceans, continent-spanning mountain ranges and forests, the swirling cloud formations of complex *weather systems, the green ribbon of coastline he crossed on the descent, and the great geometric forms of irrigated agricultural complexes further inland, just on the other side of the coastal mountains. No, this was a paradise, every bit as diverse and rich as Semhaata, and nearly as technologically sophisticated.*

Was it possible that they possessed a Sanctuary and didn't know it?

* * *

Dr. Jansen caught up with Tereza at the officers' club, at dinner. "May I sit with you?"

She appraised him. "I'd like that very much."

It was pleasant to have someone to talk to, at least somewhat freely, just a normal conversation. She asked about his background, his work and family. He had been born in a tiny Danish island village, but had spent most of his life in England and the United States; that explained his faint and unidentifiable accent. He was an astrophysicist by training, and had been involved in early exoplanet research, but for several years had been doing advisory and administrative work. A widower, with two children and, a few years ago, his first grandchild.

He asked about her family, and she didn't know where to start. She put down her fork. "Let me tell you a story, Doctor.

"I was four years old in October of 1938. My Tēvocis Arturs — my uncle — had been living abroad for many years, and he had just come home from Africa with his new wife and baby daughter. My sister Emma was born that summer, too. I remember... all of us, my aunts and uncles, and my parents and me, and my grandfather, all sitting in my grandfather's study, listening to the evening radio.

"Have you ever heard *War of the Worlds?* The radio program?"

He shook his head. "No, I remember the movie, of course. Many years ago."

"The movie was nothing like it. The radio show was absolutely terrifying. It was so — real. So vivid. I didn't understand it at all at the time, but I thought about it many times, later, over the years. What I remember most was my Tante Annika, holding Rita, my cousin, and her slow-growing horror, and understanding, and then acceptance, as she came to realize just what she had married into, what people would think of her family, and her child — if they knew. And my mother with Emmie, and these two women, holding hands and holding on to their babies and crying for their daughters. It, ah, made an impression.

"I have only known two things for certain in my life. The first is that I love my family very much, and my life's work is to protect them. The second thing is that at the heart of protecting them is *keeping the secret.* So" — she made a sweeping gesture — "can you begin to imagine what all of this is like for me?"

He leaned back, set his fork down. Folded his hands. Precise little gestures of careful consideration. He looked at her with sympathy, and shook his head. "No, I can't. I... recognize that, at least. I can sympathize, a little, though. My life's work has also been upended, but it can be nothing like the turmoil you and your family must be going through.

"Many of these military men are scientifically minded, and curious. But a few of them, some of the ones in charge here, I think, would be just as happy to throw your grandfather under a bus in service of the status quo. Hand him over to our friend out there" — a vague gesture in the direction of the dry lake — "with good riddance to them both. I can understand that you would do anything to prevent that."

"Yes, I would." Fiercely. "What is it that you want, Doctor?"

"Hm. What do I want." He chuckled a little. "That's a wonderful question. What I want... is for this thing to end up, somehow, with peace. Peaceful exchange, peaceful dialogue. I want for us to be able to learn from these people, and for them, if they like, to be able to learn from us. Interstellar spaceflight! Communications, engineering. My God. Medicine... can I back up for a moment and make a comment? Did I understand you that you were born in 1934? Ms. Darzins, I was born in 1939, and you could be my daughter."

"That's not quite true." But she smiled a little.

"Your grandfather..."

"They obviously have a different lifespan." She shrugged. "My family has inherited some of that. It's a blessing and a curse, I'll tell you."

"This is exactly what I'm talking about. It would be such a waste — such a waste to lose this opportunity. I think that once this fellow has what he wants, he's going to be, *pfft*" — a sweeping gesture of flight — "gone, and then what? We wait, hoping they might decide we're worth another visit? I would prefer an outcome with more guarantees. So. I am entirely in support of preventing him, however it's possible within the bounds of decency, from finishing what he came here to do and whooshing off before we have learned a great deal more from him about who he is, where he's from, what his people are like, how we might communicate with them further. That makes us natural allies, yes?"

She regarded him with some wariness. "Maybe."

"And yet. I am also profoundly opposed to any kind of inhumane treatment whatsoever of our first guest from another intelligent civilization. I think that the rationale for that is self-evident."

"Certainly."

"I think they have... a little problem. I think that now they have him they don't have any idea what to do with him. I think that they're making it up as they go along, and they're going to start arguing amongst themselves, soon. You have a great deal of power in this situation, simply by virtue of being the only translator at hand. You can advocate for better conditions. More access." He shrugged, smiled. "Perhaps he would appreciate the effort. Open up to you."

Tereza started laughing. "You know, I had almost this same conversation yesterday... oh, it doesn't matter. Maybe before this is over you'll meet my grandfather, for whom being the most bullheaded old SOB in the room is a virtue. I've always wondered what it would be like to see him go toe-to-toe with one of his own, and I think we're getting an idea with this one. . But yes, I will try."

* * *

Sometime after midnight, Gretchen was staring at the ceiling, trying to untangle the events of the day. On the nightstand, her phone made a soft noise; she rolled over and looked at the text message. Kate. *You ok?* She'd almost forgotten that Kate, and her phone, were back in civilization.

We're ok. She paused. *He looks rough. Tired. Anything I should know?*

Shouldn't be, unless this drags on. Call me right away if fine motor control starts to go. He'll tough out the rest.

Why aren't you here?

At my mom's. Seeing David in the am.

She didn't like that. Even the worried, unsettled Kate she'd seen that morning was so much healthier than the shadow from half a year ago. *Don't go back there,* she thought, but there was absolutely no point in saying it.

And anyway, Kate would be all right, she thought. There was a new sense of purpose about her, calm under the turmoil. Kate was the desert, beautiful and complete unto herself, as she always had been. But Goban was a river that transformed all he touched.

Too much to express. Gretchen craved time to sit and talk with Kate about all of this, face to face. Finally, she just texted back: *Be careful. Don't trust that scene.*

Yeah I know. Need to do this though. You be careful too. Love you.

Gretchen lay awake, thinking, for a while after that. Looked at the clock, did some math. She reset her alarm, much earlier than it had been, and let herself fall hard asleep for a couple of hours.

* * *

David Páez called Kate just after eight and asked her to meet him at a coffee shop near the lab. She drove straight there, taking the contract Emma had just emailed to her, excited and hopeful and ready to do business. She didn't notice his face until she was sitting down across from him.

She'd seen him in a lot of moods over the years, but never like this. Grim-jawed, white-knuckled. "Kate, you whore," he snarled. "What the hell do you think you're trying to drag me into?"

It hit her like a punch to the gut. She stared at him, too stunned to lash back. She felt as though she was falling, scrambling for footing, finding none. "I don't understand."

"You lied to me. You're lying to me right now."

"I'm not." She made a small, helpless gesture. Her head started to pound; she tried to draw a deep breath, felt the constriction of rising panic. "I don't — what is going on? What did you find out?"

"You know damned well what I found out." He shook his head. "We worked pretty well together, didn't we? I never had any reason to think that you thought I was stupid, Kate. You could have just — tried to bribe me. Brought me in. Okay, maybe I would have taken a cut, maybe I would have turned you in. Who knows? Screwing me around like this is insulting."

Her field of vision started to blur; her ears were ringing, throat tightening. She stared at him through narrowed eyes, trying to make sense of it, started to say something, retreated, tried again. "Tell me. Tell me what you think is going on here." Sharply, precisely, each word enunciated.

"I know what's going on here. You used me. You tried to use my lab to launder dirty research. And sat there and lied to my face about it. Who are you really working for?"

I don't understand, I don't understand. She dug her fingernails into her palms, concentrated on the sensation. Spoke slowly, heard the tremor in her own voice. "I told you. I am working for the Darzins family, from Chesterton, Colorado. One of the family members has an autoimmune disease. I am —" Deep breath. "I am trying to help the family doctors figure out what's causing it. It seems like what's causing it is a deficiency of this hormone. So I just —" Another deep breath. Another. Her chest hurt; she felt control spiraling out of reach. "I just need enough of it to experiment with. Please. I just need your help —" And the wave crested over her, and her throat closed over the words, and she was shaking all over, and her vision went red and then started to close in.

"That's enough," she heard the man at the next table say, as though from a distant place, through an echoing tunnel, and she was barely aware, through the sobbing, as they arrested her and half-carried her out, of her own thrashing and protesting, as David sat there watching, the fury blown off, looking tired and disappointed.

* * *

CHAPTER FIFTEEN

Tereza approached the tent smiling, hands spread, making herself appear as unthreatening as possible. Trying to project conciliation. She toggled the speaker.

"Good morning. I know that yesterday was very difficult for everyone. I'm sorry, can we start over? I realized I didn't introduce myself. My name is Tereza. May I ask your name?"

The stranger stared at her with suspicion that stopped just short of open hostility, held her eye for a long minute, and then relented. "Andessat Moret," he bit out.

"Thank you, Moret." She took a deep breath. "You have been here for one full day now, and we've had some time to discuss various things. The doctors here can find no reason to keep you in full medical isolation, so they are preparing a room for you." That had been a lively debate, but she had made the argument that he had effectively already been through quarantine, alone on his ship on his long flight. They weren't learning anything by keeping him isolated now. Exposure might bring changes; he might need a hospital quickly, or they all might need to be quarantined later, but they weren't learning anything by keeping him isolated now. "The security people still have requirements, of course. We're going to move you closer to the main part of this base. You'll have more privacy, and a little more freedom of movement. Not a lot. I could only do so much." She made a small helpless gesture. "I'm sure you're hungry, and I can't imagine you slept well here. While we wait for the vehicle, I have arranged for some better food."

His eyes narrowed, and his mouth was a thin grim line. He held his arms close to his body, shoulders a little hunched, a closed-off posture. "Why?"

She shrugged. "Why not? We have no ill intent toward you, just... questions. You came to our home, remember, uninvited."

He considered. "If I answer your questions, will you let me go to get on with my work?"

She smiled thinly. "I think you know better. There's a conflict between the two roles that I play here. As a translator, I have no authority; I converse with you, and then relay and advise. Please don't expect me to make decisions or promises.

"But my primary interest is still — and will remain — Engineer Nhoresh's wellbeing. Even if you do negotiate your release from this facility, you have no means of access to him except through me." It hung in the air between them: *remember that when you're thinking about how cooperative you want to be.* She saw his reluctant acceptance in the drop of his shoulders. So she nodded to the two SPs who had driven her out from the main base, and they stepped up, covering her, as she opened first the outer and then the inner airlock panels. She offered him her hand, and he clasped it hesitantly, and stepped out into the brisk November desert air.

* * *

The woman — Tereza, he reminded himself — handed him a flimsy cup. "These are some things that Engineer Nhoresh likes; I hope that you'll like them too." The warmth spread through his cold fingers, and he wrapped both hands around the cup reflexively, and took a sip.

He must have looked startled; she smiled. "*Coffee.* You have..." — she struggled for the Semhet word for a moment — "caffeine, yes? Cold caffeine beverages?"

"Yes. There are several caffeine-bearing fruits, and we make stimulating juice drinks. Nothing like this." It was very good.

"That's what he told me. Coffee is one of his favorite things in the world, he drinks it constantly. It's a fruit too, the seed of a fruit actually, but it's dried and roasted and then steeped in hot water." She passed him a small bag next. Some kind of cured meat sandwiched inside a savory pastry. Protein and starch, good; it wasn't too strange, and it was warm and smelled delicious. He tried to eat with dignity. It was difficult, between the awkwardness of holding the fatty, crumbling pastry in one hand, out in the open with a brisk morning breeze rising off the desert, and his sudden hunger. The preserved emergency rations from the night before had been barely palatable; he'd eaten just a few bites, late, in the dark, after everyone but the guards went away.

This, the fresh air, the conversation without the plastic barrier, and the comforting, tasty food, was calculated to lift his spirits and lower his guard, he realized. It was working — that and the prospect of being away from this barren, open, unprotected place. *Also further away from my ship,* he thought unhappily. Not that it mattered; the ship, a dozen paces from where he stood, might as well be a continent away, with the guards and their weapons between him and it. Change could only mean opportunity, if he was quick enough to snatch it.

* * *

By the time the car reached the field office, Kate had tapered off sobbing and, improbably, dozed. She sat up and climbed out of the car, blinking, numb, and meek, and they took her to a small, bland room with plastic furniture. She put her head down on the table and tried to focus on a question, a thread, but found herself utterly unable to think.

After a few minutes, a red-haired woman her own age came in and sat down across from her. She had a sympathetic face. "The agents told me what happened. I'm sorry. Did you have an anxiety attack?"

Kate rubbed her face, felt her puffy eyes, her still-shaking hands. "Yes, I must have. I don't understand what's happening." Her voice started to rise on the last word, a brittle, shrill edge to it.

The woman looked at her for a long time, looked over her red eyes and nervous fidgeting. "You know, I think I believe you." She slid a business card across the table. "My name is Amanda Dorsey. I'm the supervising agent in this case. I would like to help you, but you have to tell me the truth."

"I told David the truth." Bitterly.

"The Darzins family? Autoimmune disease?"

"They told you."

"Kate, they were recording. Of course they were." Dorsey shook her head. "You know that Henry Darzins has fled the country? Do you know who he really is?"

The blood was rushing in her ears like the sea. She took a couple of deep breaths. Felt the pressure recede a little. *Don't answer any more questions, Kate.* "Please," she said, shakily. "Please tell me what I've been arrested for. Specifically."

The agent pursed her lips and watched Kate's face carefully. "You have been arrested for unauthorized possession of classified technology, and conspiracy to manufacture and sell that technology to a foreign government."

Classified technology. The dizziness was descending again, but in the midst of the blur, the thought that had been tickling at the back of her mind for months snapped into focus with a rush. "Oh!"

"Okay, I'm waiting."

Kate closed her eyes, half-afraid, half-hopeful of the answer to her question. "It's the HPE-317, isn't it? That's what you think I stole." When she looked at Dorsey again, the other woman was staring at her, lips tight, nodding slowly.

"From what Dr. Páez told us, it is a variant. Not exactly the same variant as his lab produces. You've done some further work on it, clearly."

His awful behavior made sense; everything made sense. Kate laughed, low and bitter, a faint edge of hysteria behind a tired sigh. Rubbed her face, shook her head. *I can't get away from it. Move thirteen hundred miles, start a new life, and it just follows me.* Loathing filled her. Her fingers found the smooth angles of the pendant, her touchstone of interlocking polygons, and she calmed a little.

Serotonin uptake was one of the processes affected by HPE-317, she remembered, irrelevantly.

"No, it's not. That's not what happened. It makes sense, though. It's got to be similar enough to make the mistake understandable. What I told David is the absolute truth. I've been studying this disease. This was my breakthrough. The sample I brought to him is a naturally occurring compound that I isolated from the blood of... the target case."

"Henriks Darzins. Nhoresh Goban."

"Yes." All the secrets were coming out. She could be done with secrets, finally. It was a relief. "There is a correlation, a historical correlation, between his symptoms and the fluctuations of this compound in his body." A flashback to Rita in the lab: "*the flare-ups look like an Addison's crisis.*" *No, the flare-ups look like* 317 *withdrawal. The buildup too, just in slow motion.* That was what had derailed the Alcon project, over and over again: the drug worked like a dream, worked better than they had dreamed. But the withdrawal was horrific.

"We think that it's a hormone deficiency. Insulin deficiency causes diabetes, okay? So you give a diabetic patient synthetic insulin to correct for it. Same thing here. We isolated a sample, and we're trying to synthesize a therapeutic quantity of it for testing."

"Who is 'we'?"

"His doctor and I. I was hired to identify the cause of the disease, help her develop a treatment."

"So you show up on your old boss's doorstep, offering a contract to outsource the production of this chemical to his lab."

"Exactly."

"And it just happens to be virtually identical to the classified, experimental military performance enhancement drug that you were working on right before you quit to go work for these people."

Kate shook her head, took a deep, shaky breath. "Evidently." Not by design. Not by her intention, but not by coincidence, either, apparently. No accident.

"So your patient is an alien super soldier." Dorsey's voice dripped with skepticism.

She laughed, then, not the mad-edged laugh, but a real throaty chuckle. "Not super soldier. Super farmer. Not... exactly alien either."

"You lost me."

Kate stood up. So much nervous energy. She paced, ran her hands through her hair. "We've been chewing on this puzzle for a while now. Basically, as far as I've been able to determine, he's human, but he's stronger and smarter than anyone I've ever met. His people live two, three times as long as we do. I have been tearing my hair out for months trying to figure out how he could be so similar to us and yet so different in these key ways. I think... what this hormone does for us, what we were trying to achieve with the 317 project, is his normal state. But he really is very sick. For us, it's an enhancement, but he is adapted to it, and he needs it." She stopped, looked Dorsey straight in the eye. "Please, you have to believe me. My sample did not come from the Alcon research; it's independent and legit." *If you don't give it back, I'm back to scratch. Oh, Goban, I'm so sorry. I tried to take a shortcut and I ended up on the wrong road. Again.*

Dorsey watched her pace. There was something in her eyes — a trace of sympathy? Doubt? "Okay, Ms. Hutchins. I'm going to look into this a little. Please go with the door officer. We have a room for you." She stood up. "If you'd like a pill for the anxiety, I can arrange that for you. It might be a while. You might try to get some sleep."

Kate nodded, feeling every bit of her exhaustion. "I'd like that. Thank you." Sleep while she could, until there was work to do.

* * *

The social magic of a shared cup of coffee; Tēvs would approve, Tereza thought, amused. Or the visitor was trying yet another tactic. He was cooperating now, submitting to the decontamination without complaint, letting the medical people take the samples they wanted, answering the questions that she was being fed. He clammed up over questions about his mission, and about yesterday's weirdness about heresy; Tereza quickly got the point and steered away from those topics. After that, she was with him constantly, excepting only a ten-minute break every hour for debriefing and new instructions. And the morning went on.

Until Major Farris came striding down the hallway, and pounded on the window of the door to the small conference room. "Get her out of there!" he shouted at the SP guarding the door. "Get her out! Right now!"

The door flew open, and Farris stepped in, followed by a second guard with sidearm drawn. "You" —

to Moret — "SIT." The gesture he made left no room for doubt; Moret sat. "You" — to Tereza — "with us. Not a word." She raised her hands and backed out of the room, keeping Farris in her sight. They hustled her down the hall and into a different meeting room before he spoke. "Your access here is revoked. Your bags are being packed and your rental car is being moved to the off-base lot. You will be escorted to it. Be grateful you're not under arrest; that would have been my call."

"Major, what happened?" Tereza's shock gave way to a rising fury at his poisonous look, but she refused to give him the pleasure of a visible reaction. She spread her hands, conciliatory. "I've been right here all morning. You know that. Whatever's going on, *I don't know* about it."

He measured her up. Seemed to decide that she had a point. "I just got word that Kate Hutchins was picked up by the FBI a few hours ago. Her former boss called it in. She came to him trying to rope him into a conspiracy to manufacture and sell classified material."

Tereza cloaked her rage in dignity. Stared at him coolly, paused, counted three slow breaths. Long enough to make him nervous. Allowed a faint trace of mockery into her tone. "That's... completely ridiculous. What classified material? What was she selling? To who?"

"Well, to you, obviously." Farris jerked his head down the hall. "To him, ultimately, I assume. Or whoever he represents. You're done here. There is no way in hell you're getting another word with your friend back there."

And just like that, it was over. The SP walked her to an empty room, where she was searched — for what, she did not know — and then, a little while later, taken to a waiting patrol car. She got in, wordlessly seething, and rode to the west gate of the base, and walked through, and got into her rental car.

She sat there and analyzed the morning's events. Was there anything she could have done differently? She couldn't think of a thing; it had all been going so well. She texted Emma — *what is going on with Kate?* — and then turned the key. She had the hour's drive into Bakersfield to decide whether to go home or to Vancouver,

The cold, hard metal against her neck felt exactly how she would expect a gun to feel. "*Heta cho.*" *You will go.* Her eyes flicked to the rear view mirror. The barrel twitched. "I don't know how these things work." Moret spoke almost too softly to be heard, but with desperation; her fury and terror was threaded with pity. "How far down does the trigger go before it goes off?"

"They'll know you've escaped."

"They already do." He gestured at the stolen uniform he was wearing. "They think I am headed toward my ship. How far can we get before they realize otherwise?"

Tereza drove. Through the massed curiosity-seekers, north to Mojave, at a careful pace just below the speed limit, and then like a bat out of hell, east toward Las Vegas.

As they connected with the interstate on the other side of Barstow, Emma called her. "What's going on?"

She spoke in Semhet for Moret's benefit, watching him out of the corner of her eye, and also to bedevil any phone monitoring. "That is what I'm trying to find out. The military people said that Kate was arrested — yes, I know! I couldn't get the whole story. And then they threw me off the base. I'm coming home. I'll work out what to do next from there. Do you know anything?"

"You know about the contract." Emma had sent her the draft to review, late last night, for a one-time round of outsourcing some drug manufacturing process. Simple, straightforward. She'd tweaked it and sent it back. "I asked Rita about it, she said that Kate might have broken it. Tereza, they are very close to a testable treatment. So I sent it on to her in Seattle this morning. I haven't heard from her since."

Was it possible that Kate found something in her old research? That might explain the major's behavior. She sent another text, this one to the disposable phone that she'd arranged for Chris Carver to pick up before leaving Gunnison. *DO NOT re-enter the US. Circumstances changed. Will advise ASAP.* And then she drove as hard as she could.

They made the Nevada border in less than two hours. In Las Vegas, Tereza changed cars. Then she made a recording on her phone, describing the events of the morning, and dropped it in a FedEx pouch.

* * *

CHAPTER SIXTEEN

Kate accepted the pill with gratitude, slept off the adrenaline residue. She woke clear-headed an hour or so later, and looked around. Her jail cell was a modern, humane one: a single narrow, reasonably comfortable mattress, a small bare table attached to the wall, a chair. The room was too bright, but the quiet was soothing.

A knock on the door came almost immediately after she started stirring; she wondered if someone had been watching. It was one of the men from the car. Polite but uncommunicative, he escorted her back to the same sparse plastic interview room. More aware than she had been before, she studied the room carefully. The furniture, cheap-looking at first, was well-made but lightweight, with soft, rounded corners everywhere. There was recessed ceiling lighting, smooth tile walls. No one-way mirror, but small, flush dark glass discs high up on the walls suggested cameras. Nothing to grab onto, break, cut with, tear at; the space was designed with the expectation of trouble. She didn't plan to cause any trouble. She wanted to navigate this carefully. Make nice. Get out of here and go north.

Dorsey was there, with a short, graying, athletic man. His haircut and posture suggested military to her, but his clothes were civilian, his expression sympathetic. Confused and suspicious, Kate waited for him to speak first.

He held out a hand and she shook it, warily. His handshake was firm but not overbearing. "Ms. Hutchins. I would say nice to meet you, but these are unusual circumstances, aren't they. Inspector Michael Walsh, RCMP." He sat down, gestured for her to do the same.

"Hello, Inspector." Her breath caught in her throat; she sat, wary, watching him, feeling the panic rise again. RCMP, down here in Seattle. What had happened to Gretchen and Goban? Glanced up at Dorsey, whose expression revealed nothing.

He forged forward. "All right. So. SSA Dorsey here and her people have looked into what you told them earlier. It's pretty technical and I don't understand it at all really, but Dr. Páez has said, basically, that it's impossible to tell from your sample alone whether it was modified from a sample stolen from his lab, or recreated from data stolen from his lab, or derived from an independent source as you claim. That question is at the crux of whether or not a crime has been committed."

"Right." David must still be spitting mad.

"So let me get this straight. If you're telling the truth, then my government's problem is that we have one of the great, ah, wonders of human history — a visitor from another world with intelligent life — and he's sick, isolated, and probably scared. We need to help him, and we could use your assistance."

"Yes!" *Yes. Oh, yes, please believe me –*

He held up a hand. "If you're lying, then we still have the same problem, because it's possible that we have one of the greatest dangers to ever face humankind — a spy, a vanguard of a hostile alien invasion — in our country, maybe hopped up on military performance enhancement drugs, or coming off of them, maybe psychotic."

Her heart sank as fast as it had lifted. She sighed, tapped the table, tried to think. "I don't understand. If you think... it's so important, either way, to, what, have him in custody? Why are you here talking to me at all?" She had almost said *why aren't you at Gretchen's apartment?* but had the presence of mind to stop talking. *Don't give him that if he doesn't have it.*

"Why haven't we already picked up him and Gretchen Willoughby, you mean? Oh, we tried. They're gone. I'd like you to help me figure out where they went."

* * *

Farris watched the investigation from the sidelines, frustration blossoming into rage. He'd escaped. *She sat right there and told us he was going to try to escape. Why?* It made no sense for her to do that. There was something missing, they were all missing it.

They had found the SP who'd been knocked out and stripped, and then half an hour later found his motorcycle, a dozen yards off base, stashed in a ditch, as though the alien had intended to come back to it but never did. Wrong direction. Until that point, the search had been concentrated to the northeast. They'd found wobbling motorcycle tracks leading out into the desert toward the research base, toward the ship. Tracks left perhaps intentionally, while he figured out on the go how to work the bike, and then somewhere along the line he'd gotten confident, hopped onto pavement and doubled back, made for the west gate. He'd found a better ride, had either taken Tereza Darzins hostage or met up with her by prearrangement.

So now he was loose, off the base, off the grid, headed anywhere. Intelligent, adaptable, and determined. Dangerous. Farris thought about the Darzins family and what he'd seen in Colorado. If the aliens were all like this, he thought grimly, the world was in trouble.

The SP squadron commander hung up the phone. "That was the FBI team. They've traced her phone; it's moving on a speed and trajectory consistent with a commercial airliner. Las Vegas to SeaTac. They're trying to pin down a flight number now."

"How the hell did she get him onto a commercial airliner?"

* * *

They brought Kate a file of photographs from Gretchen's apartment. She couldn't find anything out of place. After what seemed like hours of poring over them, she asked for Walsh. "You have to let me go there. I'm sure I can figure it out, but not from these."

Dorsey didn't like it, but she wasn't getting anywhere on her own case either. There were discussions, and paperwork. It took another hour. And then Kate was northbound, in the passenger seat of Walsh's car, watching the suburbs fall away to farms and forest.

Walsh tried to make small talk, and Kate acquiesced half-heartedly, as long as he steered away from the topics dominating her thoughts: the farm, Goban, the visitor and whatever was happening with Tereza in California, Gretchen, the sample, David, the 317. She wondered how much she was revealing by what she wouldn't say. She wondered if this compassionate, competent man was more valuable as an ally than he was dangerous as an adversary.

They made the turn and crossed the bridge into Blaine, and a few minutes later, he was showing his badge and ID and the border patrol officers were waving them through. She laughed quietly. "Being a Mountie has its perks, huh?"

He glanced over at her, a little sharply, but the corners of his eyes crinkled. "You come over a lot?"

"Well, my best friend lives over there," with a vague wave to the northwest, "so yeah. Once a month, at least, until I moved to Colorado. It's a hassle for mere mortals."

"I've heard," he said dryly, and they both laughed, and she started to relax. His eyes shifted to her face again, then back to the road. "Kate, you seem like a nice woman. How are you mixed up in this?"

She shook her head, smiled. "It will all be so much easier if you quit fighting the idea that I'm telling the truth."

"Sure, right up until I'm in a hell of a mess if you're not."

"That's a fair point. How do I prove it?"

He sighed and thought about that. "Well. As I say, if you are telling the truth, then I really do want to help your guy. So how about you do your best to help me find him?"

Your guy. She was momentarily overcome by a memory. Sitting in the Vancouver apartment kitchen, sharing ice cream and making plans for an autumn road trip through the mountains, and Gretchen's laughing face. *I'm so sorry I dragged you into this.* She stared out the window. "Yeah."

* * *

One of the sergeants looked up and spoke to his CO. "Sir, the FBI reports that they've tracked down that flight information."

Farris walked over too. "And?"

The young man frowned. "It's not an airliner; it's a commercial cargo carrier. FedEx. They started LVPD canvassing the drop-offs, working southwest to northeast along the interstate. They got a hit pretty quick. Clerk had a well-dressed, middle-aged woman mailing a cell phone. International same-day delivery. The girl remembers because they don't do those very often, so she had to rummage around for the right form, and because it was right before noon. That's the cutoff for same-day delivery, so she had to run the package out to the truck."

"*Where?*"

"The recipient is a... Gretchen Willoughby, Vancouver, British Columbia."

She had played them, neatly. He grimaced. It was all he could do not to punch the computer screen. *Wouldn't you run to ground, if it were you?*

* * *

As the afternoon wore on, Moret watched out the window, the vast arid remoteness of the continent's interior passing by, southeast and then east across the bleak desert. The woman was vibrating with fury at first, but as the distance fell away, so did her anger. She seemed pensive, almost sad, as they headed up into low mountains with scrubby twisted little trees, and down onto the desert again.

They barely spoke. He held the weapon in his lap, his hand resting lightly on it. The bluff had worked, to his astonished relief; he had his freedom, and he had Tereza for a translator and guide. But he had thought no farther ahead than grabbing the opportunity, getting off the base. Now — "Where are we going?" he asked.

She glanced at him, and sighed. "Home," she said. "We're going where I have more control. What happened this morning... cannot be allowed to happen again. For your safety and for ours." She shifted over to the right, took the curving turn onto a smaller road. "We're going to stop here in Winslow for food and fuel. I need to make a call, then concentrate on moving fast, and see how close we get. If we can stay ahead of them, one more stop after this should get us home."

* * *

Walking through the apartment, Kate tried to think. What little notes would Gretchen leave that she could read and that no one else would? She was certain it would be Gretchen, not Goban, who would leave those clues, who chose the destination.

Blankets sat folded in a tidy stack on the end of the couch, where he'd slept. There were takeout containers in the trash, enough for two, but no sign they'd had breakfast. That told her they'd left this morning, perhaps very early this morning, not last night. There was no other indication that he had ever been here.

A cell phone was still on the nightstand; Walsh had mentioned that, during the drive. They hadn't taken anything with them that could be tracked. Kate picked it up, flipped through several screens. She found the text message conversation from the night before, and smiled. The last photograph taken was of Kate and Goban, just before they left the coffee shop; she hadn't realized Gretchen had shot that. No recordings, no messages.

The wallpaper was a selfie, the two women together, against a backdrop of blue water and mountains. Lunch in that mountain town, on the way to Calgary last fall. She set the phone down, walked slowly around the room, through the living room, into the kitchen. The same photograph was printed, trimmed, neatly posted on the refrigerator, held in place by a silly joke magnet, one she'd bought a couple of years before. *We'll be best friends forever because you already know too much.*

She felt a catch in her throat at that. She remembered finding it in some gift shop and dropping it in the mail a year ago, a silent thank-you. *I can't tell you*, Kate had said, the first time Gretchen drove down in the middle of the night to sit with her after a panic attack, and Gretchen had accepted that, had not judged, had not demanded anything at all. Kept whatever she was thinking to herself. Came back, a couple of times over that summer, when Kate called.

I want the whole story sometime, she'd said, in Calgary. It was time. Past time.

Kate turned away and saw the laptop left out on

the counter, carelessly. Not very Gretchen-like.

The power light was blinking: asleep, not off. She flipped open the screen. Guessed the password, an old joke, logged in on her first try.

The desktop wallpaper had changed since the last time she had been here. Ghostly washes of salmon light angling through shadows of ultramarine, The Mitre jutting up almost from a shoreline rendered in mist, the riffle of the lake's surface shimmering copper in the evening light, with the vast bulk of Mt. Victoria rising in the distance, cut by the forms of scraggly spruces.

Like an Albert Bierstadt painting, she had said of the Uncompaghre, and *too beautiful to be real* was what she had meant, because the man was famous for monumental fantastical epics, impressions of the Rockies and the Sierra Nevadas as they might have been but never quite were, except that sometimes he did paint from life.

Evening Glow, Lake Louise. Date unknown. Not a well-known painting, and small, not *Wind River Country*, but all the more enthralling for that.

She looked up at Walsh. "I know where they are."

He nodded. "Right. Let's go then."

She opened her mouth to continue, but was interrupted by the ringing doorbell. Walsh snapped around, attentive, hand on his holster. She shook her head frantically, imagining Gretchen's sociable neighbor dropping by for a cup of coffee to find Mounties with guns instead. Mountie, singular. Walsh could be scary enough by himself, if he wanted, Kate had no doubt. "*I belong here,*" she mouthed.

He gave a small, tight nod; he got it. He checked the peephole first. Then he looked puzzled. He stepped away, out of line of sight of the door, and waved for her to answer it.

It was a FedEx delivery driver. She signed for the package as Gretchen. The driver went away, and she closed the door. Walsh was looking at her, curious. She handed the package to him; he opened it.

It was empty except for a cell phone. There was a sticky note on the screen with a four-digit number, in a precise, feminine hand. Kate tried it as a password; it worked. In the recent calls, House, Office – such *helpful descriptors*, she thought, wryly – and some unsaved numbers. "Office" was a Denver number. She pulled up the main contact list. Many, many names, most of them unfamiliar, although a few popped out, enough to make a pattern. Barn. Chris. Conrad. Gatehouse. Kate. Rita.

What had happened to Tereza? And why had she sent her phone here?

* * *

CHAPTER SEVENTEEN

They closed up the apartment and headed back south, to a small government airfield where a jet was being prepped to take them to Banff. Kate found the last text message, and fretted at its terse anxiousness; then she found the recording and listened to it.

Walsh watched her face while she did. "Tell me about the phone," he said.

"I'm going to have to tell you a lot more than that for the phone to make sense." So Kate gave him a rough outline of her time on the farm and the family history, and a more detailed summary of the events of Thanksgiving night. *The day before yesterday*, she thought, overwhelmed with fatigue. She shook it off.

"The phone was intended for Goban, obviously. She put it in the mail this morning; she had no way of knowing they would already be gone by the time it got here." She played the message again, this time on speaker.

"*It's gone off the rails down here. Kate is in some kind of trouble, and the Air Force people think that she is passing some kind of military secrets to the Semhet – through us? It doesn't make a lot of sense. As soon as I can, I'm going to get into it, and see what I can do to help her. Anyway, they've kicked me out, so right now I'm driving like hell toward the farm, and hoping I get there before they decide to come after me too. I'm aiming to be there very early tomorrow, and I'll get in touch with you from there.*

"*This is what you need to know: I have Andessat*

Moret with me. Do you know this name? He says he knew you, before. He escaped from the base; he took me hostage, more or less, although he's as dependent on me as I am under his threat, and I'm in the driver's seat. That sounds scarier than it is. Don't worry.

"Do not come home. Do not come back into the country. Let me find out what's going on with Kate, and get Moret's legal status settled, and get guarantees for your safety. I'll call you in when I'm ready, and you and he can sit down and hash out this business between you. I have to mail this and get back on the road now. I love you, and I hope you're well and I hope to see you soon."

Kate looked at Walsh. His made an odd face, but he didn't say anything, just made a couple of little *hm* noises. They arrived at the airfield, boarded, and took off in silence. She fidgeted, stared out the window, fretted. She was startled when he did finally speak.

"I am very interested to meet this fellow."

"Will I regret that?"

He regarded her curiously. "Oh, I don't think so." He leaned back, steepled his fingers. "See, Kate, what I generally deal with in my line of work is on-the-ground investigation of national security threats. Terrorism, organized crime, human trafficking. The intelligence service feeds my team information, and we go out in the field and determine how credible that information is, and if necessary, we then act on that determination.

"A lot of these criminals are extremely good at what they do. They're savvy. They blend in very well. We have to be aware that false positives in the intelligence are a possibility, all the time. The most important part of what I do is to make sure my team doesn't get so hung up on taking down the bad guys that we hurt innocent people, and most especially innocent people in crisis.

"It's increasingly clear to me that the biggest threat to my country's security right now is not one sick old man. It's us — and our neighbors," he added pointedly, "making stupid overreaching mistakes."

Kate sighed, looking out the window. "It wouldn't be the first time."

"What happened to you, Kate?" She gave him a questioning look. "I saw the recording of you in the coffee shop. That wasn't defensive rage. That was flat-out blind terror."

She shifted uncomfortably in her seat. "I don't know how much I can tell you."

"I've been fully briefed on the HPE-317 project, if that's what you mean."

"Oh, Inspector." She put her head back, closed her eyes, felt the fatigue wash over her. "It was supposed to be different. The dream of performance enhancements for soldiers gave us amphetamines, LSD, MDMA. The MK Ultra experiments. The 317 project was supposed to be... a triumph, the project that made it all worthwhile. We all know how that goes, right? We should have known better.

"It was an amazing drug. It didn't enhance aggression; that's not what we were looking for. I mean, sure, a subject on 317 was tougher, sharper, harder. They had incredible energy and resilience. Fantastic immune performance and healing. And they were so smart. The drug affected their mental acuity — their problem-solving, task-switching, focus and discipline under stress, recall and execution of operant conditioning. Executive function.

"The problem that we never solved was the withdrawal. We experimented with dosage and duration, buffering, slow-release, drug combinations; we tried everything, and we were never able to break through it.

"It starts with joint and muscle pain, like the flu, the worst flu pain you can imagine. Agonizing headaches. Fluid builds up in your lungs, and you start to drown slowly. The fluid is also pressing on your heart, and causes tachycardia. You can't breathe and your heart is racing, like you've run a marathon, all the time. You develop a tremor and start to lose motor control. Fever. Then the hallucinations and delirium start, and sometimes psychosis. Major organ damage, in the worst cases. It's very bad.

"I was on the lab side and didn't work with the test subjects directly. I didn't... I read the reports, but I didn't know. There's no excuse..." She realized she was hyperventilating and closed her eyes, concentrated on slowing her breathing. When she opened her eyes again, Walsh was watching her, concerned.

"What did you find out, Kate? About the human testing?"

She looked away. "They were testing on prisoners."

"That's illegal."

"Yes."

"What did you do?"

"What could I do? Report it? They would have been forced to stop the trial immediately. Those men would have died. You don't know, you haven't seen..." she shook her head. "I still thought I could solve the withdrawal problem! Or get the project shut down, but leave the long-term care in place. Not just cut those guys off and abandon them to horrible suffering."

"It wasn't your call to make."

"Well, I realize that now." She always had; that was the problem, wasn't it? "But once I was inside, once I was read in to the clinical side, I was having a really hard time with continuing the work. I started having panic attacks, and nightmares. Crying a lot. Drinking too much. You know.

"They were volunteers. Military prisoners, lifers. Murderers and war criminals. Some of them, I think, really did want to do some good, to be involved in something that could save soldiers' lives, and some of them wanted the privileges that came with being a research subject. A few were just bored, I guess.

"That's what my boss kept telling me — you met Dr. Páez? He means well, but he has a narrow view. He thought that... my problems with the consent issues in the research were unfounded."

"This is how white-collar organized crime happens," Walsh explained gently. "Ethical sunk costs. Dragging in whoever you can, building webs of mutual deceit and dependency. Scrambling to stay one step ahead of everything falling apart. He pressured you?"

The understanding, she thought, was worse than recriminations. *Plenty of time for that later.* She nodded. "He told me to keep my eye on the ball. What the project could accomplish, and, uh, also where these guys were coming from. So he got some files. He shouldn't have had access to them, but he did. It didn't... help. It made things worse. I couldn't get out of my head some of the things they had done."

She hesitated. "I've never talked to anyone about this. There was never anyone who had all the pieces. The people I could talk to just seemed to think I was crazy for being bothered by it. And the people I would have liked to open up to — I wasn't allowed to." She shrugged. "That was part of my problem, I think." She went quiet for a moment, staring out the window.

"There was this one subject. He had, um," she swallowed. "He had tortured civilians. He had gotten it in his head that the villagers were collaborating. His file was pretty gruesome. He was paranoid even before we got ahold of him, and he never recovered from the psychological aftereffects.

"I went to see him, after. I couldn't untangle what he'd done from what we had done to him. I couldn't... get past it. I started..." She hesitated, swallowed. She had never spoken this thing out loud, she realized, horrified in hindsight.

"You were having suicidal thoughts?"

"Oh, more than thoughts." It was a relief; she laughed, shakily. "Last summer, I tried to take a dive off the Evergreen Point Bridge at seventy miles an hour. I didn't, obviously. I pulled back at the last second, but that was when I decided I needed to get my head clear. So I took a month off, and went on a long road trip. I'd been out almost three weeks, been in Wyoming seeing an old girlfriend, who was doing field research in Yellowstone. And I spent a couple of days with her, and I was thinking, *wow, why did I never go into a nice line of work sticking test tubes into hot springs?* I started feeling like maybe there could be life without nightmares. So I left Yellowstone and headed for Santa Fe, and that's how I ended up crashing my car outside of Chesterton."

"Where you found a life without nightmares."

She nodded, bit her lip. "For a while, anyway. Until two weeks ago. Ever since those men came to look for the beacon, it's been coming back."

"Men in uniforms."

Her eyes widened; she hadn't made that connection. She shook her head, stared out the window. "I think it's not that simple. You know, I've been working in defense contract work for fifteen years, I've known a lot of guys, good people. Very professional. The two on the beacon team were. But every so often... the senior officer on that team, I think he just got under my skin. Stirred up all of my uneasy feelings."

"Yes, I'm familiar enough with that type." Walsh was looking at her with great gentleness. "If the drug is so similar to this other chemical, the deficiency that Nhoresh Goban has, then his condition must also be similar. Did you recognize that?"

"Not then." Not consciously, she realized, recalling the unsettling feeling of foreboding that had haunted her on the farm, and the blinding realization in the interview room in Seattle. "In hindsight, yes. You're right, it's very similar. Much less acute, which changes the presentation. Cyclic, as it depletes and rebuilds. Not as severe, although definitely... bad enough. And getting worse."

"Hm." Walsh drummed his fingers on the armrest. He nodded a little. "You must have clung to him like he was your salvation." Kate looked at him, questioning. "You barely made it out of a very bad situation, but you left others behind, a horrific crime unreported, and your own involvement in it unresolved, to your great shame. Now here is a guy who did no wrong, but shares the same burden with the men who you — in your mind — had a hand in torturing. These men that you are carrying, in fact, a literally unbearable weight of guilt over. If you can save him, you can go back and save the others, you can redeem yourself. Am I right?"

The jet was descending. Kate closed her eyes and rested her cheek against the window. The cool pressure soothed the churning chaos in her head.

* * *

CHAPTER EIGHTEEN

Gretchen picked up some sandwiches and took them to the hotel suite, where Goban was sprawled out on the couch, sleeping hard. He'd slept much of the trip, whenever he wasn't driving. She didn't know how worried she should be. *Katie, you better finish your business in Seattle and get here, because I'm a little out of my depth.*

She nudged him awake. He wasn't a heavy sleeper; that was helpful. He muttered and stirred, and sat up. "Oh. Food. Thank you."

She pulled up a chair on the other side of the coffee table. "You have to tell me what's going on with you."

A trace of something — annoyance? "I'm just tired. Catching up. It's been a hard couple of days."

"I get that, but what you need to get is that I'm not your family, I'm not Kate, and I don't live with you day-to-day. I need to understand what's going on so I know what to expect."

He rubbed his face, ran his hands through his unkempt hair. "You're right." He sighed. "I cannot tell you how much I hate being handled." It seemed refreshing for him to say that; Gretchen wondered if he'd ever said it to his well-meaning family. "I hurt. My joints ache, and I have a blinding headache. Sleep helps. The headache will pass, and I'll be restless. I'll probably be up half the night."

"Okay." She nodded. "Thank you." She started unwrapping the sandwiches.

The disposable phone that Tereza had sent with him began to ring. They stared at it, looked at each other, and both grabbed for it as it rang again. He got to it first, fumbled a little. "Tereza. How are things in California?"

Then he went perfectly still, listening. "Right. No, you're absolutely right. Excellent. Thank you. Yes, ten minutes." A hesitation. "I love you." A flash of transcendent happiness at whatever he heard in reply.

He hung up the phone, set it down carefully, looked at Gretchen. "That was Kate. Tereza is in some kind of trouble. She mailed her phone to your apartment, and Kate picked it up there. She found your trail of breadcrumbs." A twitch of a smile. "She's here. She, ah, was brought by the RCMP inspector who was sent to apprehend me. Obviously she didn't want to give him where we're staying, so she has asked us to meet her at their hotel."

Shit. Gretchen took a deep breath. "Well, as law enforcement goes, we could do worse than the Mounties. Where are they?"

"No, no, they're *here*. They checked into this hotel, fifteen minutes ago."

* * *

Lou Farris spent what seemed like hours in meetings and on the phone, on conference calls. No one could agree who had jurisdiction over the visitor, or whether they could even pursue him. Tereza Darzins was another story. The FBI was looking for her now, on the conspiracy charge; they wanted the still-classified report on the beacon, and that was his way in. His CO called the wing commander in Maryland. The brass revived that investigation, given the new information confirming the

Darzins' connection to the tech, and attached him to the FBI team. Her hands tied, the supervising agent acquiesced to the liaison, and within the hour Farris was on a flight back to Colorado.

All he really wanted was to get in a room alone with Nhoresh Goban, to ask all the questions he hadn't gotten answers to the last time, and then some.

* * *

Kate sat at the hotel restaurant bar, warming her hands around the heavy ceramic cup. It was better for that than for drinking; the coffee wasn't very good, and she was dressed for the Pacific Northwest, not the high Rockies in the dead of winter. She laughed, and Walsh shot her a questioning glance. "Lately I seem to be forever either sitting in coffee shops and restaurants, or driving for days in the middle of nowhere." Then she was abruptly subdued, remembering the last coffee shop she'd been in.

Some small movement of air caused the hair to stand up on the back of her neck, and she turned, and there they were, standing in the doorway. She didn't realize she was holding her breath until Goban caught her eye and strode across the room. She met him halfway there.

Walsh came up behind her, waited a decorous amount of time before stepping forward. He held out a hand and introduced himself.

Goban smiled, shook the offered hand firmly. "May I call you Michael? My eldest son was named Mikels."

"Was?"

"I have outlived all of my children."

"I am so sorry, sir," Walsh answered, sincerely.

Goban shrugged it off, a practiced gesture of quiet pragmatism, warding off pain. "I have beautiful and talented grandchildren, and great-grandchildren. They're a joy to me."

"So I've heard."

Kate was fascinated, watching the parade of expressions across Walsh's face — wariness softening into curiosity, compassion, and then sudden awareness. Drawn in by Goban's formidable charisma, but only so far.

"Sir, frankly, you have a problem. *Several* arms of American law enforcement and the national security apparatus are now convinced that you, and your family, and Ms. Hutchins here are engaged in a criminal conspiracy with global implications. But I have spent the last, oh, seven hours or so in Ms. Hutchins' company, and she's spent most of that time presenting a pretty compelling argument that this is all a terrible misunderstanding.

"You're a guest in my country, and I'm prepared to bring the resources I have at my disposal to bear to resolve this. But I'm not entirely convinced. I have some questions for you."

Goban nodded. Kate could feel his pounding heart, the coolness and faint tremor of his hand clasping hers. But he was upright, clear-eyed. He was doing okay. She could let him go for a little while longer. "Of course. May I have a private moment with Kate first?"

Walsh was amused. "I think you just had a private moment, there."

"Hah. Well. A private *word*, then."

"Certainly." Walsh sketched a little bow. He

nodded to Gretchen. "Ms. Willoughby." She nodded back, smiled and gestured toward the restaurant door.

Kate wrapped her arms around his hips, rested her head on his chest, nestled in. "Ohhhh. It is *so* good to see you. It was just yesterday, right?"

"Early yesterday. It's fairly late. You could get away with calling it two days. Seems like forever. Let's not do that again, all right?" He pulled away a little, brushed her hair away from her face. "Gretchen had a bad feeling after she talked to you last night, so we were on the move very early. We had one text message from Tereza this morning, then nothing."

"I saw that. Gretchen is smart. It's good that you did run — things would be worse if you hadn't." Him in Vancouver, with Walsh; her in Seattle, with Dorsey and the FBI, both of them in jail, unable to help each other. Tereza all alone and on the run. And everyone at home cut off. The vision horrified her; it had all blown up so fast. But here, on another mountain, there was a chance to talk. A chance, maybe, to sort it out. "It's good that you don't know any of what's been going on, on my side. It makes your side more" — *credible?* — "undiluted. Work with him. I think he's our best shot."

"Okay." He studied her face, took in the faint traces of the day's strain. "Okay, I will." He brushed her cheek, leaned down, and murmured in her ear. "I hope he doesn't want to talk all night, though."

It was like the first glimpse of the sun after a long stretch of dark, rainy days. She laughed, softly, but her words had a fervent edge. "You and me both."

* * *

One thing that David Páez had learned, in his years in competitive government contract work, was that you could always shut down something that had been set in motion, but being caught unprepared meant getting left behind. Wasted resources meant less than wasted opportunities. So, in a moment of half-thought-out ass-covering, he'd given the FBI the drug sample Kate had brought to him, but held back the bacterial vector that made it possible to produce more.

Before he went out and got staggeringly rage-drunk over the humiliating betrayal of one of his best employees, he went to the lab and spent a couple of hours setting up the vector in growth medium and loading it into the incubator.

Just in case she was telling the truth after all.

* * *

With a smirk, Kate walked over to Gretchen, waiting near the door. "Hey. You lost your phone." She held it out, laughing.

Gretchen's eyes went wide. "That's all you have to say to me?" She snatched the phone, made as if to swat Kate with it, and pulled her into a hug, laughing with her. "Oh, hey, I'm so glad you're here. How about a drink?"

They sat at the bar, drinking beer and catching up, while the two men went back to Goban's room to talk.

* * *

With the visitor vanished, the ship still inaccessible, and the military people uncommunicative, there was no work to be done. Erik Jansen packed up and headed home.

Halfway to Los Angeles, his office called. "Doctor Jansen," his assistant said, "I had the oddest phone call just now, and... I mean, there have been a lot of odd phone calls the last few days..."

"I can't imagine," he interjected dryly.

She laughed. "Yes. But I thought you should hear this one."

"Go ahead."

"The woman said she knew you, that she has been working with you down at Edwards. She said her name was Tereza Darzins."

A sharp intake of breath. "That *is* an important call. Good for you. What did she say?"

"She gave me a set of GPS coordinates and told me to get them to you. She said to tell you that what you're looking for is there."

"I see. And did you look up the location?"

"I did, Doctor. It's the middle of nowhere. Western Colorado."

"I thought it might be. All right then. What I need you to do right now is to call and change my flight from San Jose to Denver. And after you've done that, you can go ahead and text me those coordinates. And then call Joel in Boulder and see if I might stay over with him tonight."

"You're not coming home?"

"It seems that what I'm looking for is in Colorado."

* * *

CHAPTER NINETEEN

Flying down a New Mexico state highway in the gathering dusk, Tereza circled back around to the question that had been bothering her. "What was it that I said last night that upset you so much? That you called heresy?"

Moret did not look at her. He was glued to the window, fascinated by the changing scenery across Arizona. "Goban is a nonbeliever. He was, at any rate. But he did not teach you anything at all? About his traditions?"

There was nuance in his question that she didn't understand. "He taught us as little as possible. I think he hoped we'd forget... we would have. Another thirty years, when my generation passes on. Our children, mostly, don't know. A few do." *They will now.*

"That is shameful. He should be proud of who he is." Tereza didn't know how to answer that. He sighed. "Thinking beings do not derive from the lesser. There is an irresolvable barrier."

"My people used to believe that too. But the evidence for natural selection is overwhelming."

He shrugged. "The evidence for natural selection proves the existence of the boundary. No category of life transcends it."

"Sorry?" She rubbed the bridge of her nose. "Explain that to me again."

He made an impatient gesture, an exasperated huff. "Natural selection, yes? The mechanism of change and diversity in biology? This is a universal principle."

"Except for thinking beings?"

"Obviously."

Tereza had read Darwin for the first time as a teenager, raiding her grandfather's library. It had struck her then, and returned to her in a rush now, how well-thumbed *The Descent of Man* was. He had read it many times; he had come back to it and chewed it like a dog with a bone. *Where would we be if Darwin had written The Origin of Species, but never gone on to write The Descent of Man? We'd still have great apes and Olduvai Gorge. Someone would have come along and filled in the gaps eventually.* "Where do your people believe that thinking beings come from?"

"Thinking beings are unique. Raised up by the gods. That is the purpose of the semhaata." Something in his tone left the word uncapitalized: a general concept, encompassing the name of his world but also something more.

"Explain that word to me."

"Semhaata? An isolated and protected place, for the purpose of preservation and contemplation."

Sanctuary. Not paradise. Sanctuary. She was almost holding her breath, now. "What do you believe about what came before the semhaata?"

"There is a very old myth. It tells how the gods brought us forth from hell, in a fragile and frightened state, and strengthened us and gave us the semhaata for our salvation. Or destroyed hell, and fashioned the semhaata in its place. There are many different writings, of course, and parts of the oldest versions are lost, and those are only echoes of older stories still. What is clear is that that the purpose of our being is to steward the semhaata. The one that we have, and the new ones that we may go forth and cultivate." He looked at her curiously. "Do you have a myth of the beginning of civilization?"

She released her breath in a great sigh. "We do. Like you, we have many versions. I would be very curious to read yours. Maybe that can be one of the great works, when full diplomatic relations are established between our people. To translate these myths for each other."

He was staring out the window again, pensive. "I don't think that would be well received. We struggle enough over fine interpretations of the one we have."

*　*　*

The night wore on, and, fueled by beer, fatigue, and adrenaline, Kate and Gretchen talked. First a practical catching up, and they spiraled outward from there. Unglued by the conversation on the plane, Kate couldn't stop herself; Gretchen, always the talkative one, just sat back and let her run. The restaurant closed at midnight, and they went to Gretchen's room, still going strong.

Half an hour later, there was a tap on the door; it was Walsh. He looked at Kate and nodded, once. She blew Gretchen a kiss, pushed past him, and flat out ran across the snowy courtyard and up the stairs.

Goban was standing on the balcony, watching, waiting for her. She was already shivering; he wrapped his arms around her. "You're cold."

"It's, like, two degrees out here. Inside, inside." She pushed him toward the door, and she was kissing him, and she fell back against the wall as the door closed behind her, and pulled him close, unbuttoning his shirt, laughing. "I am a little bit drunk."

"We'll muddle through." There was a smile in his voice.

*　*　*

Tereza was happier when they crossed into Colorado; she suspected the phone gambit had worked, buying them a few hours. Stopping for gas just over the border in Durango, she warned Moret, "The ride could get rougher here. It's winter in this hemisphere. We've been driving through the desert until now, but we're headed into the mountains, where my family home is. This time of year is unpredictable. We could have clear weather all the way, or we could find snowstorms higher up."

The roads were clear to Silverton, where they ran headlong into a storm. Tereza continued forward as far as she could, knowing that pushing through the worst of it tired but alert would be better than trying to drive still sleepy after a break. But alertness slipped into some altered anxiety state, every nerve on fire, and she started to see haloes around the reflectors, and taillights through the heavy swirling snow seemed much closer than they really were. She pulled over in an abandoned gas station parking lot in Ridgeway, the wan sodium lights dim and ghostly. *So close, so close.*

"Are you not confident?" he asked, acerbically, when she pulled over.

The exhaustion and shock and fear of the day caught up to her all at once, and she snapped, "I've been driving these roads all my life. You won't find anyone more confident than I am. But what you can't see is that mountain — right over there." She gestured out the window. Frustration bled into despair. "My family's farm is on the north slope. Not more than twenty — not far at all, anyway. But the mountain is in our way, and we have to go three times as far to get around it. In this weather. In the middle of the night, in an unfamiliar vehicle. The stretch that we just came through kills people in peak form, and I'm exhausted. I have to recover from that before I can go on.

"Here," she said, tapping the clock display. "You seem fairly smart, so keep up. Sixty of those to one of these. Twelve of these to a half-day cycle. So when this number comes up again," covering the one in 12:08 with her hand, "I'll have slept long enough. Wake me then. In the meantime," she snarled, "*leave me alone.*"

And she turned away from him and closed her eyes, thinking that at least no one with any sense of self-preservation would be out looking for them in this weather, and too drained to particularly care if they did.

* * *

Kate had drifted off, and it seemed like no time had passed at all when she woke with a start to discover the other side of the bed empty. The clock read just after 3:00. Goban was sitting at the little hotel desk, shirtless, freshly showered and wide awake, writing like mad on the cheap branded notepad. "I'm trying to get down everything that we talked about," he said, "to keep it straight in my head."

"You were in there for a long time."

"Yes." He passed her the full pages of notes. Chilled, she shrugged into his shirt. Reveled in the smell of him. She perched on the arm of his chair, draped an arm around his shoulder, and flipped through the pages.

Kate – first impressions – scope of hire – my medical history – family medical history – range & scope of farm business – farm history – crash – expectations (before & after) – early impressions – differences btwn E&S? – S economics – sociopolitical divisions – Sanctuary doctrine – tech & industry – likely S impression of state of E ecological issues – other tension points – likely diplomatic scenarios – philosophical/religious problems – who has authority? – latitude allowed to recovery team – why did they bolt?

"Oh, hell!" Kate jumped up, crossed the room, rummaged through her bag. Turned just in time to catch his admiring glance. She felt a little flush of delight. *I could get used to that.* "Yesterday was the day of collecting other people's phones. Here, I should have given this to you right away." She played Tereza's message for him, and watched his face.

Bafflement at first, replaced by blossoming recognition. "Andessat.... Moret. How very interesting."

"You knew him?"

"We were students together. Not... quite friends, certainly acquaintances. Hard worker, also liked to party. Popular." A sour face. "Good at talking people into going along with whatever scheme he was on. I'm sure he's matured into quite the negotiator. I expected much worse.

Not an accident that they sent a familiar face, I think."

"I wouldn't think so. If what they thought had happened here actually had, a familiar face would be a godsend."

"Yes. The worse for them."

* * *

When she turned off the highway and onto the long county road, Tereza relaxed a little. The last part was the hardest; mud under fresh ice under heavy wet snow under powder. No one had been this way since the storm began. She finessed the rental up the twisty road.

The final turn onto the private road, and twenty yards beyond that, the gate. She gasped a little, not quite a sob, more than a sigh. Exhausted, she botched the passcode twice, gave up, and picked up the phone to call the house.

Moret stirred, opened his eyes and watched her, a wordless question on his sleepy face. "We're here," she said, curtly, and then, more softly, "this is it." She took the hill slow and careful, up and over the ridge, and into the valley. Home. Two days after she had left, right down to the hour; she felt as though she'd been gone a year.

Conrad was standing on the front porch of her house. He hugged her, an uncharacteristic gesture. "Sis. Glad you're back." He tilted his chin toward Moret, unfolding himself from the passenger seat, stretching after the long drive. "Avots no visiem nemieru?" he asked, taking in Tereza's fatigue. *The source of all the trouble?*

"Jā, viņš ir viens."

"Tēvs called. Not half an hour ago. He wanted to let you know as soon as you got in. Kate's with him and she's fine. They're both in RCMP protective custody, it seems. He's pretty sure the FBI is on their way here."

How the hell did the Mounties get involved? It didn't displease her. The more layers of bureaucracy and jurisdictional infighting, the better. "I'm relieved I beat them here, then. They're probably holding off for daybreak."

"Won't be long, then. I'd better go rouse some of the men. You get some sleep while you can." And he brushed past Moret and headed up the hill without another word.

* * *

The sun was already up, turning the mountains a cacophony of pink and purple, when Kate stirred and smiled. "What is it, seven? I can't remember the last time I slept in this late."

"We'll make a farm girl of you yet." His eyes stayed closed, but he was smiling.

She rolled over and regarded him, sprawling, looking deeply relaxed and pleased. Not youth-smooth, but firm, a body shaped by a lifetime of hard work. She herself was not as firm, she knew, but she'd felt herself adjusting to the endless walking around the farm, tightening up, building endurance. It felt good.

He traced a hand idly down her hip, and she caught his fingers, entangled them in hers. Traced the lines on the back of his hand. "What does it mean?"

"It's my flight badge. Look. The double moon is the company logo." What she'd thought were concentric circles, the first time she'd glimpsed the tattoo, were two crescent moons, nested within each other. "Date and place of my commission. And each dot is a flight."

Two rings of dots, around the outside of the logo, and part of a third. "That's a lot of flights."

"It was a lot of fun."

"Do you miss it?"

He laughed, pulled his hand away. "Not even a little. I was young. It was different."

She shivered and settled closer, into the curve of his arm. "This is nice," she murmured. "Maybe we'll get a bit of a breather today. The last few days were hard."

"Mm." He stretched, and she tilted her chin up to kiss him, let herself get lost in it for a little while.

A loud knock at the door startled them apart. Gretchen's voice on the other side. "Kate! Are you decent?"

"No!" she shouted back, grinning.

"Are you coming to breakfast or staying in bed all day?"

"Staying in bed!" Both of them, this time, in unison. That set her to giggling, and she pulled the covers over her head, trying in vain to muffle it.

"I guess you don't want these warm clothes then!"

"Ugh." She rolled out of bed, pulled on yesterday's shirt and jeans, stumbled to the door. "Why are you bothering me?"

Gretchen stuck her tongue out. "I knew I was going to be here for a few days, but I figured you didn't have a chance to bring anything. So I brought you some of my clothes. Say thank you."

"Thank you." Kate laughed, contrite. "Yes, my stuff is still at my mother's."

"You're welcome. I'm going down to breakfast. See you there. *Soon*. Inspector Walsh is a little tightly wound." Gretchen glanced past her, at the stirring bedcovers, smirked and waved. "Bye now."

Kate showered, pulled on the thick cable sweater and leggings, found them to be loose. That was startling; a year ago, she had been a size bigger than Gretchen. She really was getting into shape.

Goban was moving more slowly; by the time she was out of the shower and dressed, he was just buttoning his shirt. She watched, with silent worry, as he struggled with the last few buttons. *Too soon, it's too soon for him to be this bad.* The stress of these last two weeks was showing in every line of his face, in the slow care of his movements. But then he looked up, and his eyes lit at the sight of her standing there, studying him. He ran a careless hand through his thick, dark hair and nodded at her. "I suppose we'd better get on with it."

They took their time, down the stairs and around to the restaurant, holding hands, getting accustomed to the feeling. He slipped a little on an icy patch of pavement, right outside the restaurant, squeezed hard and leaned into her to recover his balance, but now his hands were shaking. Anyone could slip, she told herself, anyone could be rattled from it, but she knew she was grasping at straws. Small things added up. He had another four or five days, a week at the outside, before the next flare-up. Right in the middle of all of this. She resolved to call Rita today, and cursed David bitterly.

Gretchen and Walsh were sitting at a corner booth meant for eight, and he had work spread out across the table. "Good morning, Michael," Goban said, sketching a little bow, pulling up a chair from the next table over. Walsh nodded absently, and Kate realized he was on the phone. She slipped into the booth next to Gretchen. The waitress brought two mugs and a fresh carafe of coffee, and Kate got to work on it while Walsh finished his call. It was, she discovered to her pleasure, much better than the bar coffee of the night before.

"You're at it early, Inspector," she observed.

"Oh, yes. Ottawa has been awake and at work for two hours, and therefore, so have I. I have been on the phone already with," he ticked off on his fingers, "my boss. The Commissioner. The Prime Minister. Our Ministry of Foreign Affairs. Your State Department. This is developing into an *event*. SSA Dorsey with the FBI." He looked at Goban. "Your granddaughter, who is a force of nature."

At that, Kate made a rude noise into her cup; Goban looked amused. "You know I adore Tereza," she defended herself. "It was a bit of a rocky road, getting there," she explained to Walsh.

"I can imagine; she's quite something. Anyway. This is a jurisdictional kerfuffle of monstrous proportions. Complicated, of course, by the fact that we have you, and the Americans have this Andessat fellow. 'Have' being relative. He is ensconced on your family farm, where a mixed team of law enforcement, security, and diplomatic personnel are headed as we speak. Both sides anticipate that there will be trouble if an attempt is made to remove him by force or coercion."

"I would think so," Goban interjected, mildly, but there was quiet danger in his tone.

"Right." Walsh nodded, some internal assessment confirmed. "You are not in custody in any way, as my superiors have accepted my assessment that you, yourself, are not a threat to our security. However. There is a consensus that your presence creates a high-risk atmosphere, but also an opportunity that this country might otherwise not have had, to participate in this historic process. I have been empowered to extend to you the courtesy of protective custody, the parameters of which I am to define, as appropriate to the circumstances. If you choose so, at any point, that protection may be extended to a request for political asylum, which will be taken very seriously."

That got Goban's attention. "That's... quite generous. And a comfort. But I have every intention of going home, as soon as possible."

"Of course. In the meantime, please consider yourself a guest of the Dominion of Canada, and myself your friendly local guide." Walsh made an expansive gesture. "And then there's Kate, who is still a suspect in a conspiracy case." He turned to her. "SSA Dorsey informs me that she has acquired a warrant to search your lab."

"Well, that's fine. That's great." The thought of strangers rifling through her lab made her ill, in fact. *Trust in Rita and Marina.* "They'll find the provenance, and confirm once and for all that my research isn't based on stolen samples."

"That's what Tereza said, after she spoke with her cousin. She's offered the farm as a sort of retreat to work all of this out, and appointed herself moderator. This is basically the same situation that existed at Edwards two days ago, except with the family, ah, enforcing the scenario rather than the Air Force."

"Excellent." Goban squeezed Kate's hand, under the table. She nodded. *Better than we could have hoped for.*

"There's also this to think about." Walsh pushed a tablet across the table; it displayed weather radar. There was a green-and-pink wall crossing southwestern Utah and northern Arizona, headed northeast, heralded by smaller patches scattered ahead of the leading edge. "Your folks are getting some weather already, and they're going to get pounded all to hell in about ten, twelve hours. So your granddaughter needs to make a decision by noon today about whether you ought to head home or sit tight."

* * *

CHAPTER TWENTY

Jake got the call before dawn; he and his father met the uncles on the porch of the big house. Tēvocis Pete heard the rotors first, several minutes before two helicopters came up over the ridge and headed for the empty corral nearest the road. By the time they set down, kicking up snow and dirt and straw, the men had arranged themselves around the corral, carrying rifles, with three of the big Mollos dogs following Pete. Jake took the position protecting Tante Tereza and his mother, off to Conrad's left.

Amanda Dorsey stepped out first, left hand high in a conciliatory gesture, but her right hand resting on her service pistol, and identified herself. "We don't want a standoff," she said immediately.

"Neither do we," Conrad said. "You might have come up the drive."

"We weren't confident that you would let us on the property."

"You weren't wrong. What's your business here?"

She held up a document. "I have a warrant here to search Katherine Hutchins' laboratory, and I have a team with me to do that. I also have Major Louis Farris of US Air Force Intelligence, who has some questions for you."

"We know Major Farris." Conrad looked over at Tereza; Jake glanced back. Her lips tightened. Tiny shake of her head. *I don't like it,* her face said, but she was not putting her foot down. "How about we say yes to you and no to him?"

Farris disembarked from the helicopter. Conrad raised his rifle; the dogs spread out, bristled tails, heads low, unnervingly silent. Dorsey said, warningly, "You really don't want to do that, Mr. Darzins."

"Maybe I do," Conrad growled. He locked eyes with Farris. Jake tensed, watching. Not yet pulling the slack out of the trigger, but ready.

Farris stood his ground, meeting the stare. "Is Andessat Moret on this property?" Silence. Farris' lip twitched. "He assaulted a US Air Force security police sergeant. After that, we think he may have taken your sister hostage and forced her to help him escape custody. If a violent crime was committed on your sister's person, don't you want to know about it? He's dangerous." His gaze shifted across the corral, over to Tereza; he raised his voice. "Or did you plan the escape together?"

Another silence. Conrad's rifle did not move. Long seconds passed, turned into one minute, two. Jake saw his aunt's hands, saw the blood where her nails cut into her palms. Fists clenched that hard, in rage, or fear.

Then her hands relaxed, and she called out, "Stand down, Conrad. Stāt –" this to the dogs, who immediately fell back, milled a little, and laid down, but watched the new arrivals with interest. "Yes, he's here. No, we didn't plan anything, and he didn't kidnap me. We ran into each other as we were both trying to leave the base, and... made a mutual decision on the spot to travel together."

Conrad stood his rifle up against the fence and stepped back; Jake released his breath, slowly, eased off the trigger, followed suit. Dorsey relaxed and gestured; the remaining helicopter passengers started to disembark. "There are two cars following us," she said. "They should be here within the hour. They contain representatives of the various agencies that have a stake in this situation. May I have your word that they won't be threatened?"

"Without Tēvs here, it's your show, sis," Tereza murmured. "You want these people in your house?"

Emma sighed. "I just want this to be over. Let them all talk. Why not?" Jake backed up as his mother stepped forward, watching the armed agents tensely.

She pitched her voice to carry over the open space. "My name is Emma Darzins-Kelley, and I am Head of Household of this outfit and CFO of this corporation. You may have *my* word. You are guests in my home. Please act like it. These gentlemen here are my husband, my brother, my son, and my cousin. They'll escort you where you need to go. This is a working farm, and this is one of the busiest weeks of the year for us, made busier by the storm that's coming in. Anything that interferes with operations threatens our livelihood, and will be documented for future legal action." She paused for emphasis and looked around; her eyes locked on Farris. "You caught us off guard last time, Major. Not today. Get yourselves settled and come on up to the big house."

"I'll see the lab first, if it's all the same to you," Dorsey said, with firm deference.

"Sure. Jake, take Agent Dorsey and her people down to the clinic. Stop and pick up your Tante Rita on the way. Major, you're with me." She nodded at her sister, turned on her heel and headed up the road. Farris hesitated. Jake's father picked up his rifle, opened the gate, gesturing through, and Farris followed the women, the other three men flanking him.

Dorsey looked at Jake. He shrugged, and she crossed the corral to the gate, ushered her team through, and closed it behind herself. "Lead on."

"The warrant?" She handed it to him. "Tante Tereza would kill me if I didn't look it over." He did, nodded his satisfaction, handed it back. Introduced himself. "The woman that was standing next to my mom? She's our lawyer. If you overstep your bounds, she'll fry you." There was not a trace of hostility in his conversational tone; he looked at her steadily.

Saw the *oh* in her eyes. "I don't intend to overstep my bounds." Dorsey followed him across the open space between the corral and barn, up onto the road, her boots crunching in the icy muck. "Why are we stopping for your aunt?"

"She's our doctor. It's her lab. Kate just works there."

"I see. What do you think of Kate, Jake?"

He didn't hesitate. "She's good people. She's pretty devoted to my Tante Rita and my great-grandfather."

"Devoted? That's an interesting word. She hasn't been here very long, has she?"

"It happens that way sometimes." He fell quiet, and Dorsey let the silence hang in the cold air for a moment before pressing forward.

"What do you know about how she came here? Did you ever get the feeling she was looking for something?

An out-of-the-way place where she would work on... a project?"

He stopped cold, turned to face her, as the first icy pinpricks of fine drifting snowflakes stung his cheek. "Ma'am, I don't want to be rude, but you're way off. I was the first one who met Kate. I made the decision to bring her up here." He started off walking again. "When Kate came here, she was a mess. She didn't want anybody to see it, and she did a pretty good job of covering it up, but it was bad. Whatever she was doing before, she didn't any want more of that."

"She still seemed pretty messed up when I talked to her yesterday."

"Well, then, maybe some of that's on you, because when she left here Friday morning, she was worried, but she was happy." Grim, anxious, and angry, he didn't say anything else.

* * *

"The gang's all here. Almost." Farris nodded to Tereza. "Where's Kate Hutchins? And *Henry?*"

He'd done that in California too, that particular nasty tone. She had swallowed it then, and was not taking it again.

She set her coffee cup down on the table, a slow and exaggerated gesture of controlled fury. "Major. A word, please." She stalked out the kitchen door, not bothering to look to see if he followed.

As soon as the door was closed, she turned on him. "You made an assumption, and you were wrong. My brother was a hero, and his death was a great heartache for all of us. What you said to my sister the last time you were here was very hurtful." She hadn't dared ask what he might have said to Rita.

"You have to understand – "

"I don't have to understand a damned thing. You're right. My grandfather has been lying about his name for a long time. Of course. What else was he supposed to do?" She looked away, out over the snowbound valley below. "My grandmother was a young widow when they met. He took the name of her first husband, and that is the name on the original claim for this property. My brother was, in fact, named after him."

"I see. I apologize."

"You people only ever bring bad news. Why are you so surprised that we just want you to leave us alone?" Tereza was taken aback by the raw hurt in her own voice, as if half a lifetime had not passed since that other very bad day. Her face was wet; she shivered. The snow was getting heavier, but the sky beyond the western ridge was clear. *Should clear up this afternoon, hit us with the next round tonight,* she thought reflexively, a lifelong habit of attentiveness to the sky distracting her, soothing her rattled nerves.

"I really am sorry." Farris was sincere, subdued. "I saw your brother's file. You're right; he was extraordinary. I was... offended, on his behalf, when I thought I had good reason to believe that his identity had been stolen. I didn't know."

"Well, you know now."

Reggie opened the door and stepped out on the

porch. "You doing okay out here?"

"We're fine, Reggie, thanks." She met her brother-in-law's eyes, nodded.

"You've got a call. There are three cars at the gate, not two."

Huh. She stomped back in the house, kicking the loose snow off her boots, and took the phone Em handed to her. "Hello?"

"Tereza! Good God, I'm delighted to hear your voice. I have finished the maze, do I get a prize?"

She laughed out loud. "Oh, yes, you do! Doctor, I'm so glad you came. Pass the phone back to Tommy."

After she hung up and took off her boots, she looked up to find Emma studying her. "That was the oddest expression I have ever seen on you, sister of mine."

"Dr. Jansen is a distinguished astrophysicist, and a very rational person," she said, a little stiffly. "I invited him to bring a voice of reason to the table."

"And a silly grin to your face. Right."

* * *

"Hey."

Kate joined Gretchen in the hotel laundromat. If they washed yesterday's things, they had decided over breakfast, both women could probably make do with Gretchen's clothes and what Kate had traveled in. Perhaps do a little shopping later.

She looked at her friend, usually buoyant, now subdued. "What's wrong?" she asked, softly. Gretchen didn't answer, busying herself with the washing machine. Kate waited.

"I'm just tired."

"We're all tired. You're sad."

Gretchen looked up, looked Kate full in the eyes for a moment, and then looked away. She perched up on one of the empty machines and sighed.

"Katie, you have been alone for as long as I've known you. Even when you're with someone, you're alone." A wry, unhappy twitch of a smile. "When you came to Vancouver in September... I could see that you were on the edge of something that was going to change your life, and I thought that maybe this is it, this is when you finally get to leave all the shit behind and be happy. And it's beautiful. Not just him, although he obviously adores you, but all of it.

"I want to be happy, but I'm so scared for you. I don't want this to end badly for you."

Kate hopped up to sit on the next machine, and they sat there together, side by side, dangling their feet in companionable silence. It took Kate back twenty years, to campus laundromats and late-night confessionals.

After a moment, she spoke. "You know, the farm was the last thing in the world I expected. I was bowled over. I'd settled into an idea that life was just shades of grey... I didn't know that you could be head over heels in love with a place.

"It took some time for me to sort that out from how I felt about him, and I was just getting to the point of trusting it. Jumping off that particular cliff. That's always been hard for me." *As you know.* A wave of old heartache and regret; she pushed it aside. "And now this whole thing has blown up, and I have never felt less in control of anything in my life, and Gretchen, I am so angry. I hate not knowing what's going to happen, I hate being sent off somewhere safe and out of the way, and let me tell you, it's nothing to how much he hates it, and watching him twisted up in sheer frustration is maybe the worst part.

"Yesterday, I felt like I'd ruined everything by taking that sample to David. Now... I don't know. Maybe it was the push that the whole thing needed, to jar it loose and move toward some kind of resolution."

"Maybe. I still might punch him in the face the next time I see him." A hesitation. "Not just because of that. I knew things were bad for you. I didn't know how bad. I should have."

"You couldn't! You shouldn't, now. I said too much last night. I don't know what kind of hell I'll have to pay for that, either. And, you know, I was right there. I was absolutely complicit. I wanted it to succeed as much as anyone; I doubled down right along with the others. You can't blame David or — or the team, or Alcon, or the Army, without blaming me too."

"Sure I can. Anyway, there's no keeping it contained now, it's all going to come out. The project..." Gretchen's brow furrowed. "Here's the thing that I'm still chewing over. How is it that Goban's deficient hormone and your drug are so similar, anyway?"

"I don't know. It is a puzzle, isn't it? We had an idea of what effects we were aiming for, and tailored a hormone that triggered those effects, and then it turns up that the Semhet have something so similar, naturally?

There must be a connection, but I have no idea what it is. We need to know more about their biology — their normative biology, not just what we can learn from one subject with a metabolic disease.

"The one thing that I'm convinced of, after all of this, is that when this is over, I'm going to go back and see it shut down." Regardless of the consequences. "We were never going to find a solution to the withdrawal. It doesn't exist. Just look at him."

"Yeah, he looks absolutely ragged. He's good at hiding it, though. How bad is it going to get?"

"Worse, before it gets better." There was nothing to say to that, so they sat there for a while longer, and then the machine beeped, and Gretchen stood up to change it over. Kate caught her hand. "You know..."

"Yeah?"

Kate bit her lip, working at finding the right words. "If I had just one wish." She faltered. There was too much history to distill.

Some silent understanding passed between them, a breath held for a heartbeat and released, and then Gretchen really smiled, full of warmth and life. "I know. And I love you for it." She winked. "I'll get mine. Thanks for the reminder that it's not too late."

* * *

CHAPTER TWENTY ONE

The morning passed with Walsh camped out in the restaurant, with his papers and tablet and phone. The women came and went, but Goban stayed, drinking cup after cup of coffee, making small talk. The caffeine might be the only thing keeping the old man on his feet, but it was also making him talkative. He was endlessly fascinating; Walsh found himself intrigued and unsettled in equal measure.

"You talk a lot about your family in Colorado. Did you have a family, where you came from before?" The look that Goban shot him was strange — startled, guarded, but also appreciative. "Has anyone ever asked you that?"

The green-grey eyes focused on some other place and time. "My wife, a long time ago. No one since, no."

"Well, I imagine, to everyone else, you've just always been around. She had reason to wonder what it was like where you came from, and how attached you were to it."

"Hm." Goban hesitated. "My father was a secondary school teacher. Sciences, biology and ecology. My mother was an environmental engineer, and traveled quite a lot. No siblings. We were just the two of us, most of the time. I had an aunt, my father's sister, who had several kids, but my cousins were all much older. I thought, growing up, it might be nice to have a big family like that, but I also felt out of place when we visited. I was pretty solitary. "

"Your mother was an engineer? So you were no

stranger to smart women. I notice you seem to surround yourself with them."

"Oh, yes. Smart, and brave, and ambitious. They come by it honestly. My wife came to America because she wanted both to own land and to be a schoolteacher, and that was not a balance that could be easily struck, for a woman of her class at that time.

"It's criminal, how you people waste the talents of women. And, you know, I didn't understand that, at least not at first. But she did. She taught me what to expect, the fights our girls would have. I believed I could build something different. An enclave. To some extent I think I have succeeded. But you don't know how pervasive it is, how your little bigotries bleed into everything." There was quiet, lingering anger in the old man's eyes, and shame. "It's better; it's been easier for my granddaughters than it was for my daughters. Not... easy, of course. And the current generation is doing some extraordinary things. But you have a lot of work still to do."

"The Semhet are more, what, egalitarian?" Walsh was curious, and, he could not deny, also a little defensive. Goban smirked; it must have crept into his voice.

"The Semhet have their own problems, that's for sure." He tossed back the last of his cup, fixed another, regarded Walsh thoughtfully. "Look. When I came here, this place was a mess. Reeling from centuries of endless wars. Choking on its own waste. Starvation and suffering everywhere, and devastating inequality, both civil and economic. And it got worse. We hid away, safe on our mountain, mostly, and watched two global conflicts in quick succession, and two generations living in terror of a third. Smaller wars everywhere, all the time, although no war is ever small, when you count up the human cost." A half-buried flinch, an old hurt. "Families divided, our own family divided, by politics and conflict. Ethnic cleansing and cultural eradication. Yes, there were times I thought I'd made the wrong call in staying, that maybe I should dig up that wretched beacon and call the Semhet in to impose some kind of reason on madness, or at least throw up my hands and go back to a place that was stable, clean, and calm.

"But every time, *every time* I started down that line of thought, I also saw something that made me think, *oh, let's wait and see.* The advancements in medicine and technology that you've made in just my lifetime? That took the Semhet fifteen hundred years. You unbalanced the global climate in a handful of decades, but you caught on, and you're dedicating the greatest minds of a generation to cleaning up that mess. You foul up in the most stunning ways, but you learn from your mistakes. You try new things, you reinvent yourselves constantly.

"There's a self-righteousness and a sterile arrogance to the Semhet. They are tremendously deliberate. Everything is design; nothing is art. They do everything very well, except for the universe of things they never try at all. Nothing about them would ever make you think, *let's wait and see what happens.*"

"A pox on both your houses," Walsh mused.

"Sorry?"

"You never say 'us,' except when you're talking

about your own family. It's 'them' and 'you.' You sit on the outside looking in and condemn both."

"It's not condemnation. It's... too much of each in me, to be able to rationalize away the deadly sins of the other. I can't be satisfied. I suppose that tips the balance of my heart more toward Earth than Semhaata, after all."

"Nothing to go home to, then."

"Not particularly. That's what I've been trying to explain to the kids. It's not that I'm afraid, or hostile. I just... don't care. I never looked back." Walsh wasn't sure how much he believed that; there was some more complicated emotion moving under the surface. But he nodded, and nursed his coffee. "I watched my wife struggle with it. I knew that she loved me and our children very much, and she was dedicated to the home that we built together, but I think that every day of her life she missed Malinovka right down in her bones. I never related to that. I've been content in the valley. More than content. I have never felt that I belonged anywhere else."

"And now there's Kate."

"And now there's Kate," Goban echoed. "I was completely taken by surprise, by Kate. Going back is nothing, but leaving, now — that terrifies me."

Walsh looked thoughtful. "Your granddaughter wasn't wrong, sending you up here, you know."

"Oh, I know that. Do you think she could have made me go if I didn't? This is what she trained for, and I needed to get out of her way to let her work." He held up his shaking hands. "Too valuable and not enough use. So here I sit, out of the way, hiding behind your border. She's right, but I don't have to be happy about it."

"You want to go back to Colorado."

"Damned right I do."

Walsh shook his head. "Once we step off the plane, I'm out of my jurisdiction. I can't protect you."

"See, that's the thing, Michael. Don't take this the wrong way, but I don't want your or anybody's protection. I'm sick to death of being protected. I want to go home and take care of the people who depend on me." He studied Walsh, thoughtful. "But I would welcome you as a guest in my home."

Walsh thought about that. "Sir, I would be honored."

* * *

Emma and Tereza spent the morning getting the big house set up, while Rita and Marina observed the search of the lab. The house was dead quiet, with almost everyone else out preparing for the storm. The sisters worked in companionable silence, the familiar communal labor of hospitality comforting.

The dining room made a serviceable conference room, with the leaves for the big table pulled out of storage and set up. The two studies and the parlor would do for breakout groups, and the kitchen, Emma announced, was strictly off-limits for visitors, a place for the family to retreat and converse in private. Irena took charge of the kitchen, calling some help in from the other houses, coordinating guest rooms, fixing lunch, baking coffee cakes and pulling cheeses and pickles from the pantry to serve as finger foods, and making big pots of coffee and tea.

Theo dropped by mid-morning. "Susan's telling me online orders are coming in pretty heavy, and we're not going to be able to get anything out until this clears up." He meant the blizzard. "But we need to stay on top of it. So we're taking all the kids and letting them have a big slumber party, a work party, down at our place." Theo and Susan's house was right across the ring road from the upper warehouse. "Keep them all clear of this other business, too."

"That's a good idea." Emma shook her head. "We may not be able to ship anything out till that clears up, either. I can't see the FBI agents letting a carrier truck come and go."

"That could be bad. We already have fifty thou in orders queued up, and it's only Sunday morning. A lot more will come in today, and our local wholesale orders are coming in too." Local was a two-hundred-mile radius, small gourmet shops and boutiques as far away as Taos and Boulder. "We start losing sales over this, it could hurt us pretty bad. For years to come."

"You don't have to tell me that." Emma did quick math in her head. If they could pick back up shipping on Wednesday, they would be okay. Probably. *Tereza,* she thought, *you have until this storm lifts to get your job done, so I can do mine.*

* * *

Tereza stood at the head of the table and surveyed the group. Moret was on her left, with Emma beyond him, on first translator shift. Around the table, there were two State Department representatives and two from Homeland

Security, and Leslie Thorne. An officer from the Canadian consulate in Denver. One of the 412th officers, up from Edwards, and Major Farris, and finally, Dr Jansen.

"I'd like to welcome you all to my home," she said, "and lay down some guidelines for the discussions we're going to have here over the next few days. Andessat Moret set down in California fifty-five hours ago, and his status is no closer to being clarified now than it was then. Nor, for that matter, is that of Nhoresh Goban, which is obviously an issue of some concern to his family. So I'm stepping in. I have here a list of questions; they are in three groups. These are the only questions we're going to concern ourselves with for the time being, so let's keep our eye on the target." She handed a stack of printed agendas to Dr. Jansen, who took one and passed them on.

"Let's sum up the current situation." She steadied herself. She was becoming accustomed to talking about these things, the things that nobody ever talked about, but it did not ease her visceral anxiety. She spoke in a clipped, precise tone, masking her distress. "Nhoresh Goban was born in about 1863, on the planet Semhaata, a citizen of the federated state of Bva'tat. He arrived here in 1889 as an employee of the OSTAN natural resource development corporation. The survey craft he was flying crashed just about three-quarters of a mile southwest of here. The following year, he met and married Amalija Darzina, of Philadelphia, born in 1870 and previously of Malinovka Parish in the Russian Empire, in what is now eastern Latvia. Also in that year, he began to live under the identity of Henriks Darzins, of Philadelphia and previously of Daugavpils, born 1865, died 1890." Major Farris had the good grace to look uncomfortable at that.

"He and Amalija had five children; their oldest daughter, Eleonora, was my mother. He has been a resident of the State of Colorado and Gunnison County continuously since his arrival, and was a landowner and taxpayer here until 1974, when he retired and passed ownership of this property to the Darzins' Mill Corporation. He remains a major shareholder in the corporation and chairman of the board." Pause. Emma translated, her voice low, watching Moret carefully. Tereza in turn watched her sister. It sounded so stark and strange, laid out concisely like that. *Just family. Our weird family.* The assembled company was silent, attentive, but Tereza could feel their uneasiness, echoed by her own.

"Andessat Moret, also a citizen of Bva'tat and an OSTAN employee, was sent here to investigate why Dar Nhoresh had not returned or reported in, after a remote query signal had activated an emergency beacon. His several statements to me have indicated that he intends to return to Semhaata with Dar Nhoresh, with or without his consent, for debriefing." Another pause, for impact, for the translation. Moret's eyes narrowed, but he did not argue or try to clarify.

"He entered the United States at about 5am on November 24th of this year. The craft he was flying was intercepted by F-15 aircraft out of Edwards AFB and Hickam AFB in Hawaii, and was escorted to Edwards. At Edwards, he was held in a status that was variously described as, ah, biomedical containment; custody as a suspected member of a hostile foreign force; and protective custody." The other officer shifted and frowned. *Plenty of embarrassment to go around*, Tereza thought, with grim amusement.

"Shortly before 10am yesterday, having asked several times to be released from custody and receiving no answer he found satisfactory, Dar Andessat assaulted an Air Force security policeman, stole his weapon, uniform, and vehicle, and fled the base. I had traveled to California to negotiate with him on my grandfather's behalf, and I was also asked to leave at about the same time. As I was getting into my car, he approached me and asked for my help." Her palms ached as she white-knuckled the edge of the table. *Relax.*

"I made the decision at that time to bring him here. My grandfather, being aware of Dar Andessat's imminent arrival and intentions, had already traveled to Vancouver to wait for developments and clarification. He is now in Alberta, in what we would obviously prefer to leave an unnamed location, in the protective custody of the national security investigative branch of the Royal Canadian Mounted Police. And that brings us to this morning. Any questions?

"All right then. These are my questions for all of you. First: Is Nhoresh Goban, in fact, a citizen of the United States? If so, what protections is he entitled to against the threat of detainment made by the OSTAN corporation? If not, what recourse is available to him? Is there an emergency path to a legal status that affords him some protection?

"Second: Is Andessat Moret in this country legally? Is the OSTAN claim legitimate, and is his status as their agent? What rights is he entitled to, and what are his obligations? Was his detainment by the U.S. Air Force appropriate, and is he required to remain in their custody? Or was it an illegal detainment from which he was entitled — or obligated — to seek escape?

Third: Have either of these individuals been, or are they expected to be, charged with crimes that may complicate or limit the range of rights and protections that they can claim?

"One other thing. I need to tell you that we have a major winter storm coming in. By late this afternoon the road will be impassable, and my brother tells me it's likely to stay that way for at least two days. So get comfortable." She looked around the table. "Who wants to start?"

One of the State Department people spoke up. "Why are we working from your agenda? We should start with an agenda-setting discussion."

Tereza smiled, tight-lipped and wry. "Let me welcome you all to my home," she started over. "Let's be clear. You are guests of the Darzins family. We'll resolve the questions that are of immediate concern to the family first. I understand that you're all very interested in bigger concepts too. Diplomatic relations between the United States and other nations" — a nod to the Canadian — "and the sovereign global state of Semhaata. The physical location of Semhaata in the galaxy, its sociopolitical structure and economy and culture, and the technology that allows its people to travel between there and here.

Their biology and evolutionary history, and their similarity to us, and what that means for broader questions of life in the universe. These are of course all profound and important questions. But they are not *as urgent* as the questions I've laid before you."

She looked around, and let that statement hang in the air for a moment, letting the assembled company chew on it, until the overwhelming wave of worry and fear that she felt settled and she could go on. "I'll be frank with you. My grandfather is obviously not a young man, and he is quite ill, and with all respect and gratitude to the Canadian government, he needs to come home. He needs to be able to feel safe coming home. Right now, that is the only priority on the table."

* * *

"The problem is precedent," the immigration lawyer from Homeland Security started, and Leslie Thorne interrupted.

"No, the problem is procedure. It's exactly because this situation is so without precedent that — look, we can effectively do whatever we want, as long as we do it correctly.

"I've received some instructions. The administration wants two outcomes from this meeting: first, clearing any legal obstacles to letting these two gentlemen work out their private dispute between them, and second, some assurances that there will be some sort of follow-up discussion of ongoing relations with the Semhet after Andessat Moret goes home, regardless of the outcome of his own mission. How do we get from here to there?"

Tereza smiled. "Are you saying the position of the White House is that the OSTAN claim is legitimate?"

"I'm saying our position is that we simply don't have the ability to meaningfully evaluate that question. Obviously any attempted kidnapping or other crime should be dealt with by law enforcement, but short of that..." Thorne spread her hands. "It's really not our business."

* * *

Some distance up the county road past Chesterton, tense and watchful in the back seat, Walsh asked, "Have you folks ever thought about putting in a landing strip on your property?"

Goban laughed. "It's come up a couple of times. Seemed like an extravagance."

"You know," Kate said grimly, "I've never actually driven *up* this road in decent weather." A more familiar car wouldn't have been unwelcome, either; needing more seats, they'd borrowed Chris Carver's SUV, leaving the little yellow truck behind at the airport.

"I'd love to see this gorgeous place you talk about so much," Gretchen said.

"I'd just be happy to see the road." *Or the gate.* That last turn was familiar.

Then there was some wan yellow light ahead, shining through the swirling curtain of snow; a great gust of wind cleared the view for an instant, and she could see the gate and the big truck just beyond it, headlights on, with Robbie and Tommy sitting in the cab. Kate pulled over and hopped out. "What in the world are you boys doing down here in this weather?" she shouted.

"Hey, Kate!" Robbie's face lit up as he swung down from the shotgun seat and strolled over to the gate. "It's been a pretty weird day, lotta people through. Tēvocis Conrad wanted someone sitting down here. We were about to call it off and head up, though. You want us to let the house know you're coming in?" Kate was punching in the code, the gate was swinging open, and the boy stepped through and hugged her.

"How about you don't, son?" Goban had to hang on to the car door to stand, but his face was alight with humor. "I think I want to surprise your Tante Tereza."

* * *

CHAPTER TWENTY TWO

The steady drone of these peoples' chatter wore on Moret; he was grateful for the woman sitting next to him, the translator. Tereza's sister, she had said. She had explained what Tereza had not — those of their generation were not the children, but the grandchildren. "These people," she had said, "live and die like *that*." A snap of the fingers. "Our family is somewhere in between. Longer-lived than them, not so much as you."

How strange it must be, to be neither one nor the other. And stranger still, and horrifying for Goban, to watch his children age and die while he himself was a man of middle years. How lonely. It made Moret sad and ill to think about it; he would not have been able to face such a thing, nor all these years in this unfamiliar place so far from home. Goban's core must be made of the stone from the mountains he came from.

Sometimes they asked him questions, and he listened carefully to the translations, and thereby, he was beginning to pick up bits and pieces of the language, guttural and clipped to his ears. But at other times, his mind wandered, processing the things that he had seen and heard these three strange days. He thought about his ship, powered down and silent, across the desert, out of reach, the message home left unsent.

He just wanted to talk to the man, to compare thoughts about this startlingly beautiful world and its strange, fragile people. Even the mission was secondary, now, to understanding what this place meant.

He stood and walked through the wide archway to the room beyond, to the large window, stared out at the blank wall of swirling snow obscuring the low red sun. Cold, dark, and alone. *Am I damned?*

Emma walked over, stood next to him, spoke softly. "*Do'cho?*" *How is it with you?* He had no words to answer.

* * *

"Settling the residency issue is easy enough," said the immigration lawyer from Homeland Security. "There are a couple of hurdles, but none we can't clear. I started the paperwork during the break. The question is, does he *want* to be a citizen? That's a different thing."

"Of course he does. He took the oath years ago, as Henriks."

"And we're not pressing charges on immigration fraud." A raised eyebrow.

"Well, thank you for that," Tereza retorted, wryly.

"It's no joke. The oath means something, and using someone else's name –"

"I tried to call again a while ago and couldn't get through. We'll have to sit on the question. Moving on."

"Let's not." A voice rang out from the kitchen doorway. Tereza turned, and gasped, just a little.

Her grandfather was leaning on the door frame, arms crossed; a calculated, effortless posture, as though he had been there all along. Kate stood next to him, and two strangers behind her. He was speaking to the immigration lawyer, but his entire attention was on Moret, a challenge written on his face.

"Don't think for a minute that I don't know what weight an oath carries, or that I didn't damn well mean it the first time. What I took on, and what I let go. You put it in front of me, I'll swear it again."

* * *

Moret turned from the window at the sudden hush, and froze.

Oh, my old friend, my adversary. Blood was rushing in his ears and he did not hear what Emma echoed, after gathering herself from her own surprise, but he could read that challenge. This was going to be the fight of his life.

The room was silent as death. Everyone was watching, waiting, barely breathing.

He walked across the smaller room, through the arch, around the big table, taking his time, gathering his thoughts. His next move could gain or lose the whole mission.

They stood face to face. Moret spread his hands wide, palms up. *"Gatsep'tat."* Kinsman. "It's good to see you... well." He was not at all well, Moret could see. But alive, against all odds, after all these years. "You know why I am here?"

"Of course." Goban was perfectly cool and still, his face like something sculpted of clay, but his gaze was lively. He clasped Moret's proffered hands, an intimate gesture, a greeting of close comrades. "As you can see, I don't need rescuing. And I have kin of my own." His gesture encompassed the watching faces, the house, the storm and the mountain itself, as though he owned it.

"You've done well for yourself. The company will be interested to hear your report."

"That will be a disappointment to them; I don't have any interest in making that report in person. I'll make it to you, and you can carry it back for me, if you want."

"You know you have no choice."

"I do not, in fact, know any such thing." That intent, curious expression hardened into quiet rage. "You will not dictate to me in my own home." Moret inclined his head, conceding the moment without conceding the point. Goban's tension eased a little. He dropped his voice. "You and I have a great deal to talk about. Not just now, though. Soon enough."

* * *

Kate watched the exchange, glancing at Emma across the room, trying to read her reaction. The older woman met her eyes, gave a tiny shrug, a furrow of the brow.

And then, abruptly, it was over. Both men relaxed, and Goban stalked across the room, barely pausing to nod at his granddaughters, to disappear through the study door without another word.

"Well, *that* was interesting," Gretchen said in a low voice, pitched for Kate's ears alone. Kate nodded.

Tereza was visibly unnerved, but keeping her cool. She called a break, and as people stood and milled around, stretching, looking confused, she came over and hauled Kate right back into the kitchen. "What just happened?" Kate asked.

"I was going to ask you the same thing. What are

you doing here?"

"He decided to come home." Kate made a helpless gesture.

"And you didn't..." Tereza stopped, thought better of the question she was about to ask, made an exasperated face. Smoothly changed gears. "Right. Hello, you must be Gretchen. And you are?"

Walsh stepped forward. "Michael Walsh. We spoke on the phone this morning."

"Oh, Inspector, of course. So this is your fault." There was humor in her voice, but also strain.

"Michael, please, I'm off duty. Ah, it seems so, yes." He smiled. "I was a bit afraid that if I didn't let him have the plane, he was going to steal Gretchen's car and hie off and leave us all behind. This seemed better."

"I'm sure." Tereza shook her head, and laughed. "Well, that's my grandfather for you. All right then."

"Where's Rita?" Kate asked. "The travel was rough on him. I want her to look him over."

"She's down at the clinic, watching the FBI tear your lab apart. I never got a straight answer on what they think they're looking for." That made Kate's stomach twist.

Irena spoke up then. "You all can talk in here if you're working. It's five o'clock and we have a full house to feed."

Gretchen smiled at Irena. "I'll help. What do you need?" Walsh excused himself to the dining room, and Kate followed Tereza toward the study.

Goban was sitting at the secretary desk in the

bedroom, tapping a pen, staring out the darkening window. He looked up when the two women came in, and the corner of his mouth twitched, the habit of a smile with no joy behind it. Kate came over and put her arms around his shoulders. "Hey. Are you okay?"

He sighed. "I thought I was prepared for that." He leaned into her, and she stroked his hair, not knowing what to say.

It was easy to avoid thinking about it head-on — who he was, where he came from. When you actively tried to forget, to pretend that it didn't matter. When no one ever discussed it openly, when he rebuffed questions both direct and subtle. Kate had fallen into that habit, these past few months. She could not imagine how much more difficult this must be for him, after all those years of cultivating that avoidance, to have his history quite literally standing in his dining room staring at him.

Tereza called down to the lab, and then pulled up a chair. "Rita will be up soon. Oh, Tēvi, what were you thinking? We had a plan, and it was working. I had just about got these people all on the same page."

"I wasn't thinking. I just wanted to come home." His eyes were closed, his face drawn and pale. The tension in his shoulders said, *it's complicated and I'm too tired to fight about it, so leave it be.*

Something shifted in Tereza's face; the annoyance drained away, leaving concern and compassion behind. "Jā," she replied softly. "Jā, labi, we work with what we have." She squeezed his hand. "Will you be out for dinner? There are a bunch of people out here who are keen to meet you, but they can wait for tomorrow if need be."

"No, I'll be out," he said, his voice thick with fatigue. "I... need a few minutes, that's all."

* * *

He was true to his word. He lay down and slept hard for half an hour, woke up to talk to Rita when she came in, and headed for the kitchen. Two coffees and a brandy later, he was ready to face the crowd, and did, with grace and charm, telling entertaining stories about the history of the farm, and answering questions as fast as people threw them at him.

After dinner, Conrad's sons started shuttling people to the other houses. A small group remained, gathering in the study. Reggie lit a fire and Tereza opened a few bottles of wine, but after one glass declared herself done.

Rita and Marina followed, not long after. As the evening wound down, it was just Goban, Kate, Gretchen, and Dr. Jansen in the study.

"How is he still going?" Gretchen asked, slightly in awe. Goban and Dr. Jansen had been talking intensely for over an hour, while she and Kate worked on finishing the last bottle of wine.

"I don't know. I'm so tired I can hardly see. He did sleep on the plane." Kate rested her head, closed her eyes. Then something changed in the timbre of Jansen's voice, and she sat back up.

He was just standing, shaking Goban's hand. "It has been a delightful evening. I'm sure we'll talk more tomorrow." He nodded and smiled, gave a hint of a bow.

"Ladies, good night."

Gretchen stretched, tipped back her glass. "Me too." She and Kate both stood, and embraced, and she walked across the room to Goban. "Thank you for inviting me here," she said. "I never had a chance to say that before."

He looked surprised, and then seemed about to say something, but she smiled and stepped out before he had a chance, shutting the door behind her with a delicate click.

Kate sat on the hearth next to his chair. His hand fondled her hair, his fingers wrapping around a strand. She made a little happy noise and looked up at him. "I didn't want to assume –"

The corner of his mouth twitched up. "And I didn't want to push. No, please stay." He started to lean down to kiss her, but at the ripple of pain through his body, she jumped up. She sat on the arm of the chair instead, arranging herself as though in his lap but carefully not leaning any weight on him, and draped her arms around his neck. His hands rested lightly on her hips. For a moment, she could forget everything beyond the study door — the house full of strange people, the tense conversations of the day, the travel exhaustion, and all of her churning fear.

For just a moment. And then she pulled back and looked at him seriously. "You should *sleep.*"

"Yes. You too. Come on." He stood, wincing. She realized that he had sat down when they all came in from dinner and never moved from that spot; he'd dominated the gathering with his presence and charisma, and people had arranged themselves around him, allowing him to gracefully downplay how much pain he was in. He leaned on her as they walked into the bedroom, and acquiesced to her help getting settled.

Finally she slid under the covers herself, and he turned toward her, and a wave of warmth and comfort and fatigue washed over her and pulled her down.

* * *

Driving in the blinding rain, and crying, there are monsters chasing after her, and she can't see them but she knows they're there and she cannot get away, and the lightning is as steady as a strobe, disorienting, the road narrow and curving, and she is so afraid. And up out of the darkness, a moment of clarity as the sheets of rain shift in the wind, a sign, and the sign says ← CHESTERTON 2 MI and she swings a hard left, down and up again, a twisted dirt road with trees overhanging it, filtering the lightning, pulse, pulse, and she thinks she may have shaken them and everything goes white and –

Running down a hallway, lights too bright, a set of crash doors at the end of the hall. Runs through it, and stops short, because Jake is there, in a hospital bed, in Army hospital pajamas, surrounded by machines, but he is alone, and he is writhing in pain, and he looks at her accusingly – and then it's not Jake but someone wearing his face, and she tries to read the chart hanging from the end of the bed, but she can't see what it says, and —

And the monsters are through the door, and she knows their faces, and she is trying to protect not-Jake but they overcome her and down she goes —

She woke with a start, felt his hand on her belly, his cheek against her shoulder. "*Do'cho?*" he asked, muzzily.

"Bad dreams. It's fine, go back to sleep." She laid her hand on top of his, closed her eyes. The drive up the mountain, she thought, must have shaken her up more than she realized. She couldn't remember the details of the dream, just a sense of road and terror and bright whiteness.

* * *

CHAPTER TWENTY THREE

Kate tossed and turned until the first threads of grey daybreak lit the window, and then left him sleeping. There was a crowd in the kitchen; the light and human warmth comforted her. She gratefully accepted a mug of coffee and a cheerful greeting from Jake, and when she met his eyes, sea-green and bright, her gut twisted with some inexplicable unease. She flinched and pulled away, found a piece of wall to hold up near the door, and settled in.

"How is he doing?" asked Rita, coming over to stand next to her. Pitching her voice low, just for Kate's ears.

"Not so good; his cycle is accelerating. I want to do bloodwork. Can I even get into the lab?"

"I just came from there. They said they might be finished this morning. I'll go ahead and take a sample, and you can get to it when you can."

"Let him sleep for a while, though. Yesterday wrung him out."

Tereza heard that, looked up from the table. "He dragged you back here in defiance of all common sense and reason because he couldn't stand not to be in the middle of it. He'll be pissed if we don't get him on his feet."

Kate shook her head. "He'll be in the middle of something, all right, if he doesn't slow down a little." Despair filled her. "Oh, Rita, I lost the sample. My old boss gave the damned thing to the FBI. I have to get to the lab and see how far the new batch has gotten while I've been gone, if they haven't fouled it or taken it."

"It's okay." It was not okay, but what else was there to say? "We'll do what we can with whatever we have." There was much of her grandfather in Rita's offhand, pragmatic shrug, Kate thought. Then Rita looked up and smiled, amused at something, and stepped out.

It was Robbie, looking star-struck. "Good morning, ma'am," he was saying. "Would you like some coffee? How do you take it?"

"Oh, bless you, darling; double-double, please and thank you." Gretchen slid in next to Kate, leaning against the wall, running a hand through her tousled hair. "That is a very nice young man."

"Yes, he is, and you should not encourage his crush," Kate replied, laughing.

"Oh, is that —" Gretchen looked faintly dismayed. "It's a curse." She accepted the mug with subdued gratitude, and then Robbie was gone again, helping his mother pull pans out of the oven. "The 'ma'am' threw me. Are we at the age where puppies with crushes call us ma'am? How did that happen?" They stood there together, in companionable silence.

Kate immersed herself in that moment, luxuriated in it. The kitchen full of people and light and decadent smells was everything she loved about the farm, and the improbable delight of introducing Gretchen to it made her so happy her skin tingled. The unrelenting worry of the past few days started to fall away, and she felt at ease. She wasn't ready to let go of the feeling.

A tall, warm presence fell into place next to her, and she tilted her chin up for a kiss. "Good morning," she murmured fervently.

Goban pulled up a stool and sat down, leaned against the wall. She frowned. He was winded and drained just from the walk through the study and dining room. But he also looked content, pleased even; the nervous energy that had enveloped him in Canada had drained away. He regarded her. Softly, he asked, "How are you doing?"

"I'm fine." She took a sip of coffee. "I'm okay. What about you?"

He shrugged. "Better than last night." A little worse than yesterday morning, then.

Gretchen was studying her, she realized. There was no wriggling out of it; she'd just get caught off guard later. "Bad dreams last night," she said, shortly.

"What about?" Her friend's tone was alert, penetrating.

"Driving. Just my subconscious blowing off that awful drive, or whatever. It's nothing."

"Yeah." Gretchen looked away. "How many nightmares have you had since you came here? It's all this Alcon shit being dredged up."

Please, leave it alone. "You're probably right." *Crash doors.* She flinched, blinked, shook off the impression. "Let's not dredge it up more, okay?" She walked away, over to the stove, fixed a cup for Goban and topped off her own. When she turned back, Gretchen was still watching her, but left it alone.

And then there was no chance to say anything else, because Tereza was standing up, calling the room to attend, going over the order of the day, and then everyone pitched in to set up the guests' buffet.

Dr. Jansen wandered in and promptly cornered Kate. "As you know, I was with our delightful host last night, and he tells me that you have run genome sequencing on him, is that right? I was suggesting that I might send it to a colleague who works in archaeogenetics."

Kate blinked. "Archaeogenetics? That's interesting."

"Yes, I have a theory."

Kate thought back to her first days on the farm. "You know what else I have? A genome sequence for a plant."

His eyes widened. "A Semhet plant? How did you manage that? Yes, that would be... very useful indeed."

She had copied those files to the laptop here at the house, and it seemed no one had mentioned the laptop to the FBI. It still sat right where it had been when she left for Bellingham, on the secretary desk in the small study. After clearing the request with Tereza, she logged Jansen in, pointed him to the right directory, and left him there, typing and humming happily away.

The morning passed, busy but quiet. She stayed in the big study, directing traffic, running messages and errands with Gretchen's help, making sure that Goban took breaks when he signaled that he needed them. A few minutes before the lunch break, a stack of paperwork came through on the fax machine down at the warehouse. Theo brought it up, and he and Goban spent a few minutes catching up. "Gonna be a good Christmas, if this damn storm breaks anytime soon," he grumbled on his way out.

"Anybody need anything from down the hill?"

"Check in with the clinic!" Kate called out. "Find out when they're going to be done down there!"

* * *

"When do I speak with Goban alone?" Moret asked, during a break in the parade of questioning visitors.

"Maybe tomorrow." Tereza frowned. "I understand that you're frustrated—"

"You don't." He glowered and paced, all nervous energy and suppressed rage. "All of these people have questions I do not have answers to. And I don't care. I am not a negotiator, Tereza. I am not a transit physicist, or a security specialist, or any of the other things they seem to expect me to be. I am here to do one job, and you are all wasting my time."

"I sympathize. I really do. But you must understand that these questions are important, and you're the best we've got."

"That doesn't have to be! Let me go back to my ship. I can send a message asking for the experts you need."

Tereza shrugged, made a small dismissive gesture. "You know that's not within my control."

He stopped and stared at her, a horrifying thought crossing his mind, not for the first time. "You would... tell me the truth, yes?"

"The best I can. I don't have all the information either."

"Am I trapped here? Are these people going to let me leave at all? Tereza... that would go very badly for you. One missing survey ship is important enough to investigate, but not worrisome. Two missing ships, in the same system — if you want to see for yourselves what our weapons look like, keep me here until an expeditionary force comes looking for me." He realized, as the words left his mouth, that it might come across as a threat, but she didn't seem to read it that way.

She just looked at him, cool and thoughtful. "I understand that, and I think they do too. I have no doubt that everything will be fine, and you'll be able to go home whenever you're ready to. But we need... to be able to establish some parameters. To have some reassurances. I think it's best that we take care of all of that first, so that the obstacles are cleared when you and Goban sit down to talk. Don't you?"

* * *

The faxed paperwork was for the immigration lawyer: a declaration of Goban's legal residency, backdated all the way to 1890, the date of the original homestead claim, his first appearance in the public record. His name was corrected, and Henriks Darzins was finally laid to rest. "That's a little more than the five years you need," the lawyer said, laughing. "You still want to do this?"

"Absolutely."

Everyone else had to leave the study during the citizenship test, and Kate took the chance to go track down Dr. Jansen and ask about his theory. "Oh, yes," he said, his ice-blue eyes full of laughter. "There are some very excited young people in Santa Clara this morning. I should have something for you by the end of the day."

The study door stayed closed for almost an hour, all

through the lunch break. When the two men finally came out, Emma winked and asked, "Did you pass?"

The lawyer answered. "If this guy took up teaching high school civics, I'd want my kids to go to that school."

Em laughed. "I did go to that school. Right here in this room."

The family gathered around, and watched as the citizenship oath was solemnly recited and repeated and the certificate signed, and then everybody cheered. Kate saw Tereza hanging back by herself, watching the proceedings from the kitchen doorway, and drifted over. "Glad that's done?"

"So glad," Tereza murmured. "We should have made sure that was cleaned up years ago."

"How could you?"

"I'm not convinced anymore... that keeping the secret has served us as well as we thought it did. We should have come forward before now, in a controlled way, on our own terms. The time just never seemed right." Kate could see how much that admission rattled her, and stirred up some old pain, but she couldn't think of anything to say.

Goban caught Kate's eye from across the room, made a discreet gesture, as though discarding an invisible object. Old cowboy sign language, he had taught her this morning. *Abort.* "He needs a break. Time to go play bouncer."

She made her way around to him as he reached the study door, and guided him through and into the bedroom. "I just need an hour," he sighed, leaning into her.

She rubbed his shoulders. "Okay. How about two?

That was the one big thing that Tereza wanted to accomplish today."

He shook his head. "State and military people want some time this afternoon."

"You're not much use to them if you can't think." *And screw Farris anyway. He's spent his goodwill credit; he can just cool his heels.* It was unfair for the poor propulsion engineer from Edwards, who seemed like a decent sort, to be saddled with that history, but the two officers did seem to stick together.

"Fair point." He lay down and sprawled, and was out almost instantly. Kate sat with him for a few minutes, then sighed and stepped out.

Emma was coming into the study, looking for her. "Marina called. They want you down at the lab; the FBI is finished. Jake said he'd drive you down. He's going to do another run on the snowplow anyway."

"Oh, that's fantastic news." Kate exhaled with relief. "He asked for an hour. More wouldn't hurt. Okay?"

"I'll take care of it."

* * *

The lab didn't look like it had been tossed. It looked exactly as Kate had left it, five days before. The team had been thorough, professional, and considerate, and she had no idea where to start.

Gretchen looked around approvingly. "This is a nice little setup you've got here." She strolled through the lab, looking at all the equipment labels. "Seems like about ten years old?"

"Mostly. They bought a lot of stuff on the cheap

during the recession. A few newer things." Kate booted computers, reviewed the sample storage. It didn't look like anything was missing, although she'd have to do an inventory to be sure.

Then she gasped. "Oh, they didn't shut down the incubator." Gretchen came over and looked over her shoulder. "Look at that. They've been busy, haven't they? Happy little 317 factories just churning away. It's been almost a week. I was so afraid the batch would be fouled." The two women worked steadily for the next hour, setting up the extraction kit and preparing the cultures for purification.

"So how long does it take to get from the culture to the drug?" Gretchen asked, as they washed up.

"Fifty hours or so. And then we start again. I'm going to go ahead and start another culture right away, in fact. This process is so labor-intensive, and the production quantity is so small..." Kate tossed up her hands in frustration. "I got four cc's from the last batch. Four. If the drug works, and I really think it will, I'll be running as hard as I can just to stay ahead. I need a production line." *I needed David.* Better left unsaid; the last thing that Kate wanted was a fight with Gretchen.

"But what I *really* need," she continued, "is a self-monitoring system." She perched on the counter. "I don't want to talk to Rita, or — or anybody else about this yet, but Gretchen, if he leaves, and I'm desperately hoping that we can hold that off until I have production quantities of a usable drug, but if he goes, it will be just the two of them alone in the ship and far from any kind of help for months.

He needs to be able to self-test and self-dose."

"You think he will? Leave?" Gretchen looked worried. Not for Goban, Kate realized; for her. *I don't want this to end badly for you.*

"I think... we have to consider the possibility that he won't have a choice. This Moret guy was on this planet for one day, and he hit a military policeman over the head and stole his gun and motorcycle, you know? You think he won't do it again if he has the chance? That he hasn't been learning from everything he's touched and seen since then?"

"Hm." Gretchen frowned. "Kate, user-friendly medical tests are *hard.* Any kind of end-use product is hard. There's a huge amount of development that goes into them. This is my field, okay? Take testing strips, for example. To make a testing strip, you have to find a chemical that reacts to your test target in such a way to give a useful visual, or combine with a colorant that does, but also that doesn't react to anything else in the sample, right? And that is soluble enough and chemically stable enough to bond to a substrate, and be, you know, still usable after months or years of storage. It's complicated."

Kate stood up and paced. "It doesn't have to be all that user-friendly in the interpretation, just in the process. He's one of us."

Gretchen looked up, surprised. "Right. He was, what, a geologist before he was a farmer? You told me that."

"Geologic survey engineer."

Gretchen snapped her fingers. "You have an

internet connection down here? I was reading about something... recently..." She went over to the computer Kate pointed out, and puttered at it while Kate set up the next round of cultures. "Got it," she said, ten minutes later. "I need a pure 317 sample for calibration and, oh, three blood samples from different stages of the disease."

"I can do better than that. I've got a complete array."

"If this works, that's the next step."

So she mounted the samples that Kate pulled for her, and took her phone and snapped a picture of the first one. "What in the world are you doing?" Kate asked.

Gretchen grinned, pleased with herself, and held up the phone, a makeshift filter taped to the camera. "Spectrometer smartphone app. It will take some tweaking, but the basic tools are there, and it's a type of data output he'd be familiar with."

Kate stared at her, openmouthed.

* * *

Two hours later, Gretchen was still silently engrossed with her phone hack, and Kate had gone as far as she could. "I'll take a break soon," Gretchen promised. "Let me get the data load done and I can cry off here and work from the house." So Kate went upstairs and puttered around in the clinic, ending up in Rita's office, making small talk.

There was a grouping of family photos on the wall opposite the desk. She studied them, delighted at times to recognize a face, or an event she'd heard a story about.

She was struck by one photo, a formal portrait of a

beautiful, smiling man, in a mid-century Army uniform with major's leaves, his face too young for his rank. Wing-wreathed red cross and quite a lot of ribbons. She could not stop staring; he haunted her. "Who is this?" she asked.

Rita glanced up. "Oh, that's Henry."

Of course, it would have to be. "I'm not sure I've ever seen a picture of him. Wow, he looks like Jake."

"He really does, doesn't he? There are pictures around. There's a print hanging in the big house of all of us cousins together. That one below it is him and me."

The snapshot below the portrait was taken in front of a helicopter, prefab buildings in the background, lush forest beyond. The pilot was hugging a pretty black-haired young woman, both of them in fatigues, sleeves rolled up, looking tired but happy. "You were in the Army?" Kate remembered suddenly; Major Farris had mentioned that. She'd meant to ask about it but hadn't had a chance. There had been so much else going on, and it had slipped away.

"Yes. It was Henry's doing, actually. I grew up on his stories of Korea — he was eight years older than me. There was a huge fight between him and Tēvs, after it was over, because he wanted Henry to quit and come home to stay. They always fought a lot, they were so much alike! And it was always, next year, after this station, after this promotion. After his twenty." Rita came over to stand next to Kate, and looked at the picture.

"So I was finishing ER residency and he had just come back from his first tour, and we were both able to come home for Christmas in 1967, and he spent the whole four days talking at me. You know how Tēvs can be when he's all fired up about something? Like that. *Rita, you've got to go, you'll love it, it's important work.* And it was: he was flying dustoff flights, the most difficult, urgent type of medical evacuations. He just absolutely loved it. And he was uncanny good. He could get in and out of anywhere, which was why they sent him into the most dangerous areas, of course." There was some naked vulnerability in her voice, in the set of her shoulders.

"You never forget, but you move on. You have to. You have to get up in the morning and do the work. My mother told me once — *you will outlive every person you ever love who wasn't born in this valley.* She wasn't wrong, and that's an awful burden to carry. You know I was fifty-six years old when I met Marina? And she was thirty-two. I was... waiting for someone I could grow old with, I think. But Henry was one of our own, and it was not supposed to be that way."

Kate looked from the picture to Rita's face, the grief still vivid, and didn't know what to offer. "He sounds like someone I would have liked to have known. I've never heard anybody talk much about him."

"Oh, you would have loved him. It was hard on all of us, when he died. More than forty years on and it's still hard even to talk about. Especially for Conrad. They were very close, and he changed, after Henry and... after we lost Julia. Colder. Too focused on protecting people to think much about taking care of them." Rita offered that small gift of grace, not quite as an apology, but as a plea for understanding.

Kate thought about the cracks she'd seen in his

façade, from time to time, the hurt and fear underneath the brusqueness. "I've never thought badly of Conrad. I admire him. I've just... *felt* badly, that I seem to make things difficult for him a lot of the time."

"Oh, it's not you. All of this" — Rita made a gesture that encompassed the agents recently gone, the other strangers up the hill, all of the stress and uncertainty of the past few weeks — "it was all coming anyway. We've had a few quiet years, you know? The turn of the century devastated us. My parents' generation passing on, seven funerals in ten years. After that... we withdrew from the world even more. We're all getting older, slowing down. We have a pretty quiet and comfortable life here, and we value that, and leave the adventuring to the younger ones now.

"I think you were a harbinger. You shook us all out of our complacency, and when all of this other business happened, we were paying attention. You've started us talking about things we don't talk about. That's not a bad thing."

Kate was still pondering that when Gretchen finally came upstairs. They all piled into Rita's truck and headed up the hill together.

* * *

CHAPTER TWENTY FOUR

Goban and Dr. Jansen were sequestered in the study when the women arrived at the house, so Kate and Gretchen headed to the kitchen to lend a hand with dinner. With the guest buffet set up, the kitchen crew sat to catch their breath while the last few pans of casserole finished baking.

Tereza popped in a few minutes later. "Do you all have a few minutes? Tēvs wants everybody in the study. Ah, you might go ahead and turn off the oven," she added, and disappeared.

The room, though large, was already packed, and people were still drifting in. Kate looked around, making note of the faces present. Goban was sitting at his desk, pale and strained.

Walsh and Thorne were standing together by the fireplace, but none of the other government people were present. Moret hovered just inside the door, uncomfortable, looking around at the crowd, with Tereza next to him. Everyone else in the room was family. Gretchen leaned close and asked, very quietly, "Should I be here?"

"I have no idea," Kate whispered back, "but don't you dare leave."

Dr. Jansen was perched on the edge of the desk, looking for all the world like he was about to launch into a lecture. He stood up, looked around, and smiled. The chatter ceased and the room was silent.

"Good evening. Thank you all for taking this time; I think you'll find it worthwhile. When our guest arrived here on Friday," gesturing to Moret, "one of the first questions that occupied my mind was — how is it that he is so amazingly similar to us? This is, of course, a question that has occupied the Darzins family for much longer, and is in fact central to your very existence." The translation caught up and Moret tensed, asked a sharp question; Tereza shushed him.

"Kate was generous enough to share some of her research with me, and to allow me to share it in turn with a very enthusiastic postgraduate student of my acquaintance whose area of study is in archaeogenetics." He paused, silently offering a chance for questions. "All right. So I sent to him three gene sequences: that of our gracious host; of a preserved flower that he brought with him from Semhaata; and of an unknown but apparently benign bacteria that turned up in the digestive tracts of both of these gentlemen, and therefore, we think, can reasonably assume to also have originated on Semhaata rather than here on Earth."

Another pause. The room was silent except for the low murmur of Tereza translating.

"I just had an email back from Alonzo, that's this young student I know, and he and his team have been running computer models. I want to emphasize that these are extremely preliminary results. There's a great deal of work still to be done, but some clear patterns have emerged. Do I need to explain the term 'last common ancestor' to this crowd?" A glance around. "Very well. Please bear with me; this isn't my own field of expertise, obviously. Alonzo has explained this to me with very small words, and I shall attempt to do the same." A smattering of laughter.

"Let's start with the least surprising result. The, ah, inferred time to last common ancestor between the bacteria and the plant turns up at around two billion years, which is perhaps a little older than one might expect, but not outside of the range of the plausible. But this is where it gets interesting. The bacteria and the plant, when each was run against Goban's genome, *broke the model*. The most reasonable answer that can be taken from the results — the results, by the way, were that the time estimate exceeded the age of the Earth, and then the software crashed, repeatedly — the best answer is that no common ancestor exists, full stop. Put simply, there is no common evolutionary history. If the plant and the bacteria are native to Semhaata, then the Semhet themselves are not."

Tereza was stumbling over a slow and careful translation. Jansen waited patiently. Kate watched Goban's face; his entire attention was on Moret. Finally, Tereza stopped. Moret was still, silent, frowning.

"So of course the obvious next step is to run Goban's genome against an archived human one. It's amazing what's available on the Internet these days. That result came back much faster, and did not crash the computers, so they ran it against three different data sets." Kate gripped Gretchen's hand. "Seventy-two thousand years, people. Somehow, seventy-two thousand years ago, a breeding population of early modern humans found themselves on a world around another sun many hundreds of light-years from the Earth. Clearly, they had help.

"The Semhet are not aliens; they are our long-lost cousins who have found their way home. But I think that there can be no further doubt that real aliens do exist in the universe. At this point, we have reached the end of what science can tell us, and as one does, we turn to religion."

Moret's face was bloodless; he looked like he might bolt from the room. Tereza gripped his elbow and hissed something in his ear.

Jansen stepped aside, and Goban stood and took over the perch on the corner of the desk. "*'In the beginning God created the heaven, and the earth, and the earth was without form, and void, and darkness was upon the face of the deep: and the Spirit of God moved upon the face of the waters,'*" he recited. "I am not religious, but Amja was, and I was content to leave her to teach the children in the ways of her faith, and I learned enough to hold my own in a conversation. That is why, to whatever extent each of you has embraced it, we are, on the whole, a Lutheran family.

"But the Semhet also have a rich and complex religious heritage and a great body of myth. In recent days, I've been thinking about the oldest written creation myths. In the beginning, the story goes, the gods of the dawn of time came upon the damned ones, weak, frightened, and starving in the cold and dark outer wilderness. The gods saw good and potential in these people, so they gave them strength and raised them up, gave them a paradise for their use, and called them the blessed.

"There are many, differing and sometimes conflicting, beliefs about what this origin means for right action and life's purpose. One common belief is that the destiny of the Semhet is to go out into the universe to find and cultivate new sanctuaries wherever we go." That was, Kate realized, the first time she had heard him say we and Semhet in the same sentence.

"You have to understand that this is an absolutely literal belief; evolutionary biology, after all, supports the doctrine that the Semhet cannot exist without the intervention of a higher power. The question of whether Semhaata is the only sanctuary is also an open one. So when I first came here, and found people like myself, that's what I assumed — that this was a second, unknown sanctuary. This was not... a difficult idea to accept.

"But my wife was always bringing home books, the works of the greatest minds of the age, to help me find my footing in this world. Among the books she brought back from one trip to Denver were the two seminal works of Charles Darwin. These were very challenging for me, and I struggled with them for a long time; I wasn't the only one, of course. In Berlin, in 1922, I saw a chimpanzee for the first time, and I knew. You can't... you cannot look into the eyes of these creatures and not feel a kinship.

"It was just a few years later that the work of Dart and Leakey reached the public, and it ignited a fascination in me, and I have followed the science ever since, as it developed. The second generation of Leakeys, and Johanson and Tattersall, and these brilliant young scientists like Alonzo Olavarria, combining disciplines to create entirely new fields of study.

"So, when Dr. Jansen mentioned this number to

me, seventy-two thousand years, it rang a bell, and we looked it up. In the late 1990s, an anthropologist named Stanley Ambrose wrote two papers in which he linked a massive volcanic eruption in Indonesia to an apparent substantial drop in human population."

Goban paused and looked around, let Tereza catch up. The room was silent, attentive. There was a quiet reverence in his voice, and the audience was riveted. "I would like for you all to just sit with me for a minute and think about how life was for those people, under the shadow of the supervolcano. A thousand years of cold dark. A thousand years of hunger and fear, of the lingering nearness of death. Perhaps... some faint cultural memory that it was not always like this. A sense that catastrophe could descend from the sky at any moment, that the great powers of the universe are capricious, even malignant. The very landscape of hell.

"In time, the environment healed itself, but that fundamental human experience remained. These are our common ancestors. This is your legacy.

"But there is another legacy, another history. In that history, great powers descended from the sky again, but this time in compassion, bringing hope and a golden world of possibility. This is not a legacy of fear; this is a legacy of pride, of genetically engineered excellence, and of absolute certainty in one's own worth and rightness of purpose. Arrogance is the Semhet birthright; there was never any possibility we could be anything else. Only in the last few thousand years has life on Earth become safe enough to allow you to begin to develop belief systems with anything approaching that arrogance. But like some smaller sibling, you have worked so hard to catch up.

"And that brings us full circle, from religion back to science. I look around and I can already see a hundred questions on your faces. We don't have answers now, but we will. Working together, I have... faith that we can answer all of these questions. Maybe even discover the true nature of the gods."

* * *

It took half an hour for the room to settle down. Finally, people started drifting out, in twos and threes, still talking. Kate stayed where she was, arms crossed, watching.

When they had the room to themselves, she strolled over, trying to project calm in spite of the upheaval she felt. "Can we talk?" she asked, mildly.

"Of course." Goban looked exhausted; that performance, and the day, had left him ragged. She thought about not saying anything. But if she brought it up later, and he realized she had swallowed her own distress in order to not be a bother while he was sick, he'd be furious — and she would deserve it. And she was not going to let it go altogether.

So she offered him a hand, and he leaned on her a little, and they walked into the bedroom and sat down on the edge of the bed together. She turned and faced him.

"You kept this from me." He just looked at her, not grasping her point. She threw up her hands. "Goban, you *kept this* from me! You knew –"

Realization dawned on his face. "I suspected. I

knew that Earth had to be the home world, but I had no idea how. How long ago the split was. How it could have happened, why, any of it. All of that, Erik and I put together an hour ago."

"And you didn't think that would be of use to me? That little tidbit?"

"You figured it out on your own! You told Emma, months ago."

"But I didn't –" Kate stopped, so furious she was tripping over her own words. "Before I was your lover, I was your employee. I still am. I am trying to solve a problem here, and I needed to know what you knew. It could have helped me. I might have broken this already, if I had known what I was looking for! If keeping your damned secrets wasn't more important than your wellbeing..." She brushed tears away, roughly. "Well, all the secrets are all out now. All of them. Was it worth it? Is there anything else you haven't told me?"

"Kate..." He made a helpless gesture.

She stared at him, gray-faced and in pain, and knew that it wasn't fair, but she was too mad to back out now. Sat silently, trying to sort out her head, and a small, nasty thought rose up unbidden and would not be banished. She stood up and paced.

She almost walked out then, but she turned at the door and came back. She felt the tears start to well up again, and pushed them down. "You want to go with him," she whispered.

"No." He reached for her, caught her hand.

"Don't lie to me." She pulled away. "Don't lie to

yourself."

He sighed and looked away. "Yes. Okay? Yes. There is some part of me that wants to go back to the place where I was born. To a place where everyone speaks the language I hear in dreams. Does that surprise you? Did you think I wouldn't feel anything?"

"*You told me* you didn't feel anything. More than once."

"I was wrong."

A saving grace: he had not said *I lied*. Being wrong, she could accept. But she could not overcome, not that easily, not without a little time and solitude to think. *I just don't know what to say to you.* She mustered the self-control not to say it aloud. Kate had never been angry at him before, and she didn't know what to do with that feeling. So she bolted.

Not wanting to face the crowd in the dining room, she cut through the bathroom, up the stairs, and into the old suite.

She almost ran smack into Walsh, on his way out. "Oh, I'm sorry," she mumbled. "I didn't realize Emma had put anyone in here."

"Hey, hey." He caught her by the arm before she could flee back down the stairs. "Are you all right? You look like you need a quiet place to sit for a few minutes. Come on in here, there's a little library here in the corner – "

"I know." She laughed, startled by the sharpness of it. "This was my room for a few weeks." She let him walk her to the turret library and sit her down, and gratefully accepted the glass of water he brought.

He regarded her for a moment. "Listen. I'm a farm kid too. New Brunswick. I know how oppressive these big close-knit families can be, even though you love 'em, eh? You need anything and you don't feel like talking to them, you come find me."

"Thank you." She bit her lip. He nodded and slipped out, leaving her there, blessedly alone.

* * *

It only took a few minutes to calm down, and then she was angry at herself, and then she was sad, and finally just tired.

She found *The Descent of Man* on the shelf and flipped through it, stroking the yellowed, foxed pages, trying to wrap her head around the new reality he'd had to adapt to. She'd struggled to come to terms with a reality with Goban in it, with the Semhet; but she'd never contemplated how it had been from the other direction. *Why did I assume it was easier for him? He's just had... more time.*

She took the water glass back to the bathroom and rinsed it out, then went down the way she came, avoiding everyone. The bedside lamp was on, but Goban was asleep. She undressed and slid into bed, and in his sleep he shifted closer to her. She pulled him close, and found herself soothed enough by his nearness to sleep, fitfully.

Just before four, Kate stirred, uncomfortably hot, throwing off covers, and then she realized that the heat was pouring off of him. Sometime during the night, he had crashed and flared.

She sat up, which caused him to stir restlessly, reaching for her. She stroked his hair and murmured soft words until he was quiescent again, and then slipped out and padded upstairs to Irena's room.

"Oh, hell," Irena muttered groggily, when Kate told her. "We knew it was coming. All right. You've been through it twice; you know what to do. Set up the ice packs. I'll be down in a few minutes. Tante Rita thinks starting IV fluids earlier might help... you think anybody's in the kitchen yet?"

"How about I stop on the way and put the kettle on, and you come along behind me and fix us both a cup?"

"Sounds good to me." Irena waved her off, and she headed back downstairs.

On her way out of the kitchen, she stopped and looked out the window for a moment. Stars, and a blush of false dawn. The storm had broken.

* * *

CHAPTER TWENTY FIVE

Tereza fled the kitchen for the small study to think, and holed up with her coffee in the turret sitting room, looking out over the valley, serene with its deep blanket of fresh snow, pink-streaked in the early morning light. The morning was going to be about damage control, but it still could be productive.

She sensed a presence, and looked up. "Good morning, Doctor."

Jansen made a dismissive gesture. "Erik, please. I think we've been through enough by now to be past formality." He came over and stood next to her, looked out the window. "My God, it's beautiful. That cliff, I had no idea. That storm was astonishing. Winters here must be tremendously isolating."

He knew something about that, she was sure, given where he'd grown up. "It can be brutal, that's for sure," she said. "You should see it in the summer, though."

He glanced at her, looking for something, it seemed. "I'd like that." A pleasant silence settled. Then he said, "I'd like to spend some time with Moret this morning."

"You'll have to find someone who has time to translate. I can't, I need to sit with the diplomats."

"I thought your grandfather was going to do that?"

Tereza flinched. She sipped her coffee, pondering, then looked at him. "Erik, I'm going to tell you what I'm not ready to tell the others, not yet. My grandfather is in the acute phase of his disease. All this stress has caught up with him, and he collapsed during the night. He'll be bedridden for the next few days. We will have to do the best we can without him."

He looked shocked, but did not speak for a moment. Finally, "How awful, I'm sorry. Will he recover?"

"He always has before, but we hold our breath and wonder every time." Tereza was so tired. She could hardly bear to look at him, did not want him to see how fragile she felt, but when she looked up she realized that he saw right through her armor.

He laid his hand over hers. "Oh, dear girl," he sighed. No one had called her *girl* in half a century. From someone else it might have been condescending, but from him, just now, it was strangely comforting. "Please, if there is any way at all I can help, do tell me."

* * *

Boys on tractors were out before dawn, clearing the snow from the ring road and starting to work their way down the long drive and the county road. Emma called the shipping depot to let them know the road would be open. The truck rolled over the ridge just after nine o'clock, greeted by a bundled, cheering warehouse crew. The FBI and Homeland Security people were packing up and heading out; Thorne and the State team hoped to wrap up in the afternoon, and the Canadian envoy was already gone. Dr. Jansen was holed up with Moret and whatever Semhet-speaking family member stood still long enough to be roped into translating. The whole thing was just... evaporating.

Susan called up from the warehouse an hour later with the message that Kate had a package, and one of the teenagers ran it up the hill. Kate met the girl at the study door, looked at the return address on the small box, and almost dropped it. She set it down carefully on Goban's desk, sat down, and stared at it for a moment.

Then she took an antique silver letter opener from the drawer and slit the tape. There was file folder on top, with a note attached, dated the day before.

> *Kate,*
>
> *I hope that when this gets to you, it's not too little too late. SSA Dorsey called me this morning and told me what her team found. I'm sorry.*
>
> *I couldn't remember what bothered me about what you said in the cafe, until I went back and looked at some old files. Before you came on the project, before it had the HPE-317 designation, it was given the code designation Chesterton. The file I've included here explains why. Maybe it will answer your questions.*
>
> *Look me up the next time you're in town. I owe you.*
>
> *David*

Kate had a sudden, sharp headache. (← *CHESTERTON* 2 *MI*) She shook her head, took a couple of slow breaths, and set the file aside.

She removed the layer of insulating foam. There

was a miniature medical cooler. Inside it were twenty-four 20cc vials, neatly labeled "HPE-317/Chesterton Variant".

She froze. *David, you lovely bastard. All is forgiven.*

She picked up the phone and called the clinic, and as calmly as she could told Sylvia that everything was fine but she needed Rita back up to the house, yes, right now please. Then she picked up the file and opened it.

There were two document folders inside.

FINAL AUTOPSY REPORT --
DARZINS HENRIKS J MAJ
DATE OF BIRTH 7 NOV 1930
DATE OF DEATH 17 JUN 1969
DATE OF AUTOPSY 19 JUN 1969

CHESTERTON PROTOCOL
STUDY PROPOSAL
1 MAR 2002

Kate set aside the first folder, opened the second.

I've seen this, she remembered in a rush. Right there on top, a fact sheet, Henry's photograph, everything. She had a vivid recollection of the first night, in the rain, looking at Jake, finding something familiar in his face. Yesterday, and the photos in the clinic.

She turned the page, and there was Rita's photo, too.

Just as she finished reading, Rita strode in, in a hurry. "Sylvia told me to get up here. What's going on?"

Kate pushed the box across the desk; Rita looked

inside and her eyes widened. "Oh!" She pulled the cooler out; there was another sheaf of papers under it. "Oh, look, dosing histories. Let's get to work."

So they did. It only took a few minutes to read through the material David had sent, calculate a dosage, and prep a syringe. Kate followed Rita into the bedroom, washed his face and held his hand while the other woman administered the injection. "Now we wait."

"I have something else to show you." She brought back the file back from the study, and watched the clock while Rita read.

Rita did not speak, but the parade of emotions on her face spoke volumes: confusion, clarity, heartbreak, silent weeping rage. *The answer was here all the time. If they'd asked for consent, if they'd shared this information* – Kate felt ill. She was outraged for what had been taken from Rita and from Henry, and what had been done with it, and her own role. For all of it.

Finally, quietly, Rita said, "So it's no accident that you ended up here."

"No. Not... planned, but not coincidence either. I don't remember seeing the sign that night, but I've looked at maps half a dozen times and there's no other reason I would have made that turnoff. And I've seen it in dreams, since." *If you can save him, you can redeem yourself.*

Seventeen minutes after the injection, Kate felt a rush of heat blossom and recede under her hand, resting on Goban's forehead. The fever broke, and he slept.

* * *

Moret had asked for writing implements the night

before. He went back to the room he'd been given, and wrote, and thought, and paced, and wrote some more, trying to sort it all out. He'd had an idea of what was coming almost from the beginning of the old scientist's story, but it had been a shock anyway.

He was not a religious scholar any more than he was a diplomat, but he was all alone.

The intense young woman named Thorne had made one thing clear, yesterday. He would be returned to his ship, but he would not be allowed to take off without first sending a message detailing what he'd found here. "Channels must be opened," she said. "You must understand our position. We cannot sit here and wait, not knowing whether the Semhet will come back in a year or a generation. We have to know. We have to go all in and deal with the consequences, sooner rather than later, as much on our terms as possible."

The military advisors, she said, would prefer to hold him here until a reply came. She had some sympathy for that position. "A hostage?" he asked.

"A guarantor." Tereza had stumbled over the translation, and later told him that in her language, the two words were identical.

These people terrified him. So inconsistent. So *feral.* The truth of the revelation was sinking in: this world was Onovet, the hell of myth; these people were the damned, the abandoned ones, and what the Semhet would have become, but for the gift of the gods.

So here he was, trying to compose that message, trying to parse his options, when a knock came on the door.

It was the old astrophysicist, with Emma in tow. Moret muttered some half-hearted greeting, and she asked how he was doing. "Contemplating suicide," he said blandly, and, at her alarmed look, added quickly, "Not worth it, in the end. That military engineer assures me you people would puzzle out how to work my ship. Or the company would send another. Or some other thing."

"Is it really that bad?" she asked, her voice warm with sympathy.

He sighed, long and glum. "I would wish that Goban had died in his crash, except some other poor soul would have stumbled over this place anyway. There is no going back. So, we go forward."

She relayed the conversation to the old scientist, and they spoke for a minute. She held out a hand. "Come downstairs and get some food, and then maybe we can help you figure out how to make the best of it."

* * *

"Hi," Kate whispered, when his eyes opened.

She had laid down a few minutes before, sensing that Goban might stir soon. She was stretched out on top of the covers, her face a few inches from his, and she smiled, waiting for the sleep fog to clear.

He blinked. Stretched gingerly, and then with more vigor. "How long was I out?"

She laughed out loud. "Six hours," she said. "Not even that. What time is it? You slept for a couple of hours. Oh, it's noon."

He stared at her, stunned. "Noon... Monday? What happened?"

"My old boss had second thoughts, I guess. I have to call him and get the whole story. He ran the synthesis, anyway. It came on the FedEx truck this morning."

"It worked? Your drug worked." His eyes widened.

"Like magic. Took about twenty minutes. It was a beautiful thing."

"*You're* a beautiful thing." He rolled over, pinned her down, kissed her hard.

She laughed again, freed a hand, slid it down his hip. "Feeling good?"

"I feel *fantastic.*"

Kate flashed back to the last time she'd seen him like this, in the first blush of euphoria. He'd wanted her to stay, then, and she'd walked away. *Not this time.*

* * *

A little while later, her head on his shoulder, she asked, "What are you thinking?"

"Mm. Just that... before you wandered in last summer, I was settling in and getting comfortable with the idea of getting old."

"Huh. I was just building up to getting angry with it." For a heartbeat, she thought he was going to make fun of her. *Forty turns on this earth and she feels old, how quaint.*

But he didn't. He turned toward her, pulled her close. "Lend me some of that rage," he whispered. "We'll go down fighting together."

* * *

CHAPTER TWENTY SIX

"This was never supposed to be me, running this show," Tereza said, her chin resting on her cupped hands, staring out the window, restless and pensive. She shook her head and smiled; a small, wry, regretful thing. The negotiators had broken for lunch, and almost everyone was out getting a bit of fresh air and a look around the farm. She'd had the little study to herself, until Leslie Thorne walked in.

"How so?" Thorne pulled up a chair.

"There was a big family dispute in the late sixties about coming forward. My brother was very much in favor, very vocal about it. He'd suspended work on his PhD when the Vietnam War broke out — aeronautical engineering. He was due to come home and get back to that work, and he was being groomed to be the family spokesperson. My sister-in-law Julia was opposed."

"He was the one who was killed in action?"

"Yes. And after that, it was Jules my grandfather looked to for advice. She was an astronomer, she knew how to talk to the public about the science... when she died, I was next in line, and I just hoped it would never happen."

"And yet here we are."

"Here we are."

"When was that?"

"1996." She shook her head, sighed. "That's why you haven't seen Conrad around much during all of this. It's a just lot for him to take."

"A lot for you, too. This isn't only about dragging

all these secrets out into the open for strangers to paw over, after you worked so hard to keep them. This is all tied up in grief for you, too." The other woman's brow furrowed, thoughtful and sympathetic. Her hands folded, unconsciously echoing Tereza's own. "But for what it's worth, I think you've handled things very well. Differently, maybe, than either of them would have done, but there's nothing wrong with that. I think that we all wish there were someone else to hand this off to — someone smarter, more qualified, more experienced — but there isn't. We are the best we have.

"We're all here for a reason, and regardless if the reasons that brought us were serendipitous, or even misguided, we bring with us the perspective of that experience. I do believe that our best hope lies in that."

Tereza nodded. "That's what I was trying to tell Moret yesterday. I think he's out of his depth, and very frightened, and resents being put in the position he's in. We've been so focused on how this discovery is going to change our world, and my grandfather has been away from that place for so long, and his loyalties are so tied up here — Moret feels like he's the only one who is thinking at all about what's going to happen to Semhaata when the news gets home." Emma had relayed the morning's unsettling conversation to her. For all the time she'd spent with him, he was unreadable to her; she'd had no idea he felt that bleak.

"Well, he's not altogether wrong. He's the only one who has an understanding of it, anyway."

A shadow fell across the arched doorway; Kate,

walking quietly through the dining room to the kitchen, catching Tereza's eye as she passed and nodding a brief greeting. Tereza stood. "I'm sorry, excuse me for a moment."

* * *

When Kate walked in, Gretchen set aside washing up from lunch, and came over to give her a hug. Kate just hung on for a minute, letting the morning's emotional rollercoaster slow and still.

Tereza had noticed her, and followed. "How's he doing?" she asked.

Kate smiled to herself, filling the kettle, setting up the French press. She turned and looked up at the other women, grinning broadly. "He's... getting dressed. He'll be out in five minutes or so. So, coffee." Kate summed up the events of the morning.

After a moment, Tereza broke the stunned silence. "You said you were close, but I had no idea."

"Yes, if all of this other business hadn't happened, I would have been going to Seattle in the next week or so to set up the production outsourcing." Kate shrugged. "It... worked out, weirdly enough." They all sat for a moment, absorbing the revelation.

The kettle whistled. Kate switched it off, absentmindedly. "Who's still here?" she asked.

Emma answered. "The State people and Ms. Thorne. The two Air Force officers. Dr. Jansen and Michael Walsh. Everyone else has gone."

"That's why the house seems so quiet."

"It's almost over," Tereza said, hope threaded

together with fatigue in her voice.

It's barely beginning, Kate thought.

* * *

After two days of storm, the sight of the sun had Michael Walsh feeling energized. Everyone he wanted to talk to was busy, and so he thought he might just take a stroll. On his way out, he ran into the American officer standing on the front porch, and made small talk, and invited the man to walk with him. "Are you heading out today with the others?" he asked.

Major Farris shook his head. "I'm here until this thing is settled; I'm Andessat's escort back to his ship. You? I never figured out your role in all of this."

"Hm. It started out as threat assessment, and then protecting Goban, when it became clear that he was more likely to be a catalyst for trouble than a perpetrator. That job ended when we came to the States, officially, but I still feel the need to have his back. So yes, I suppose I'll be here until it's done, one way or another." Michael looked at the pretty little houses on the outside of the ring road, and the snowy woods beyond, against their granite backdrop. "You haven't said much, these last few days. I've seen you around, of course."

A grimace. "I've been trying to shut up and learn. This place confounded me, the first time I came here. Every instinct I had, and every conclusion that my training led me to, turned out to be wrong. I made a lot of mistakes. Did more harm to my own mission than anything else. So this time around, I'm just observing, trying to make sense of it."

"That's the best you can do, I suppose. Nothing that any of us has ever known could have prepared us for these last few days."

"You've done all right." Farris was staring off in the distance. "What made you decide to stand with them?"

"Oh, it was Kate. I had a sense of her basically good intentions... almost instantly. Then I spent some time with her and became more convinced, rather than less, as I learned more. I never trust a first impression, but I do pay attention to it. How I feel about the first impression after I've had a little time to observe, that's the key, for me."

Farris did not speak for a long time. Squinted, looking out over the blanketed buildings, the sharp, blue-shadowed cut of the snowbank on the edge of the freshly plowed road. "I kept asking myself, *What doesn't connect?* I couldn't find a framework for what I could observe. The harder I looked for what was being withheld, the more convinced I was that I was missing something — the less anything made sense. I never considered the simplest..." He shook his head. "I couldn't let myself seriously consider the possibility that they are all exactly who they appear to be. That was the missing piece." They reached the bend at the bottom of the valley, continued around the vineyard, and back up toward the big house. The crust of compressed snow crunched under their boots as they walked in silence, each caught up in his own thoughts. Sky and earth blurred into a saturated field of blue and white, broken only by lavender shadows and the rust-grey wall of stone.

* * *

Kate took the coffee and some leftovers to Goban in

the study, and sat cross-legged on the hearth and watched him while he ate, enjoying the sight of him rambling around.

"You ready for this?" she asked.

He looked up, startled, and grinned. "Oh, yes. I'm looking forward to it. I wanted to be in the thick of it from the beginning, but – the last few days have been rough." The grin faltered, and then settled into a deeper smile, full of wonder and delight. "You did it. I'm in awe, Kate."

She smiled back. "I told Rita at the beginning I couldn't possibly do it by myself, and that was true; I had a lot of help. Years of her work to build on, Gretchen's help... and David's, in the end, after all. And the job's only half done. As long as we can keep the drug in production, you never have to get sick again" — *never again!* — "but we still don't know what caused it. I want a *cure*, Goban, I want a *fix*. Maybe now that everything's public, we can recruit a really good team to work on that; it doesn't have to be me and Rita all alone out here." *Maybe I can still help the trial patients.* Kate toyed with her pendant. For the first time, the thought of going back didn't fill her with panic.

He nodded. "There's time enough to talk about it, now."

* * *

Everyone looked up when he strode in, tall and straight-shouldered and alert. He dipped his head and gave a little bow when he shook Leslie Thorne's hand, all cowboy charm. "My granddaughter tells me you folks have questions. I haven't been myself these last few days, but

I'm here now. Where do you want to start?" He pulled up a chair.

Thorne smiled warmly, her eyebrows raised. "It's good to see you looking so well." He gave a slight nod, a slight smile. "We've taken care of all of the technicalities. The... irregular circumstances of Dar Andessat's arrival caused some consternation, but it was really just a matter of applying established procedure to the situation on the ground. That's not so hard.

"But tomorrow, the three of us need to go back to Washington and advise others on how to be prepared when your diplomats arrive, how to strike the balance between protecting ourselves and being open to all the possibilities that we can't yet imagine.

"I really have only one question for you, and it's this: what do you think we need to know?"

He considered that. "That's quite a question. I really am not the right—"

"Dar Andessat keeps saying the same thing. Help us out here."

It was, in fact, the very question he'd hoped she would ask. Lying in bed after Kate had left, his head clear for the first time, really, since this whole business had started, he had been hashing this out. Choosing what he most urgently needed to get across, if he had only this one chance to get a message to the people who would shape the world to come.

"All right, then. You were in the study last night?"

"I was. These men weren't, but we talked about it, afterward."

"What you have to understand is that the Semhet have not faced any real challenges in... a long time. We never had a true industrial revolution such as you've had, a sustained period of rapid innovation and population explosion. The closest thing — rebuilding after the final wars — that was a thousand years ago. The planet is geologically stable, the civilization very nearly so. There have been scientific advances, of course, and refinements in philosophy and religion and historiography, but essentially, there is very little motivation for change. Very little to have to adapt to."

"A thousand-year global peace." *We could learn from you,* Thorne's face said.

Goban grimaced. "You don't know what it's taken to maintain that. This is what I'm saying. You need to be careful of falling into that trap, right there."

"You told Inspector Walsh that Semhaata has..."

"... Its own problems. Yes. Our system of government is effective, but it's not just. Not in any sense you could consider it to be so. We, of course, have different ideas of justice. Human rights, quality of life... we didn't have an Age of Enlightenment either. Or, rather, we did, but our philosophers came to some quite different conclusions."

"Do you think they will try to impose their ideas of justice on us?"

"No," he said, quickly, dismissively, and hesitated. Nodded. "Yes."

"By force?"

"No." With more confidence. "Why would they

feel the need to use force? You don't have transit technology; you don't have any way to exert any influence on them at all, really. They have no need to conquer if they can just overwhelm and control. No. They won't impose their values on you, so much, as on the cultural boundary. They will police the boundary ruthlessly."

"It sounds like you think they'll be afraid of us."

He laughed, mirthless. "Of course they will."

"Why?"

"This will be an upheaval the likes of which Semhaata has not seen since the final wars. This will challenge everything they think they know. You will. The fact of your existence, which is one thing, but also yourselves. You have the most tremendous capacity to tolerate discomfort, and you have such short memory, individually, and on greater scales. Which allows you to do astonishing things — make ambitious attempts despite great personal hardship, sacrifice much on a gamble and win — but also causes you to tolerate suffering and conflict to a degree that will be incomprehensible to them.

"We've lost something you never did. And most Semhet would say that we have never missed it, and wouldn't know what to do with it if we had it."

"What's that?"

He hesitated, looked at her seriously. Made sure she was paying attention. "Autonomy."

She tilted her head a little, considering that. "You're proof that that's not true."

"I am... neither here nor there. As I have been reminded, more than once this week. You can't draw conclusions from me. No. Every society is a compromise, right? A social contract. Every society figures out for itself where it draws the line between the greater good and the individual, and has systems for policing that line. For culling those who don't conform, can't comply. This is one of the functions that space travel serves for the Semhet. I never fit in, and I found my way out. But I did not fit in here either. So I retreated to my mountain, built something different for my children. A third axis. A middle path.

"But you see, I could not have done that until I came here; I had no exposure to such an idea. Every society draws its own line, and you have practice at living with neighbors who draw a different line. Not easily, not without conflict, but the reality of that difference is your world. That thousand-year global peace you mentioned? That thousand-year global unity? It has made the idea of any alternative path antithetical to them. If they ever had any understanding of how to live in the face of a *different way of doing things*, they've long since forgotten it. They will fight like hell to keep you from reintroducing that idea." *They.* He'd slipped back, he noticed, distantly. Distancing himself, again. He wondered if Thorne had noticed, or what she took from it. She was writing quite a lot of notes.

"So that's the challenge. The Semhet response to such a challenge — the human response, really, but even more so — will be to control, to shape the circumstances rather than adapting to them. They will try to gain the upper hand in everything. Diplomacy, economic exchange, scientific exchange. Everything. They will do so bluntly, with shows of force, and subtly, by undercutting your own perceptions of what you have to bring to the negotiation."

"They'll come in, rich and flush with seductive technologies, and tell you everything that's wrong with you. Your civilization. They'll turn up their noses at your burgeoning sustainable energy tech base, and offer more powerful systems — at a high price, and on their terms. Same with medicine, computing and communications, agriculture, everything. They are going to offer a very attractive and appealing future, by way of stroking their own egos and demonstrating their own superiority. Yes, they will be afraid of you.

"The Semhet are not going to be able to see beyond Earth's problems. And it will be hard for Earth to look beyond the opportunities, what they can offer, what... transformations are possible. So take care. Don't let them act on the assumption that they have all of the advantages; they don't. Take your time to sort out what you have to bring to the table, and what you have at stake.

"There are lessons to be taken from your history, and from ours. I come from a small mountain city, a provincial capital remote from the big urban centers, one of the last holdouts of the last war. My people have assimilated, integrated, but we've never quite forgotten how it was in the days after the war. How it was imported food and cheap energy and the restructuring of civil government that conquered us in the end, even as the walls held.

"Don't be seduced. That's all. Remember who you are, and don't let them make you ashamed of it. Don't ever forget that you're the ones who survived on your own. That doesn't make you better than them either, but it doesn't make you worse. Just different. There's strength in difference, and that will be a hard lesson for both worlds to learn."

She was nodding earnestly, writing fast. She was so young. *You will learn a little faster, I think, and in that is your power, and your only hope.* Goban watched her, overwhelmed with inchoate sadness. Felt Kate's gaze on him, looked over, and met her eyes briefly. Remembered, with sudden vividness, that first day out riding up on the mountain. *Turmoil, for two worlds.*

Then Thorne looked up. "Right. That's... very helpful. I wish we had more time."

"We'll be doing this work for the rest of our lives."

"I suppose that's true." She stood, and her colleagues took the cue. She held out a hand. "Sir, thank you, and the best of luck to you. I hope we meet again."

* * *

When Emma couldn't stay anymore, she sent Robbie in her place. He had always taken an interest in the old language, she said, the most fluent of the great-grandchildren; he was clearly fascinated with the visitor, and had intelligent questions of his own to add to those he relayed. So they sat in the little study through the morning, the three of them, just talking, and Erik Jansen called on every bit of experience and training he had to navigate the middle path, drawing out as much as he could while also practicing compassion and gentleness.

Others came and went: the Air Force engineer for

a while, and one of the diplomats. Robbie's sister brought some lunch, and chided him teasingly for losing track of time.

Sometime later, Robbie looked up at the opening of the door, stopped in midsentence and jumped up. Erik turned, surprised and delighted to see Goban crossing the room. He rose and shook the other man's hand. "It's good to see you on your feet," he said. "I heard otherwise."

"Ah, yes." Goban smiled. "I was ill, earlier, but I had a stroke of luck. The medication I needed came in the mail as soon as the storm broke."

"That's excellent news."

"Robbie, thank you. I'll take over from here."

"Jā, Tēvi." The young man said something to Moret, held his hands out, palms up. The visitor looked surprised, smiled, and laid both hands over them. The two nodded at each other, and Robbie retreated.

Goban was delighted. "Amazing that he remembered that... a toddlers' game of pat-a-cake turned into a secret handshake between a little boy and his old granddad."

"I think you'll find yourself surprised by that sort of thing as your family interacts with more Semhet. You leave your homeland, you raise your children somewhere else, but you take it with you, and somehow, they absorb it. My own children were raised in England and America. I know how it is."

A sideways look, a laugh. "Hm. Well. I have business with our friend here."

"So you do." Erik sketched a little half-bow, and

stepped out. A moment later, the other two men followed, already speaking in rapid-fire Semhet, and cut through the parlor and dining room into the larger study, and there they stayed.

The afternoon passed, with the door closed. From time to time there were raised voices, and Tereza looked alarmed, but then they quieted again. Thorne and the State people left, soon followed by the Air Force engineer. Family business, gradually, returned to normal.

Mid-afternoon, Erik sought Tereza out. "This has been one of the great adventures of my life," he told her. "I'm so grateful to you for inviting me here."

She smiled a little, hesitated, embraced him. Her cheek against his, she whispered in his ear. "Stay in touch." She walked down to the motor pool with him, and when he crested the ridge and took one last look back, she looked very small, walking up the ring road alone.

* * *

CHAPTER TWENTY SEVEN

As the descending sun set the cliff wall afire, Goban went to the credenza and poured a golden liquid into two glasses, and held one out. Moret sipped it, tentatively. "This is fascinating. What is it?"

"Mead." Goban laughed. "Just enjoy it; you might not want to drink it if you know what it's made from." He watched his guest, a steady long stare. "You torment me."

"There's a solution to that problem." Moret matched the stare, held it. Held it until Goban looked away. "You must go back. This is the best way. If I don't return — or if I return without you — it will be much worse for them."

"You could tell the company that I'm dead."

A low, bitter laugh. "You know I would love to do that. We both know how it will go, when word of what we've found here spreads."

"Yes. Why don't you?" Moret had told him of the circumstances of his departure: the speed and secrecy, the company undercutting the government conspiracy of silence. *We know now*, Moret had said, *what is out here. And why it was kept quiet. But the secret will come out.* As all secrets had, over these strange few days.

"I have a job to do." Moret sighed. "So do you. You have a debt, you know that."

"I don't owe them my *life*!"

Now Moret was the one who glanced away; he seemed embarrassed at bearing witness to this anguish. But he was resolute. "You *do*, in fact, owe them *your life*. Your life's work, lost. The benefits of it, denied.

"You've had a good retirement out here, haven't you? Not the way you planned it — yes, I understand, something like this was always your plan, wasn't it? An early retirement, a well-padded savings, a place in the backcountry. That was the bargain you made when you swore the oath and they put their mark on you. You gave the company your *work*, and they gave you the means to have all of this.

"They upheld their end of the contract. Not in the way anyone could have imagined, but they did. You need to uphold your end."

Goban drank down the glass, poured another. Took a large swallow and savored it. Sighed. "I am going to miss this." He did not bother to contain the naked heartache in his voice. "Can I have until the morning?"

Moret breathed out relief. "That military officer tells me it will take... a quarter day, perhaps half a day, to travel back to my ship. There is some work to do there. I can be gone for a day. When I return, you need to be ready to go."

Conversation stopped cold when the two men walked into the dining room. "Emmie," Goban said, and Emma lifted her chin, caught his eye, held it steadily. "Let's have Christmas early."

* * *

So they did. Emma sent her boys out to cut a tree, and went herself to pull her grandmother's antique glass and woven-straw ornaments from the attic, with help from Kate and Gretchen. Jake and Robbie came back two hours later as the last of the twilight faded, with a perfect little Douglas fir, and also a yearling doe. Emma laughed and hugged them both, and set Reggie and Walsh to butchering.

Susan brought some sausages and cheeses up from the warehouse. Candles were lit. Bottles were opened, wine and brandy and mead flowed freely, and stories and songs were shared. Kate found herself drifting toward Gretchen and Walsh, who hung together, outside observers to an intimate, emotional family gathering.

Walsh was intrigued. "You'd think this was false cheer, or denial. It's not. It's just... indefatigable determination to be joyful in the moment."

"Yes. Because tomorrow, everything changes." Kate bit her lip to hold back tears.

Over the course of the afternoon and evening, Goban found time to pull each family member and guest aside for a private conversation. When the clock struck midnight, he rose from where he had been talking with Conrad, and strode over to stop in front of Kate. He paused, dramatically, for a moment; then bowed low, took her hand in his, turned it over, and kissed the inside of her wrist. She shivered and tossed back the last of her mead, and grinned at Gretchen. "Bedtime." Gretchen grinned back and blew her a kiss.

Joyful in the moment. It was sweet, and slow, and they spent a lot of time just exploring each others' bodies. When it was over, she finally sobbed, and he held her, and had the good grace not to speak at all.

She half-woke once to find herself alone, but drifted

back down, and the next time she stirred, he was there, fast asleep.

* * *

In true Old West fashion, people had rummaged through their own treasured mementos to find gifts, or had written letters. Kate found a small pile in front of her, when the gifts were all sorted.

The first was from Jake — a small framed photograph of the little mare she'd so enjoyed riding all through the fall. He opened up the back of the frame; tucked in behind the picture were copies of her pedigree papers. "I'd like to breed her next year," he said. "The first foal would be yours, too." She teared up and hugged him.

There was a beautiful silver art deco seagull pin, from Tereza and Emma — for when Kate missed the coast, Emma said. It had been their mother's, a gift from one of the uncles after a long-ago visit to San Francisco.

Last, Goban handed her a small, heavy square package. She hesitated, then carefully slit the tape from the wrapping paper, turned it over, lifted the paper away.

It was the pair of iridescent pressed-flower glass pieces that she had found in the old trunk, her second night on the farm. "Oh," she gasped, and looked up at him.

The whole of the past four and a half months passed between them. She wanted to say something, like *why don't you bring some of these back to plant behind the house,* or *take me with you and show me where they grow* or *I should have left the damned things in the bottom of the trunk.* She saw the same thoughts behind his eyes. *I wish we had more time.* But time wasn't going to make this anything but harder.

* * *

Gretchen and Rita spent some time with him, teaching him how to take a sample, use the phone and app to calculate dosages. "If you only test every two or three days," Gretchen said, "and keep it shut off the rest of the time, the battery might last the trip. If you can hack a way to recharge it, that'd be better. *See someone* as soon as you get there."

"I think that getting away from the doctors will be the bigger problem, for a little while."

There were some pieces of farm business to attend to, and some packing. He didn't take much. A few changes of clothes, books and photographs. The medical supplies that Kate and Rita packed up. Amalija's little cross, and Kate's serotonin pendant, strung together on a silver chain.

The sun was low when the ship appeared, looking like a meteor in slow motion, bright against the purple-grey sky and shifting into shadow as it dropped down onto the big meadow, up beyond the cliff rim and the wind turbines. Everyone went outside and watched. A few minutes later, Moret emerged from the orchard, walking up the road.

Goban walked through the crowd, exchanging some touch and word with each of the assembled — a hug, a hand on the shoulder, a murmur, a laugh — and stopped in front of Kate. Though she had braced herself for rage, or fear, or sadness, there was only emptiness. Despair so encompassing it felt like nothing at all.

He spoke softly enough that only she could hear, feeling his breath against her neck. "I have enjoyed these days with you. I'm grateful for them."

The torrent of hurt crashed over her then, threatening to pull her under. She shied away from the edge of panic. Touched his face, let her fingers linger along the lines of his cheek. "Come back." Desperation tinged her voice.

"I can't promise." She saw his flinch, and immediately regretted it. "Please don't, you know I can't." He laid his hand over hers, his long fingers wrapping around hers. Kissed her, slow, and stared at her hungrily, as if he were fixing her face in his memory to carry for a lifetime. In the end, neither of them could bear to speak the last word.

He walked away without hesitation, met his traveling companion on the road, and the two of them disappeared into the orchard. Kate stayed and watched until that shining light reappeared over the cliff wall, shrank, and vanished among the gathering stars.

* * *

EPILOGUE

1-20

Amalija,

We have a thing in common, now. There's a gulf too wide to cross, separating each of us from him. Is it strange that it's you I think of, whose council I crave?

Life goes on. The farm is as strong as ever; you would be so proud. I don't know how they do it; they've lost their stable center, their heart, and I've only lost a dream, a maybe, a might-have-been. But they get up every day and do the work, and, inspired by that, so do I.

Jake and Marina are teaching me to work with horses. I think I'd like to learn about breeding. I'll never be a mother, but the idea of having a hand in creating a life is something that has unexpectedly taken hold of me and shaken me. I have spent my life living lightly on the earth, barely leaving a trace behind me, but you've taught me about a different way to live, and I want to give it a try.

I feel your presence in the wind in the orchard, in the patterns woven in the wool, in the smell of the old books that you brought here all those years ago. I see you in their faces, hear you in their songs. I wish you could see the mark you've left.

I am so alone, Amalija, so alone. I don't know how he did it, all those years without you. You get up every day and do the work.

2-4

 Amalija,

 Irena has had her baby. Her husband got home just in time. He rolled in yesterday morning, and with a lovely surprise in hand: orders to rotate back stateside, to Fort Carson. She will go to be with him, of course, but they'll only be a few hours away, home every couple of weekends. She's ecstatic.

 He's a nice kid, and obviously adores her, and they are so sweet together, the three of them. A little boy, blond like his daddy, although who knows how long that will last? Henriks Arturs, after his uncle and his great-uncle. A good name for a soldier's son; I hope you would approve.

4-18

 Amalija,

 The Semhet ships came yesterday — three great big ones, full of diplomats and bureaucrats and economists and all that. Just like when Moret came — a great electromagnetic flash yesterday, far out at the edge of the solar system, and in orbit this morning. The first shuttles landed in Delaware a few hours ago, and others are coming down in major cities all over the world.

 The news is a constant, unending stream. Reporters come to the farm and are turned away; the county commissioners and sheriff were here earlier, talking to Conrad about closing the road.

 The State Department called to invite the family to send representatives. Robbie is going; he'll be fast-tracked into George Washington University in the fall, and interning at the new embassy they'll be building. I think he has some of Goban's wanderlust in him, and I wonder where it will take him, and where he will eventually put down roots.

It's strange. All those years of quiet reserve, keeping the secret, keeping the sanctuary — Goban never did stray too far from his roots, after all — and for what? Everyone in the world knows the family's name. It's deeply unsettling, especially to the older generation, who lived with the secrecy for so long. There is an overwhelming, heart-aching, pervasive sense of "please let us just go back to normal." Normal isn't coming back. Nothing will ever be the same.

At least they had those years, and we still have this land.

4-24

Amalija,

Another blizzard. I wonder if this damned winter will ever end. It keeps the press away, anyway.

5-8

Amalija,

Lambing is on! I don't see that much of the real work of farming, but it's all hands, so I'm doing a lot of driving up to the west meadow and back again, and running errands, and holding things. Trying to stay out of the way while watching and learning. There are so many lambs! A nuzzling, bleating, running, stumbling invasion.

I've never seen anything like it.

6-10

> Amalija,
>
> Home from a strange, emotional trip to Seattle. Not nearly enough time with Gretchen, although she's planning to come down in the fall sometime, for a week or so. We talk almost every day now, more often than we did when I lived in Seattle, but it's not the same.
>
> I spent a few days at Alcon to consult on new protocols. The family is suing, the IRB people from Fort Detrick have come in and shut down new research, but they are continuing to work with the remaining subjects. A couple of the guys will simply have to be on the drug for the rest of their lives, because the danger of weaning them off of it is too great.
>
> On the last day, I went up to Madigan and visited one of the subjects. He should never have been in the program in the first place; just a scared and angry kid who went into the Army because some juvie judge decided he needed discipline. He had gotten in a fight and killed a lieutenant, and that's how he ended up in the prisoner group we recruited from. He was one of the guys who tried to suicide during withdrawal, and when I talked to him, I found out why. During the time he was on the drug, he said, he was sorting out his problems, thinking clearly for the first time in his life, making connections between the injustices he'd struggled with, his own choices, and how those things conspired to drag him down. He felt all of that slipping away from him when we took the drug

away, and he couldn't take it.

Now, on the new variant, he's getting better again. The impact on executive function is real; this young man's brain is healing itself, repairing damage done by childhood malnutrition and neglect. This is what makes this research seductive: if the drug can do so much good, how can we bear to quit trying to find a way to make it safe? We flung ourselves against that wall so many times, and it wasn't just ourselves we were leaving bloody. It terrifies me. I want no part of it, but I have a responsibility to these men, forever.

7·21

Amalija,

It is a year ago today since I came here. Can you believe it? I would not have recognized myself. The whole world has changed; it's not just me. Tereza came home for the weekend and said there were clusters of goggling Semhet tourists in downtown Denver; her command of their language impressed them very much, and they bought her an expensive dinner. She was bemused, but isn't, it seems, tempted to give up her law practice for translator work; there's a hell of a lot of money to be made in commercial contract law these days, and she's having fun getting in on it.

Dr. Jansen also took her out to dinner while he was in Boulder last week, and she seemed very pleased about that.

They haven't opened travel in the other direction, though. Some nights I lie awake and think about that day, about driving down to New Mexico with nothing more than I can carry, and walking onto a ship to carry me to the stars, and not stopping until I find him. And starting over again, again.

But in the meantime, they have the money, and money is power, and the power makes the rules that the rest of us have to live with. As it ever has been. So here I am.

* * *

She left before dawn on a golden October morning, with the last of the roses from Emma's arbor and a backcountry pack — food and water for a few days, first-aid kit, radio, popup tent. She intended only a half-day ride, but she was alone, and you could never know, in these mountains. The difference between the glorious seduction of autumn and killing winter balanced on the edge of a knife. She headed up through the big meadow and across the ridge, laid the roses on Amalija's grave, and continued on up, beyond the property line and into the national forest, over the snow-patched, barren, moonscape saddle between the peaks, onto the west flank of the Uncompaghre. The barren ruggedness above the tree line was beautiful, so high up that she could see the broken vastness of the ancient lava field to the south, and the curve of the earth. She took her time.

You could lose yourself up here, but you could not escape. Even here, the tracks of civilization were visible, in the contrails of airliners and the military planes on maneuvers out of Colorado Springs, and more recently, the high-atmosphere pinpoints of Semhet shuttles — not common, but becoming less remarkable. They crossed the sky as tiny dots of light, bright enough to see in daylight, but just barely.

One caught her eye, far on the western horizon. She watched it idly as it crossed the great bowl of the sky, too directly eastbound to be headed for Holloman; it must be bound for the east coast, she thought, or for Europe. So tiny, so distant, but impossibly bright, disproportionate in the space it took up in her sky.

It was not her imagination. It was brighter, twice as bright, ten times as bright, as it should have been. It was going to pass not more than a handful of miles to the north. *And it was descending.* The eastward progress of the burning track across the sky was overtaken by its plummet; it was not going to pass at all, it was coming down right into her mountains. Right into her valley.

"Come on, bright eyes, take me home." She leaned forward and rode like hell.

* * *

Coming November 2017
Darzins Mill Trilogy

Book Two

Refuge

Ashare loved the maglev, for coming home. The suborbital could take her to the provincial capital in less time than it took to walk from her flat to the station, but the half-day journey near ground level let her see the mountains fall away, the grasslands open up, the great river Moreta shimmer on the horizon and then bend close to pass right under the track at the Moret'anaa Bridge, proliferate into the many-coursed Braid with its wetlands full of wildlife and salt flowers, the soil of a continent filtering through its fingers to build up the fragile delta. That was where the train turned south, and she knew that she would be home soon.

The sun was setting when she disembarked, the evening sky filling with stars. The great shimmering arc of the Mother River passed overhead, dazzling out here on the coast. That sight always surprised and delighted

Ashare anew; the light pollution in Bva'tat City's dense center made the Mother River a pale ghost of herself. She strolled slowly, her satchel tossed carelessly over her shoulder, enjoying the cool spring breeze carrying the smell of the ocean, debating supper. There was street food, there were restaurants, but there was also her own kitchen and a quiet meal alone. That last choice won out over the others, finally, as she crossed the threshold of her complex.

A man was sitting on her front step.

He was a little older than her, pleasant-looking enough in a bland bureaucratic fashion, hunched a little in what seemed to her boredom and something else. *Visitor*, was what it was; he was out of place, and making no effort to be anything else, a passing stranger. Not getting comfortable. He had something of Oro'atva about him, in his broad face and stocky form, the layered greys and greens of his clothing blending into the shadows. She wondered how long he had been sitting there.

He saw her coming, rose to greet her. Held out a single hand, palm-up. A brusque and overly-familiar greeting, she thought, for a stranger on her doorstep in the evening. She tapped the open palm with her fingertips, equally brusque, refusing him the courtesy of palm-to-palm. "Doret Ashare," she introduced herself briefly.

He smiled. "I know who you are. Kassa Roje."

"Is that supposed to mean something to me, Dar Kassa?" At his raised eyebrow, she huffed a little in exasperation. "I'm sorry, I'm tired and hungry, I've been traveling all day. Let's toss off the pleasantries and just get to who you are and why you're here, can we?"

He nodded. "Certainly. I'm up from Semhoshe." *The* capital; he was a long way from home, in truth. "Over the next few days, some surprising and disturbing news is going to come out. I'm here to share it with you before it all becomes public, because it starts with your cousin."

Now she was really confused. "I don't have any cousins." *And you still haven't told me who you are.*

"Nhoresh Goban. Do you know that name?"

She did, although she hadn't heard it since she was a child. "Goban? My father's cousin. He died... oh, years ago. Before I was born, I think. He was some kind of deep-space surveyer, wasn't he? He was lost in the field?"

"Not dead. He's coming home. And what he found is going to change everything, forever."

* * *

TYPSETTING NOTE

The text is set in Goudy Bookletter 1911. Designed by
Barry Schwartz, it is based on master designer
Frederic Goudy's 1911 Kennerly Old Style,
which draws on Dutch and
Ventian traditions.

Goudy Bookletter 1911 is open source.
You can find it and Barry's other work at
https://www.theleagueofmoveabletype.com/
members/crudfactory .

The chapter headings, leaders and page numbers, title page,
and cover are set in Cinzel and Cinzel Decorative. Designed
by Natanael Gama for the Google Font Library,
"this font family is inspired in first century Roman
inscriptions and based on classical proportions.
However it's not a simple revivalism.
While it conveys all the ancient history
of the Latin alphabet it also merges a
contemporary
feel onto it."

Cinzel and Cinzel Decorative are
donationware. You can find it and atanael's
other work at http://ndiscovered.com/ .

Thank you for supporting independent
artists and designers.

ELIZABETH BIEHL writes and makes art in
the gorgeous historic City Park West neighborhood of
Denver, Colorado.